GOLDEN HARVEST

Generation's Journey

GOLDEN HARVEST

Generation's Journey

ROSANNA C. SHARPS

Word Sower Publishing

ISBN: Softcover   978-1-7364833-4-3
          Hardcover   978-1-7364833-5-0
          eBook   978-1-7364833-6-7

Word Sower Publishing
Columbia, California

www.wordsowerpublishing.com

I would like to extend my gratitude to
those who assisted in my efforts in
publishing the "Golden Harvest Trilogy."

To God, for His inspiration.
To my husband, Michael for his support.
To Margaret, for providing the historical resources for Snelling.

Contents

1

New Year, New Inventions

Sower Farms, Snelling, California
January 1873

"Why don't you sit down, Jon, before you wear a hole in the wood floors?" Jonathan Sower's wife, Mary, said with a forever engrained Kentuckian accent. Her hazel eyes glistened as she sat in front of his office hearth embroidering a pillowcase. His eighteen-year-old daughter, Naomi, sat next to her as she evaluated numbers in an accounting ledger. David, his seventeen-year-old son, sat across from them, with Bible study notes in hand.

Jonathan inhaled the rich, sweet, aromatic tobacco scent from his clay pipe as he paced by the window. The 2,500 acres of unseeded fields were rain-soaked. The rapid expansion of his wheat business affirmed his decision to follow God's direction to move to California eight years earlier after the Civil War had ravaged his inherited farm in Kentucky.

Another year had gone by without a visit from his eldest son and daughter, Samuel and Sarah. The unwelcomed vice-like pressure in his chest manifested when worry for his children's welfare consumed him and further aggravated his old war wound to his right shoulder.

Jonathan hoped to see either one of them approach the long wayside path to his farmhouse, happy to be home. *Why? Why can't you both receive what I have to offer: a home, a secure life, and an abundance of love from your family?*

The silhouette of Samuel with shoulders slumped, as he trotted up the path on his horse Christmas of 1870, was still vivid in Jonathan's mind. That was the last he had seen his eldest son, rightful heir to his estate.

"Pa, I need to borrow money." Sam choked on his words. "I need just a little to tide me over until I can find work on the railroad. The Central Pacific only has maintenance jobs available, and they've hired men with families to support first." There was a quiver in his voice and his eyes reddened. "I suppose I can still try my hand at gold prospectin'. But I think that season has passed me by now that big companies have taken over using hydraulic mining."

After a week, he journeyed again. Sam was determined to make his mark in the world on his own. A letter from him arrived the following January and stated that the employment lines were swollen with men desperate for jobs. He hoped to contact their old friend, Patrick Fay, for any possible hauling work.

Countless times Jonathan's wife contacted the Sheriffs' offices and railroad stations throughout the outlying counties to inquire of any information on Samuel's whereabouts. The answers would always return to her void.

He'd be twenty-four now. *Ah, son, where are you? I hope you're alive.* His heart ached, and his spirit groaned for an answer.

Dear Pa and Ma, the children are growin' up strong. I'm pregnant again. This baby is due in April. But as usual, Lad will be gone again. Pa, would you mind if I borrowed Ma again to help me deliver your next grandchild? Sarah's annual letters always seemed to read the same. *I'm pregnant. Please send Ma.*

Sarah's sweet, youthful face lingered in his thoughts. He had not seen her since she eloped in the summer of 1869. She moved to Mariposa on a one-acre farm that belonged to her husband, Lad, whom Jonathan had never met.

The last time he sent Mary to Sarah was about a year ago. Mary had told him that she met Lad as he headed out the door for another three-month cattle drive, leaving his pregnant wife and two toddlers to fend for themselves.

When Mary returned from that visit, she was frustrated with Sarah's stressful home situation: raising three children by herself and disheartened by the endless arguments she had with Lad when he came home. Mary had begged Sarah and her family to return to their farm, but she refused because of the grief-stricken memories of her first love, Joshua, throughout Snelling. His tragic death from cholera while he assisted his father's itinerant ministry impacted the direction of her life and tested her faith's condition.

Twenty-two with three young'uns that I've never seen. Abigail, three, Billy, two, and Isabelle, one. Oh, daughter, what has become of you?

"I wish I could, dear." Jonathan continued to pace, finally answering his wife's request.

The rays of the mid-January sun peeked through the scattered rain clouds and filtered in the office's wood shutters and cast a soft light on his family who remained. A peaceful ambiance compared to the thoughts that agitated his mind. He met with them to discuss the implementation of the new farm equipment for their crescive wheat business. He couldn't wrap his mind around machines designed to perform the detailed work that men and animal can do. *Old age has me bent. This new generation is much too fast for me. I've gotta keep up if I want my business to thrive.*

"No matter how many times I keep hashin' the figures in my brain, I still can't help but be anxious 'bout usin' the twenty-two-mule harvester and steam-powered threshin' machines. I'd rather do things the old-fashioned way and hire more farmworkers," Jonathan said while he rubbed his neatly cropped beard.

"Pa, I do believe the math is correct. The new equipment will do the majority of the hard labor so we won't need to hire more workers. These machines will save us plenty of money in the long run. Three dozen farmhands are all we need," Naomi said as she ran her fingers over the ledger's pages.

"I guess I'm a bit nervous now that we've added another 1,000 acres after the last harvest. Two thousand five hundred acres is a lot of land. We've more than quadrupled our growth since 1864. This is the most property my family has ever owned." Jonathan stared out the window and took a deep breath.

David shifted his weight. "And I think growth is inevitable. Not only must we meet the East's demands for transported produce through the transcontinental railroad, but we also need to supply California's growin' population."

Jonathan sat down in his wing-back chair, placed his elbows on his knees, and scraped at the soil under his fingernails. "In fact, the topic of conversation these days amongst other farmers is the need for fruits and vegetables. The fair-weather climate in California gives us an advantage over our Midwestern and Eastern competitors. Many are switchin' over to this lucrative market. We may also want to consider doin' the same." He clasped his palms, lifted his head, and locked eyes with each of them. "The railroads have invented ice-cooled railcars, usin' frozen brine blocks to keep the produce from spoil on the eight-day journey back East. Modern technology is simply amazin'." Jonathan stood and returned to the window, where he visualized what his fields would look like with fruit trees instead of wheat.

"Sweetheart, I admire your foresight. However, can we pray 'bout this proposition? I'm still gettin' accustomed to the idea of utilizin' the latest farm inventions, too, let alone a different industry." Mary put her embroidery down, eyes glued on her husband. "I speculate you already made plans to proceed in this new direction?"

"The thought keeps crossin' my mind ever since I delivered the wheat to Nielsen's flour mill last season. By happenstance, Fred Maxfield and Eustace and Marlena Kelly were there also." Jonathan glanced at his wife's knit brows and pierced stare then returned to his seat. "I believe you've met them before, dear. Fred owns the 3,500-acre wheat farm on the southwest side of Snelling, and the Kellys are the owners of the 8,000 acres of grazing land near Merced Falls.

"After concludin' business with Mr. Nielsen, we all had a chance to discuss what the future holds for the agricultural industry now that the railroads factor into the picture. Fruits and vegetables seem to be the growin' commodity.

"Mary, I'm not expectin' this to take place immediately. However, we should start givin' it some thought."

Jonathan shifted in his seat and clenched his pipe between his teeth, smoke escaping as he spoke. "I'd like to stay ahead of my competitors, mainly Mr. Maxfield. Unfortunately for Fred, he did not receive an inheritance as I have from my family." Removing his pipe from his lips, he turned to his wife to assert confidence. "Word around town is that he acquired an enormous capital loan from the bank to establish his wheat business. He purchased the acreage, farming equipment and livestock, and paid the first three years of employee's salary with these funds. My gumption tells me his financial situation will not afford him to improve his outdated equipment and aging livestock, let alone try to change his industry." Sensing his wife's anxiety, Jonathan languished his vision in smaller steps, not to overwhelm her, and settle back in his chair. "So I do count my blessin's, darlin'. God is on our side preparin' every step of our way."

The whites of Naomi's eyes enlarged. "My goodness … that's a tremendous endeavor indeed, Pa. I presume you'll need to review our budget first before makin' any changes. Let me know when you want a financial statement. Fruit trees require a large investment. However, I do see your point. We won't have to worry 'bout planting a new crop year after year." She sauntered to her father, placed the ledger in his hands, tugged at her blouse over her bustle, and returned to her seat.

Naomi turned to her mother. "Our family garden and small fruit orchard are thrivin' in this blessed California weather, Ma. It produces more than enough to feed our employees and us. Imagine what 2,500 acres will do for this country." She pointed toward the wheat fields. "Thank the Lord for blessin' us with the Suen family to manage our domestic needs and teach us the Chinese technique of growin' fruits and vegetables. Fondness has grown in my heart for them. Jia-Li and I are the best of friends." Nodding at her mother, she then smiled at him.

"You are correct, Naomi. Indeed, you're your father's daughter, always havin' an eye for the future." Mary sat erect and reached for the small bell on the coffee table. "Yes, the Suens are a blessin' to this household. If not for Huang-Fu's brother's tragedy, they'd still be servin' him on the open seas, and we wouldn't be as far along in our business as we are today. They are the bridge we needed to communicate the needs of our Chinese workers and ourselves." She shook the bell.

"I am so thankful the Lord gave you and Pa the wisdom to take them in as our domestic help after I spoke to you about their plight. I can't believe they've been with us three years now." David's eyes sparkled as he grinned.

The clay pipe clung between Jonathan's clenched teeth as he grinned in agreement. "Yes, indeed. The almighty and all-knowing God does work all things together for good for those who love Him." He puffed out some smoke. "Lettin' our cabin to the Suens is a fair trade for their domestic services and a small salary. Without them, we wouldn't have known how to feed these men, but they do. God is good."

Jonathan winked at his beloved wife and hoped to assure her with a warm smile. His decision to hire the Chinese farmhands caused a divide between them and the townspeople who despised the job-invading foreigners. His family's true friends were the pastor and his wife and a hauling business associate from another town who also employed the Chinese men. The hidden current of the town folk's prejudice was restrained by a thin stream of civility driven by his Chinese-employee-based business's success.

He recalled when the railroad was completed. Many of the unemployed Chinese rail workers had transitioned to farm work as a natural choice of employment. Snelling grew a quarter of its size to 1,200 residents as the Chinese laborers sought work at the wheat farms in their small town. Unfortunately, not all the farm owners were inclined to employ them, even after they proved their worth on the railroads. Most white citizens had ill sentiments toward the vast population of Chinese who migrated to California because the "Coolies," as the Caucasians derogatorily called them, took these jobs for much less pay.

From Jonathan's perspective, they were the best farm workers he had ever employed. They were hardworking and humble. They did not complain much and were affordable. *Hmm. Should I continue to do what is best for my expandin' business, or do I follow the growin' anti-Chinese masses and keep hatred from erupting in my town?*

The middle-aged butler dressed in a dark cotton Chinese attire entered the office and bowed. His waist-length queue swung beneath his black cap as he moved.

"Did someone call?" he asked with an accent.

"Yes, Huang-Fu. We were just talking amongst ourselves about how blessed we are to have you, Liang, and Jia-Li as part of our household," Mary said.

"Ah, I understand. The feeling is mutual."

"Would you mind fetchin' a pot of tea for us?"

"Not at all, madam."

"Thank you, Huang-Fu," Naomi said.

"Most certainly, Miss Naomi." He bowed and excused himself.

David leaned forward in his chair. "All right, Pa, let's go back to the subject of plantin' fruit trees. You haven't forgotten that I'm hopin' to attend Taylor University in Upland, Indiana next year. Won't you need my assistance for this endeavor? This change may have to take place next spring or when I return in four years after I get my theology degree."

"Yes, son, I've considered this. Next spring is much too soon. It'll have to wait until you return, unless, by some great miracle, Sam comes home." Jonathan glanced involuntarily at the wayside path again. "My first concern is to find someone to oversee the livestock when you leave. This position would be perfect for that husband of Sarah's, should he be inclined to accept. I must deal with both situations when the right time approaches."

Jonathan's mind raced as he thought about all he owned and operated: the harvester, threshing machines, twenty-two mules, eight horses, six oxen, twelve heifers, five milk cows, forty hens, two roosters, and four turkeys. He employed over three dozen Chinese farmhands from the immigrant camp on the west end of Lewis Street and the Suen family who rented their two-room cabin next to the farmhouse. *And now David is leaving for college. What am I doin' wrong that my children despise their inheritance?*

Liang and her nineteen-year-old daughter, Jia-Li, entered the office and placed a pot of tea, four cups, and a plate of almond cookies on the table.

"May we get you anything else?" Liang asked.

"Oh, this is mighty fine. Thank you," Mary said.

"We will be in the kitchen if you need us." Jia-Li's young voice rang as she and her mother returned to their chores.

"Well, Pa, you'll need to hire more workers next year if I'm the only one left to help you on this farm. I may be made of strong Sower stock, but it's a bit much to handle all the chores of my bubs and sis and accomplish the accountin', too." Naomi poured the hot beverage and grabbed a cookie. "Besides, why should I pour my heart and soul into this fine estate if Sam is goin' to inherit the whole lot?"

Stunned at Naomi's comment, Jonathan stopped pacing. *What would I do without Naomi?* She had taken on the majority of the chores since Samuel and Sarah left home and always had a smile on her face and a song in her heart while she worked. Never once did he contemplate her role on the farm should Samuel not return. "My dear girl. Don't think that your efforts have gone unnoticed. Your ma and I appreciate your hard work. Our plans are for y'all to divide a portion of the inheritance, Samuel havin' the greater since he is the eldest male. However, if he chooses not to return, then surely your portion will increase if you choose to stay."

"I don't plan on goin' anywhere else. I love farm life, Pa and Ma."

Ah, only one chooses to stay — the least likely of all four, the middle child. I would've thought Naomi to be the first to leave the roost, squeezed out by her elder and younger siblings.

David stood and stretched. "Good. Now that that is settled and if this meetin' has concluded, I've got to finish preparin' the Bible lesson for tonight with the Suen's."

"Well, that's all I had on my mind," Jonathan said as he tried to relax his shoulders.

"Oh, and Pa, trust in the Lord with all your heart and lean not on your own understandin'. In all your ways acknowledge Him, and He shall direct your paths." David quoted Proverbs 3:5-6, his genial countenance lifting the conclave's gravity.

Jonathan's heart swelled as he observed his level-headed son leave the room with his Bible in hand. *All right, Lord. I pray Your word will continue to be a lamp to my feet and a light to my path. Show me the way I am to go.*

2

Good News, Cold Trail

The daybreak's light crept in through the master bedroom's wood shutters. The rooster's crow announced another glorious day at Sower Farms. Mary propped herself up in her bed, pushed back her handcrafted quilt, and, as usual, watched her husband dress into his dusty dungarees, cotton shirt, boots, and Boss of the Plains Stetson. After dressing, he never failed to kiss her before he retreated to the kitchen for a stout country breakfast.

"Have a splendid day, my love. I'll be down soon after my mornin' prayers and quiet time with God," she said. This was her special time to pray for her family, and she never skipped a day without the Lord first in her life. "Today is Tuesday. I'll be headin' into town for my weekly visit to the Mercantile and the courthouse. Do you need anythin' while I'm there?" After the market, she made it her aim to drop-in on Marshal Warner at the Snelling Courthouse for any possible news about Samuel. She had sent posters to neighboring town's sheriffs and county marshals with a sketch of his likeness and her contact information. For three years she waited, but the small tidings resulted in cold trails.

"Yes, dear. Would you mind pickin' up another tin of pipe tobacco? Be sure it's my favorite brand, Kentucky Club."

"Why, of course. Will there be anythin' else?"

"No, dear. That'll do. You also enjoy your day." He kissed her on her forehead and trotted downstairs where the pleasant voices of their family and the domestic helpers chattered.

"Dear Lord, I thank You for Your watchful eye and preservin' hand upon my family. Please protect my son Samuel from danger wherever he may be. Send Your angels to take charge of his life and help guide him. Draw him back to You in the way You find fittin' so he may return to You with a sincere and contrite heart.

"As for Sarah, Lord give her the measure of strength needed to care for her young children. And for Jonathan, Naomi, and David, I request your guidance and blessings as they commence with their daily routines at the farm. Thank You, Father, for all You do in our lives. May we give You glory through our actions today. Amen."

After she prayed and meditated on Scripture, a myriad of thoughts and items to do for the day passed through her mind. She donned her working corset, corded petticoat, and apple-green-and-saffron plaid day dress. She wrapped her faded russet braids into a bun, grabbed a straw bonnet from the wall rack, and headed downstairs for breakfast.

"Good morning, madam," Liang said as she poured hot coffee into Mary's cup and brought her a plate of scrambled eggs and biscuit.

"Good mornin', Liang." Mary blessed her food then devoured it. "I'm headin' to the market today. Do you need anythin'?"

"No, madam. Husband at Chinese Camp buying supplies for farmworkers. Naomi, David, and Jia-Li plant in garden seeds that husband will purchase. They already outside to till soil."

"How wonderful. I would love to work in the garden with them, too." Mary finished her biscuit and gulped down her coffee. "All right. I must skedaddle and do my errands if I want to get back in time to join them." She adjusted her bonnet and headed to the foyer to grab her shawl.

"Basket of bread and fruit for Marshal on foyer table." Liang followed her to the door. "Mr. Sower said he prepare carriage for you by corral."

"Thank you, Liang." Mary high-stepped out the door, hopped into the carriage, and rode into town.

THE TWO-STORY SNELLING COURTHOUSE became a familiar sight to Mary as often as circumstances allowed her to visit. The initial day was when she and her husband purchased the first 500 acres for Sower farms in 1864, and after that additional increments totaling 2000 acres. Next came the regular Sunday church services moderated by the itinerant pastor, Daniel McSwan, before he acquired the church on Green Street. Then, upon Naomi's mock arrest when she was in grade school to teach her a lesson for thieving at Jacobi's Mercantile. And now to seek the law's assistance to locate her wandering eldest son. Seventeen steps to the second floor. Heaven forbid, she will ever have to call upon her family in the first-floor jail. She shook the dreaded thought from her mind as she entered the courthouse doors.

"Well, if it isn't Mrs. Sower, come to visit me again. You are just the person I wanted to see." The marshal's teeth glistened beneath his thick mustache, and his eyes sparkled brighter than usual, outshining the star-shaped badge above his shirt's chest pocket.

"Good afternoon, Marshal Warner. You want to see me? Whatever for? Am I in some sort of trouble?" She placed the small basket emanating the bread's fresh-baked aroma on the marshal's overloaded desk. For the past three years, her visits became a drudgery, sensing she was an annoyance to the marshal and his deputy as she inquired of her son. She knew the basket of pabulum always kept the doors open for her.

"Trouble? Oh no, ma'am. Please take a seat." He searched for a piece of paper amongst his files as she sat down. "This telegraph came in this mornin' from the jailhouse in Jamestown." He passed it to her to read.

Samuel Sower arrested last night for intoxication and instigating a brawl at the National Hotel Saloon. Released this morning after he sobered. Currently employed as a roustabout at pig farm in Columbia. No address given. Sheriff Bourlain, Tuolumne County Jail.

Her ecstatic heart sent bursts of joy throughout her body. "Oh, Marshal Warner. Besides givin' birth to my son, this is the best news I've heard about him in a long time. Thank you so much for your patience with me all these years." Tears clouded her vision.

Strange enough, the image of Samuel inebriated, battered, bruised, and chained to a jailhouse cot brought her joy. Despite his unfortunate circumstances, his whereabouts put an end to the mystery and Mary's misery.

"Ma'am, does this mean we won't be meeting like this anymore? We sure will miss the weekly comestibles."

ELATED, MARY RETURNED TO THE FARM, ran to her husband's office, and leaped into his arms. "Jonathan, our boy's been found!" She shoved the telegram into his hands.

Her husband scanned the document, his jaws dropping. "Well, thank the Lord he is alive and livin' in Columbia."

"Yes. On a pig farm of all places. And he told us he doesn't want anythin' to do with farmin'." Mary grinned as she clutched his elbows.

"It's amazin' how life's situations come back 'round. First, his gold pannin' dreams didn't come to fruition, and then the railroad work was short lived. From what I hear from Patrick Fay, his haulin' business has been sufferin' ever since the railroads came. So he must've not had enough work for Sam." Jonathan shook his head. "Rock bottom. He must be desperate."

Mary's soul swelled with excitement, bolstering a hymn from William Cowper, "God Moves in a Mysterious Way."

> "God moves in a mysterious way
> His wonders to perform;
> He plants His footsteps in the sea
> And rides upon the storm.
>
> Deep in unfathomable mines
> Of never failing skill
> He treasures up His bright designs
> And works His sovereign will.

Ye fearful saints, fresh courage take;
The clouds ye so much dread
Are big with mercy and shall break
In blessings on your head.

Judge not the Lord by feeble sense,
But trust Him for His grace;
Behind a frowning providence
He hides a smiling face.

His purposes will ripen fast,
Unfolding every hour;
The bud may have a bitter taste,
But sweet will be the flower.

Blind unbelief is sure to err
And scan His work in vain;
God is His own interpreter,
And He will make it plain."

Jonathan rubbed the back of his neck as if relieving pressure. "Pride is what's keepin' Sam from returnin'. It seems to run in the Sower men along with a ramblin' spirit, wantin' to discover the world. Grandpa had it when he left England, Pa had it when he left Virginia, and I had it when we left Kentucky. And now Sam has it," Jonathan said as he sauntered to his office window to peer at the wayside path which led to La Grange Road. "This cycle must stop if I am to pass on our wheat farmin' business." Turning, he gazed at her. "Pack your bags, Mary. We shall leave tomorrow mornin' and head over to Columbia to search for him. Someone must know his whereabouts."

"ARE YOU SURE WE WANT TO BE STAYIN' AT MORGAN'S HOTEL, JON? Not too long ago there was news of a woman stabbin' her two-timin' husband to death in one of the rooms." Mary shuttered as their carriage rolled along the dirt road of Columbia's Main Street lined with red brick stores with iron-clad doors and windows.

"Well, darlin', I don't think we have much choice. It's either this hotel or the Fallon. I reckon you don't want to be near the crowds and noise of the Fallon Theater next door. And I know you won't want to stay in the roomin' house at their Chinese camp, either." He pulled on the reins and stopped the horse in front of the infamous lodging. "Besides, I can request a room far from where that incident happened."

"Yes, dear. Please do. All I know is I can use a warm meal and a good night's rest in the same bed after travelin' for three days. Sleepin' in a different room every night is quite unnervin'." Mary winced as she viewed the two-story structure with a green awning that stretched the entire length of the windows. She stepped onto the boardwalk, adjusted her traveling jacket and skirt bustle, and her sight was drawn to a farcical young couple who sipped an inebriant of some sort on the balcony of one of the rooms adjacent to the street.

The gentleman tipped his derby to her as he leaned over the ornate, black iron railing. "Good day to you folks down below!"

"Good day to you, sir." Jonathan grabbed their bags from the carriage, and handed the valet coins to park at the livery down a block across the street. "Right this way, darlin'." He led her into the charming lobby graced with a spray of mountain flowers in a large ivory vase to the left on a window table. A door to the right led into the spacious dining hall with stairs that ascended to the second-floor rooms.

"Welcome to Morgan's Hotel. My name is Geoffrey. My wife, Marjorie and I are the sole proprietors of this fine establishment." The young man stood from behind a roll-top desk and approached the front counter made of fine dark mahogany. His eyes peered down at the bulging carpet bags in her husband's hands. "Let me guess. You folks need a room for a few nights."

"Yes, sir. We would like a quiet room, please, away from the street noise, and preferably far from the room where the murder occurred."

The owner rolled his eyes. "Ugh. You've heard of the tragic news. It happened well over five years ago. Some people come to stay here and request this room for that very reason. Like the couple staying in it now." He pointed to the room upstairs on the north side close to the street. "The thrill of a good ghost story is something they must enjoy." He chuckled and shook his head.

"Ah, I think they greeted us as we entered. They were havin' a fine time on the balcony and didn't seem shaken," Mary said, then bit her lip.

"Well, I can give you room ten." The clerk handed Jonathan a map. "It's on the same side of the hotel but the opposite end in the back. There is only one adjoining room between it and the shared bathroom. I can assure you it is peaceful and quiet there. If you hear anything bump in the night, please notify me and I will reimburse you in full." The clerk knocked on the counter as if carrying out the superstition to knock on wood for good luck, and winked at his wide-eyed wife.

"That'll be just fine. We'll take it for three nights to start and may need it longer, dependin' on how much time is needed to locate our son," Jonathan said.

"Oh?" The owner tilted his head. "Lost your son, have you now? Is he here in this neck of the woods?"

"Yes. In fact, last we heard he was workin' on a pig farm in the outskirts of Columbia," Mary said as she moved close to the man for more information.

"Oooo." He let out a slow, diminishing whistle. "There are several farms west on Parrots Ferry Road, north on Italian Bar Road, and east on Jackson Street." He scratched his head. "Why don't I block this room out for a week, just in case you may be here a while? Do you have a name for this young man?"

"Samuel Sower. Almost the spittin' image of my handsome husband. Darker hair, though." Mary giggled as she glanced at Jonathan.

"*Hmm*. Don't recall the name. But then again, he probably has no need to stay in a place like this if he is workin' on a pig farm. You might inquire at Kline's What Cheer and Coffee Saloon next door or Jack Douglas Restaurant and Saloon down the street. Many of the locals frequent those bars. They may know of your son there."

"Thank you, Mr. Morgan. We shall." Jonathan reached for the room keys on the counter.

"All right. Please let me know if you need anything. There are plenty of books to read in the parlor upstairs, and the dining room downstairs is open for breakfast, lunch, and dinner."

MARY AND JONATHAN SIPPED ON SARSAPARILLA TEA at a window table in the Jack Douglas Restaurant and Saloon while they observed the cluster of men who entered and exited Columbia's dusty streets. All appeared alike in their dirt-laden attire and worn-out slouch hats as they returned from their gold diggings or a hard day of work at the backwoods farms. Their faces were cracked and sun-drenched beneath their lengthy and scraggly mustaches and beards. Samuel may have gone right past them, yet they would not have known him. She hoped their son would recognize them instead.

"The past six days have been discouragin' at best without one clue to direct us. No one seems to know him. We must be missin' somethin', Jon. Maybe we should be lookin' in Jamestown. After all, that's where he did most of his gold prospectin' and was found intoxicated in their saloon."

Jonathan placed his hand over hers as he poured consolation and wisdom into her anxious, aching soul. "Sweetheart, he's out there. I can feel it in my bones. You're right. Perhaps we aren't lookin' in the right place. We've visited as many pig farms and saloons as we could on this go 'round. But alas, our time has run out, and we must go home. We've our own farm to run. Don't worry, darlin'. He'll show up. The Lord is watchin' over him." Ambling to the bar, he settled his tab, and they returned to the hotel.

Sadness and longing for her son filled the hole in her heart once again as they drove home the next day. Thoughts of Samuel as a wide-eyed, fearless, and competitive young boy flooded her mind. He was always one to live for the moment in search of new experiences, oftentimes not thinking through the consequences of his decision.

She recalled Samuel when he was five as he donned Jonathan's muddy work boots and tripped every step. Then at twelve, when she spied him mimicking his father at his desk while he aspirated on his clay pipe. She chuckled as he dizzied at the tobacco's potency. He gagged and spat and quickly doused its fiery content. Then at fifteen, when he and his father returned from a hunt, minified by his father's grand and numerous trophies.

Yet on countless occasions, Samuel rectified his visage by oppressing his younger brother with challenges too absurd for a boy almost half his age. They climbed tall trees, raced through the wheat fields, swam across the creeks, and wrestled in the barn's loft.

Oh, Samuel. Do you run from home for fear of being a mere shadow of your father? Are you afraid you won't be able to fill his shoes? Trophies are not the mark of manhood, scars are. Please return to us. Endure and finish the race with the joy of knowing all that your father has is your inheritance. We are your parents, and we will not give up on you.

3

Swollen Storm Clouds

"Ow, ow, ow!" Sarah jerked her right hand as she pushed the cast iron skillet's scorching handle toward the back of the wood-burning stove away from three-year-old Amanda's reach while she held Billy, her two-year-old, on her left hip. She had no time to grab her pot holder and run to the stove to avoid a potential accident.

"Don't touch, Amanda. Hot." Her stern eyes met her daughter's. "Come, sit down for some breakfast." She nudged her toward the four-seat pine table in the two-room cabin and placed a terry bib over her white cotton short clothes. "I need to change your brother's and sister's nappies. Just stay there and eat, all right? Don't leave your chair for one moment," she said as gentle but insistent as possible.

"Yes, Mama." Amanda forked into her scrambled eggs.

Sarah rushed to her bedroom, grabbed a couple of clean terry napkins from the children's dresser drawer, and lay Billy on her bed to change him. As soon as she unpinned and removed his soiled diaper, a steady stream fountained in an arc toward her, wetting her apron. "Ha, you naughty boy!" She placed the used napkin over his private part until he stopped urinating.

He giggled, drooled, and clapped his chubby hands.

"You think that's funny, do you?" She tickled his tummy as he rolled and laughed. Turning him, she wiped his bottom, pinned his fresh nappie in place, and adjusted his short clothes. They returned to the kitchen, and she placed him in his wood high chair. "All right, Billy, here's your breakfast." She turned to pat her daughter's head. "How you doin', Amanda?"

"Good, Mama."

"All right, continue eatin', the both of you, while I change Izzy." Sarah marched over to the crib near the stove where one-year-old Isabelle lay staring toward her direction. She peered down at her lethargic daughter, removed her quilt blanket, and scooped her into her arms. "Come on, baby girl, let's get you out of these wet nappies." Returning to her bedroom, Sarah repeated the same routine she did with her son, minus the giggles and laughter.

Amanda was colicky, Billy mischievous, and Isabelle … unresponsive. Each of her children has a personality of their own. Isabelle's character, however, lacked definition. Sarah's pent-up emotions, which ranged from joy to frustration, accumulated inside her like swollen storm clouds that sucked moisture as they moved across rugged plains. The effects of her moodiness manifested itself in her body. *You need to calm yourself, so your milk won't sour. It's hard enough to force-feed Isabelle, but to try to give her unsavory lactation would diminish any chance of increasing her appetite.*

After she changed and readjusted Isabelle's long dress, Sarah unpinned her apron top and unbuttoned her blouse. She gathered Isabelle in her arms and returned to the front room and settled into her rocking chair by the stove.

"Okay, Izzy, are you ready for your breakfast? I sure hope you're goin' ta have a better appetite today." An open jar of honey sat atop the end table, and Sarah dipped her right index finger into it and slathered the sweetness on her baby's tongue. She pushed her blouse aside and positioned Isabelle's head so she could suckle. The warmth of her lips pressed into her breast, but the suckling motion was not there, unlike her first two children.

"Come on, sweetheart. You've gotta eat." She hugged her baby's frail body close to hers and rubbed her cheek. Instinct caused her milk to drip, and Isabelle had no choice but to swallow.

"There you go. Drink, sweetheart."

Sarah relaxed into the creaky rocker as she hummed a soft lullaby and allowed thoughts to stream through her mind. She viewed the dirt path outside the window and imagined Lad returning home from his long four-month cattle drive, which began in early spring.

The drive started from the Goodnight-Loving Trail in Texas, down through New Mexico, Arizona, and finally, California. Lad connected with the wranglers at the second leg in San Diego. The drovers would relocate the livestock to one of the many watering hole locations in Northern California owned by his wealthy employer, Jackson Montana. She expected her husband to return mid-July.

Sarah was still not used to him being away for so long, even though they had been married four years. The truth was she had grown to despise his job and his cowboy friends. Loathsome visions never failed to trouble her of Lad and his comrades as they drifted in and out of small towns to rest and replenish in saloons, intoxicated, and having their way with the saloon girls. In fact, this is how she met Lad at Snelling's dance hall called The Barn. His rough cowpoke friends were not about to change their lifestyles just because he was newly married.

The frustrated thoughts caused her blood to boil. Izzy writhed in her arms and gagged.

"I'm sorry, darlin'. Are you done?" She lifted her daughter to her shoulder and tapped on her back till she burped. Cradling her again, she continued to rock her to sleep.

Aw, sleep. "I wish I could close my eyes like you." Sarah could never get a good night of rest while Lad was gone. She worried about thieves or Indians trespassing their small farm on the outskirts of Mariposa. Why her husband chose to live out here, far away from large communities, baffled her. *I suppose it works for a cowboy who loves open ranges, despite the area's notorious reputation of battling occasional raids instigated by disgruntled Indians.* The thought ran a shiver down her spine. She glanced toward her bedroom at the shotgun that hung over her dresser, hoping she would never have to use it.

However difficult the town was, for Sarah, Mariposa was a reprieve from the painful memories she hoped to leave behind in Snelling. The dangers of this small town taxed less on her than having to deal with the heartbreaking recollections of Joshua, her first love, rekindled at the sight of various landmarks in her family's hometown.

Despite the anamnesis of her first love, she did miss her family something fierce and yearned to return home while Lad was away. But someone had to maintain the small vegetable garden, the half dozen chickens, the pig, milk cow, and horse. They couldn't afford a ranch hand. Besides, Sarah still sensed her parent's resentment toward her because of her unruly and rebellious behavior after Joshua's death. She added to their ill sentiments after she decided to elope with Lad to Mariposa in the spring of 1869.

And now, here she was, alone and miserable with three young children to defend. It was a miracle she wasn't pregnant again when he left in April. Otherwise, she'd be writing home requesting her mother, who helped afford the care needed from a midwife.

Every time Lad had come back, her mother returned home, and the dreaded love-hate cycle began between her and her husband again. For the first few months of his return, they would express intense passion for one another. Then their moods would settle for a stretch of blissful family life, which alleviated her morning sickness. Finally, upon the last month, contention and hurtful arguments would erupt before he departed for the next drive.

Sarah visualized the maddening drama in her mind.

"Sarah, I'll be leaving in a few weeks for San Diego," he'd say.

"How long will you be away this time?"

"I don't know, darlin'. Probably the usual four months."

"Are you goin' to pass by the gamblin' saloons?" She figured her suspicious and fearful interrogations would cause Lad to spin into a fury. Many times, his fists were clenched, ready to plant it across her jaw, but he restrained himself. The watering-hole towns attracted the unrefined, disorderly, ruffian sort of people by providing the finest of debauchery, covetous-filled saloons, avarice, and gambling casinos to fulfill the lusts of the flesh, much of which her cow-poking husband was once accustomed to. She prayed that his love for her would have changed his behavior and wanton desire.

"We will, more than likely. Dag-nab-it, woman, I know what you're drivin' at. What do you want me to do? I can quit work. Is that your answer to our problems? Then how are we goin' to feed our children?"

The weight of his words caused Sarah guilt, confusion, and tears, producing in her a false sense of selfishness. The wails of her toddlers' cries followed shortly after. The entire household would tremble in anguish.

Her focus would turn to the needs of their children. The wages that Lad earned were enough to maintain their small farm. She had to be strong to care for them in his absence. Every ounce of her time and energy seemed to be spent either caring for the livestock or nursing her infants.

Sarah's life assimilated peaks and valleys, never a stable moment. Still buried deep in her heart were acrid feelings toward God, as she blamed Him for Joshua's death. The furthest consideration in her mind was to call upon the Lord for His help. Bittersweet emotions blistered her thoughts as she awaited Lad's return.

Oh, my love, come home to me safe and with a sound mind. She longed for his embrace, yet she was panic-stricken about the thought of another argument.

Soon Lad would be home. The hope of the few months of bliss suppressed her lonesome feelings. However, the anxiety of the repercussions from the melodramatic cycle caused her apprehension. Sarah ached for resolution but did not know where to find it.

4

More Precious Than Gold

"Oh, man … my head. I think I'm gonna be sick." Samuel's temples throbbed, the effects of last night's whiskey. He quivered, clumsily rolled out of his straw and gum blanket bed, and heaved into his washbowl lying on the ground. He wiped his mouth and beard on his long underwear sleeve and lay down.

As Samuel closed his eyes to steady himself, he sensed his blood rush back to his head. The trickling of the small creek in the holler a few yards away triggered another wave of nausea. But he inhaled deep, which forced it to retreat. He began to drift to sleep when he discerned the familiar sound of his horse Fire as he neighed outside of his cold, damp, and shabby wall tent.

"All right, Fire. Wait a moment. We'll get there when we get there."

At least at the pig farm, his horse could graze with the other horses while he worked part-time feeding the livestock. It was located a good two miles outside of the town of Columbia. He begged farmer Pete for a job, aware that the old man did not need nor could he afford to hire help on his small farm. Graciously, out of the mercy of the farmer's heart, he offered him part-time hours, three days a week, at fifty cents a day, enough to purchase his whiskey and a little bread. He also allowed

Sam to pitch his tent next to the creek on his property.

Shaking from lack of food and hungover, he felt defeated and stumbled onto his feet to dress for work.

Neigh, neigh. The hungry horse scratched at the dirt beneath his hooves.

"Okay … okay. I'm starvin', too." Samuel steadied his wobbly legs and slipped them into his dusty trousers and suspenders. He scrounged around his tent, looking for any morsel of bread to calm his queasy stomach. All he was able to find were a couple of corn cobs with a few kernels remaining, which he had taken out of the pig slop two days earlier, and an empty whiskey bottle. Disgusted with his bony reflection on the smoky glass container, he realized the worthless wretch he had become, and a sudden fit of rage raced through his body. In anguish, he took the container and threw it to the ground as he fell to his knees and cried aloud.

"Oh, dear God. What am I doing here? What have I become? Even the pigs are fed better than I am. Please help me." He could not bear the thought of another cold winter without any food in his belly and sleeping in his wet canvas wall tent.

Like the arms of his loving mother, he received a sense of comfort he had not felt before. Returning home to his family had crossed his mind at other times. This was never an option for him before because it meant he would have to lose his pride and accept the fact that he failed at his dream to strike gold and become rich. However, this time, the idea of home seemed appropriate and comforting, now that he had accepted the truth of his wretchedness. He sensed God had forgiven him, and without a shadow of a doubt, his parents would forgive him for his mistake of squandering his inheritance on a covetous lifestyle.

Thank you, Lord. Yep. It's time I go home. This aspiration mustered up energy from some hidden storage room within his wasted being. Enthusiastically, he knew what he had to do. Instead of reporting to work, he decided to tear down camp.

He and Fire rode into Columbia, where Samuel sold his wall tent and cot to one of the gold miners. With the money, he purchased enough food for the three-day journey back to his parents' farmhouse in Snelling.

Samuel gave his horse a carrot as he reminisced. "I betcha Pa is fattenin' up the turkey, and Ma is preparin' all the fixin's for her pumpkin and apple pies."

He figured the mood at the farm would be festive as they prepared for the holidays. November 1866 was the last time he spent Thanksgiving with his family. He returned home for Christmas in 1868 when his gold panning dreams fell apart. Then his last visit was Christmas in 1870, after the completion of the railroad.

This unexpected visit would surprise his parents because he had not written in a long while. His longing to go home burned in his heart and pushed aside his guilty feelings.

"Come on, Fire. Let's go home." Samuel patted his faithful friend's neck and mounted his back for the sobering journey ahead.

AS THE AFTERNOON SHADOWS BEGAN TO LENGTHEN, Mary sat in her oak rocking chair on the farmhouse porch and noticed a silhouette of a horse and its slouched rider who slowly approached along the main wayside path from La Grange Road. The autumn field was dry, leaving a trail of dust behind the unexpected visitor as the steed's hooves kicked up the dirt. Mary recognized the distant, *clip-clop* rhythm that occasionally paused as the hungry animal took a nibble of wheat stubble from the harvested fields.

"Jonny." Mary addressed her husband, who sat with *the San Joaquin Valley Argus* near pressed to his nose. "Someone is comin'."

Peering over the edge of the newspaper, Jonathan squinted, then his jaw dropped. He seemed to recognize the slump of the shadowy and lean figure who sat upon the dark horse.

"Oh, my Lord, I believe that stranger is our long-lost son, Mary." Jonathan stood. He threw the paper down and leaned on the front porch rail. "Yes, it has to be him. Even his slouch hat looks familiar." Jonathan placed his hand across his brows to shade his eyes from the golden rays of the low sun. "It *is* him. Samuel, Samuel!" Jonathan ran down the steps and across the long wayside path to meet their son.

Tears welled up in Mary's eyes as she watched Jonathan run

to Samuel. Her heart leaped and danced inside her chest as goosebumps flitted on her forearms. She grabbed her crocheted shawl off the back of the rocking chair and wrapped it around her trembling shoulders. She had prayed for this moment.

UPON RECOGNITION OF HIS FATHER'S WELCOMING VOICE, Samuel gave Fire a little kick with his spurs to quicken his stride toward him. As soon as they were close enough, Samuel dismounted his horse and ran to his father.

"Oh, my son, you're home. We've missed you so much."

Samuel did not expect his father to greet him so warmly. Conviction grieved him for his lack of communication in the last few years.

"Pa, will you forgive me? I'm so sorry. I apologize for leavin' and not visitin' or writin' you in a while. But I'm back, if you'll take me."

His father reached out and wrapped his arms around him. Samuel immersed himself in his loving embrace as his father patted his shoulders and rubbed his fingers across his bony back. Malnutrition ravaged his once sturdy body. He knew his downcast countenance projected the same lack of sustenance.

The look in his father's eyes expressed his thoughts. *I told you so.* But he never criticized or judged him. Sam hoped his words of repentance were enough to satisfy his father's chastisement.

"You're my son, Sam, and our door is forever open to you. You'll always have a place to lay down your head here. Now, come on, I believe your Ma is as anxious to hug you."

His father placed his arm around his shoulder as they walked toward the farmhouse, and Fire followed.

As soon as they were several yards from the house, his mother ran to them and embraced him.

"Oh, Samuel, we're so glad to have you back. Please tell me you're home to stay."

"I am, Ma. I'm so sorry I failed you both and left when you needed me most. My plans didn't turn out as I hoped, and now, I have nothin' that can make you proud of me. Will you let me come back and work for you?"

"Samuel, you are our eldest son, and all of this is your inheritance, if you want it," his mother said, pointing to the farmhouse and fields.

Straightaway, his father removed the gold band on his right hand, leaving his wedding band on his left, and placed it on Samuel's right ring finger.

I've always admired this ring.

"This ring was passed down to me from your grandfather before he went to be with the Lord. He wanted me to remember I was carryin' the family name. Now I'm goin' to pass this heirloom to you, Samuel, as the eldest son of the Sower clan and heir to this estate. This is my promise to you."

A lump formed in Samuel's throat as he revered the band of gold on his finger. Amongst all the gold nuggets he panned for the last few years, none of those stones could compare in value to the ring, which was now in his possession.

"But Pa, I don't deserve this." Samuel sobbed as he stumbled on the words.

"It doesn't matter whether you deserve it or not. I'm doin' this because I love you, son. So, say no more. Why don't you get your things and take your old bed in David's room while I put Fire in his stall in the barn. David and Naomi will be excited to have you home," his father said with sternness in his voice.

Huang-Fu, shuffled out the front door and immediately proceeded to assist his father, removing Samuel's saddlebags and personal effects from Fire's back. Huang-Fu followed behind Samuel and his mother as they entered the farmhouse and walked up the staircase to the bedroom of his youth. He placed his belongings on the floor at the foot of his old bed, now utilized as a spare when visitors came.

"Why don't you get settled in and take a hot bath before supper? I'll bring you some of your father's clean clothes for you to wear until Liang can wash yours. Naomi an' David should be home soon an' would be very surprised to see you."

"Thank you, Ma, for everythin'."

Samuel kissed his mother on her lightly powdered cheek before she exited the room. She requested Huang-Fu to fetch the kettle of boiling water on the stove and a bucket of cool water from the artesian pump in the kitchen for the bath.

While Samuel perused the familiar farmhouse bedroom, he mused at David's Bible and belongings gathered on the dresser bureau. On the floor perched against the wall beside the spare bed was his old fiddle case, which he had not touched since the last Christmas he visited. He dared not take it with him to work, simply because he had no time to play or practice and for fear of it being destroyed.

Samuel removed the fiddle from its case and softly plucked at the strings to tune it. He sat on the bed, grabbed the bow, and rubbed it with rosin. As the instrument rested under his chin, he closed his eyes and began to play the warm melody "Home Sweet Home," taking in every note of his dear old companion that reclined in his arms again.

WHILE SHE POURED A GLASS OF LEMONADE in the kitchen, Mary paused as the soft, familiar music wafted through the once-active rooms of the farmhouse, reminding her of the memorable moments when the entire family engulfed themselves in the songs they played. She, too, closed her eyes and allowed the song to reach the deepest of warm past recollections of her children's adolescence. Samuel's return brought about a sense of completion and an end to an unsolved mystery, which had plagued her every thought. Now she could rest, and her mind and spirit were finally at ease. *Thank you, Lord, for bringing Samuel home safe. I do pray his wanderin' days are over, and he can envision his destiny here on the farm. Open his eyes to appreciate the value of his inheritance.*

SAMUEL PLACED HIS PRECIOUS FIDDLE and bow into its case. Then he removed his dusty boots, gun belt, and worn-out hat and piled them on the floor at the foot of his bed. As he opened his saddlebags, he unpacked what few items of dirty clothes he had and dropped them in the wicker basket by the doorway.

He could hear Huang-Fu pouring the hot and cool water into the slipper-shaped tin tub. Afterward, the butler gently knocked on the bedroom door. "Mr. Samuel, your bath is ready. I will take your laundry when you are done."

His mother came upstairs with a glass of lemonade and handed the tangy refreshment to him as she held his hand.

"It's so wonderful to have you home, son." She hugged him as her eyes teared, then she proceeded to her bedroom to gather some of his father's clothes as Samuel followed. After she placed the clothing on the small table next to the tub, she turned and held his face. "Take your time and relax, son. You're home now."

Samuel sank into the warm, soothing bath, stretched out, leaned back, and closed his eyes. He soaked in all the pleasantries of home again as he listened to the sound of laughter and chatter from his parents, the smell of supper cooking, the taste of fresh lemonade, and the thought of slumber in the comfort of his soft, cozy bed. His mind drifted as he reminisced, blissfully falling asleep in the temperate water.

5

Welcome Back

Footsteps clamoring up the staircase interrupted Samuel's restful moment as he soaked in the tin tub. He did not realize how long he had been asleep. Dreaming seemed like only seconds, but half an hour had passed, and the bath had become lukewarm.

Tap, tap, tap. The rugged knocks on the bathroom door intensified, followed by the cheerful, anxious, and familiar voices of Samuel's sister, Naomi, and brother, David.

"Sam … Sam, are you in there? Welcome home!"

Still in a daze, Samuel splashed his face with water. "Yeah, I'm back. Give me a moment. I'll be right out."

He grabbed the bar of soap and finished his bath, dried himself, and put on his borrowed clothing. In anticipation of what would occur once he swung the door open, Sam took a deep breath. David and Naomi pushed the portal open after he twisted the knob. His siblings stood with wide-eyes and grinned like bright beacons of light. They leaped into his arms with enormous bear hugs and laughter. Tears of joy pooled in their eyes.

"We were so worried about you, Sam. We've been prayin' for you day and night hopin' we'd hear *from* you, instead of hearin' *about* you." Naomi expelled kind chastisement.

"I apologize for puttin' y'all through the agony of not being made aware of my whereabouts," Samuel said, frowning. "After the railroad, half the time I wasn't sure which direction my feet would take me and where to fetch my next meal. I thank you for prayin' for me. I think your prayers kept me alive. If I weren't dead from someone else's hand, I would've been from my own." Samuel stared at the floor, ashamed to look at them in their eyes.

"Well, you're home now, Sam, and we love you. God does the savin', not us. We make avail our requests to Him and accredit Him for His works." David comforted him as he gave the Lord credit. "Come on. Let's go downstairs for supper."

MARY AND JONATHAN OVERHEARD their adult children's conversation from his office. She also wept to experience their laughter once again. The trio's bantering triggered a flood of memories and emotions hidden deep within herself.

Often she wished time would reverse to when her children attended grade school. The age of innocence. Carefree, yet trusting and dependent on their parents and their wisdom. The words she or her husband spoke weighed as gospel truth and her children's obedience instantaneous.

The age of accountability began when her children reached middle to high school age. Each of her children struggled with this formidable time as they discover their strengths and push the grade school boundaries she and her husband set. Samuel found himself wanting material wealth. Sarah is discovering love's difficulties. Naomi lacks discernment when choosing friends. And David desires to preach before becoming an adult. They are aware of right from wrong. However, they resent their parents telling them what to do, so they must experience life's proverbial challenges first hand.

Mary relaxed into her chair, and her spirit lifted as she reflected upon the age of responsibility. Her children are experiencing personal challenges and coming into adulthood. They will realize the old sages' proverbs are true to life as they remember what was taught them in their youth and apply the adages to their life situations. Isaiah 55:11 came to her mind.

So shall my word be that goeth forth out of my mouth: it shall not return unto me void, but it shall accomplish that which I please, and it shall prosper in the thing whereto I sent it.

Oh, Lord, I do pray this is true for my children. Bring scripture back to their remembrance when they encounter struggles. As difficult as they may be, I do look forward to this time when my children will become responsible adults and once again recognize and appreciate me and Jonathan and the decisions we've made as parents. Samuel is crossing this hurdle. Sarah, I pray will be the next. The thought of her eldest daughter apart from her siblings rekindled Mary's maternal longing.

"If only Sarah could be here, too," her thoughts poured from her lips.

"She will be soon enough after news of Sam's return reaches her." Jonathan stood from his wingback chair by the fireplace and extended his hand to Mary. "Shall we join our family for supper?"

SAMUEL'S EYES ENLARGED, AND HIS STOMACH GROWLED as Liang and her nineteen-year-old daughter, Jia-Li, laid platters of food before him.

Jia-Li was almost sixteen when Sam saw her briefly during his last Christmas visit. Although a teenager at that time, she had a ten-year-old stature. The Suens' were new employees then, and Sam was too preoccupied with his instability to recognize them.

His senses dulled by the ache in his belly, Samuel glanced at Jia-Li's blossomed beauty then diverted his attention to the exotic cuisine. As usual, the family joined hands as his father lead the prayer.

"Heavenly Father, we thank You for Your grace and mercy toward us and especially for watchin' after our son, Samuel. We are ever so grateful for his return, Lord. We continue to pray for our daughter, Sarah, and her family. We also ask for your blessin's upon our entire household, farmhands, and employees, and this wonderful meal set before us. In Jesus' name. Amen."

Exotic spices and seasonings tantalized his taste buds. Ginger, cinnamon, cardamom, curry powder, Sichuan pepper stir-fried into vegetables not yet discovered by Western civilization. Bok choy cabbage, snow peas, Chinese eggplant, dried mushrooms, and silk squash.

Samuel recalled the first time he had tasted Chinese food at Mr. Chung's general store in Chinese Camp near LaGrange eight years ago, then during the holidays when he last visited home, and also while having supper with his Chinese railroad gang in Promontory, Utah. He had not had a healthy, home-cooked meal in what seemed like ages. He was ravenous and was not ashamed to demonstrate his delight in the delectable sensation. "Umm, umm. Delicious. I think I can live on this food for the rest of my life."

"Welcome home, Mr. Samuel." Jia-Li giggled, and her eyes twinkled. "We are happy you like our cooking."

After supper, he gathered with his family around the sitting room fireplace to reacquaint themselves as they shared the events that occurred while apart. Samuel shivered as he recalled difficult moments working the railroad. He wrapped a crocheted throw around his shoulders and pulled his chair close to the hearth.

"On many occasions, I wanted to write to y'all, but the numbness in my fingers prohibited me. I'm capable of sledging a hammer for ten hours, but holdin' a delicate instrument like a dip pen at the end of a cold, hard day deemed too difficult for these calloused hands." Samuel opened and closed his fists as he demonstrated the lack of refined agility.

Mary pouted. "A simple note tellin' us you were fine and alive would've sufficed."

"I tried, Ma. But by the end of the day, hunger and exhaustion reaped the best of my Chinese gang and me. After a meal, we barely had enough time to take care of personal business before fatigue set in, and sleep became a priority."

Comparing roughened palms, Jonathan shook his head in agreement. "I'm quite familiar with exhaustion workin' the fields under the sun's extreme heat. However, I've yet to experience, nor do I desire the gruelin' conditions the railroad requires of their employees.”

“You’re correct, Pa. The mountain ranges of the Sierras are harsh and unforgivin’. The heat from blastin’ didn’t affect the frigid cold one bit. My men and I worked in three continuous shifts, day and night so that the snow did not build up around our work. The men slaved without rest to meet the railroad’s deadlines.” Water filled Sam’s eyes. “I lost several good men in blasts, on steep ravines, and yes to the freezin’ cold temperatures.”

David placed his comforting arm around Samuel’s shoulder. “One’s heart grows fond of these dedicated and industrious people.”

“And scarce do they complain too.” Jonathan leaned into his chair and puffed on his pipe.

The Suen family entered the room and bowed. “Mr. Sower, if you no longer need us, we will retire now,” the butler said.

“Thank you once again, Huang-Fu, Liang, and Jia-Li.” Jonathan paused then snapped his finger. “Come to think of it, I do want to share for a moment what is on my mind. How ‘bout we plan a grand Thanksgiving celebration to welcome my son home? I thank President Lincoln for makin’ this an official holiday. We’ve been celebratin’ this time of gatherin’ to express our gratitude to our good Lord for ten years now. Samuel’s homecomin’ gives us much to be thankful for.

“Huang-Fu, you may select a prime heifer and turkeys from our stock and prepare an extravagant meal for our guests. I’m sure my wife will assist you by providin’ some of our Thanksgivin’ recipes. Hire as many farmhands as needed to organize this event. Of course, I plan to compensate you and those who help.” His father’s eyes sparkled as his siblings responded, mouths gaped at the wonderful idea.

Samuel stood from the sofa and knelt by his father’s chair to extend him a handshake. The gold band on his finger reflected the room’s candlelight. No words came to his mind to express the overwhelming emotion in his heart.

The sudden hush in the room caused Samuel to draw attention to Naomi, whose intent focus glared at the ring. The countenance on her face changed to a gloomy frown and emanated a distressed, unspoken tension that deflated his joy like a dagger. He realized Naomi must have been the only sibling who labored on the farm alongside their parents after he and Sarah left home, and David fixated on church ministry. *Ah, sister, I bet you're wishin' I never came back. This place means a lot to you, and I bet you hoped to inherit the farm.* Cringing at the thought of contention between them, he turned to his father and hoped she didn't catch his observance of her.

"Oh, of course, Mr. Sower, we would be honored to do this for you," the butler said. "Allow me a day to think about the preparations, and I will discuss it with you later. Is this all for now?"

"Yes, Huang-Fu. Thank you. Have a good evenin'."

"The same to you, Mr. Sower. Again, welcome back, Mr. Samuel."

The Suen family bowed and left the room.

His mother placed her knitting on her lap, nodded at the Suens', and then turned to him to share their story.

"You may recall, Sam, we hired this wonderful family to do all the cookin' for our entire household. They came to America as servants for Huang-Fu's brother, who was a wealthy international merchant. Some anti-Chinese thugs murdered him, ransacked his cargo, and set fire to his vessel while Huang-Fu and his family purchased provisions on shore.

"Mr. Suen had to find a safe place right away for his family, in particular for his daughter. If not for his brother's respectable reputation amongst the Chinese aristocrats, Jia-Li would've been abducted from them by some powerful Tong community in the United States, brought into slavery, and then forced into prostitution. Jia-Li is Huang-Fu and Liang's only child and the only grandchild in his family.

"After his brother's murder, the Suen family found refuge at a Methodist church in San Francisco." She stopped for a moment.

David stepped in to continue their story. "Pastor McSwan explained to me that this Protestant denomination had sent missionaries to Nanking, China, in 1847, and developed an indigenous leadership. Seven men amongst these leaders were ordained as deacons and four as elders. These four had converted from Confucianism to Christianity. The gospel reached the Suens' for the first time while at Nanking, through one of the preachers named Hu Yong-Mi.

"Well, the church in San Francisco contacted our church to notify us of their plight and that their distant relative resided at

Snelling's China camp.

"If I hadn't been workin' with Pastor McSwan in our church office that day, I would've not intercepted the telegraph from San Francisco by the courier that afternoon. That was God's plan for me to receive that message," David said lambent, sharing his testimony about God's orchestration of events in their lives.

"Pastor McSwan and I knew all too well the China camp was not conducive for a husband and wife with a young daughter, not when ninety-five percent of the population is male, and the remaining are women of ill repute. I didn't have the heart to send them to live at the camp. Then the thought occurred to me that their services may be useful to our family and our Chinese workers. So I informed Pa and Ma straight away." His younger brother glanced over to their mother, who continued the story.

"So we offered them food, a small wage, and the use and security of our cabin in trade of their household services. Huang-Fu needed to protect his womenfolk from the Chinese men in California. Single Chinese women are not safe in the camps.

"They do a splendid job maintainin' our farmhouse and the small garden and fruit trees I planted in the backyard a few years ago. We have a meaningful and trustworthy relationship with them. Aren't they wonderful?" Samuel's mother said.

"Yes, they are a delightful family." Samuel realized he had not met women of this nationality elsewhere on his journey. He had always labored with Chinese men, whether they were farmhands or railroad workers. The women seemed as polite and humble as their male counterparts but with an ounce more gentleness and acquiescence. Their meekness added a sense of mystery about them. Sam understood Huang-Fu's desire to protect his precious possessions.

"So, Sam, tell us more of your experiences workin' on the railroad." His father interrupted his thoughts. The family continued to share stories until the fire burnt to embers. Soon, they, too, retired for the evening. Sam's heart and mind filled to overflowing with visions of what lay ahead for him on the farm.

THE FOLLOWING TWO WEEKS before Thanksgiving were an adjustment period for Jonathan's eldest son. He realized Samuel did not know how successful he had become in the wheat industry. They rode the horses around the perimeter of the 2,500 acres of grain land. Afterward, Jonathan gave Samuel an orientation of the grounds and the two barns, one he remodeled and the other he built since Sam's last visit.

Sam's jaw dropped as he viewed the new barn. It was double the size of the first and housed the farming equipment and some of the livestock steers, heifers, and milking cows, along with the hens and turkeys. "Golly, Pa. You must be one of the wealthiest land barons on this side of California."

"No, not quite. There's another fella on the other side of town that owns 3,500 acres of wheat land." Jonathan snickered. "However, we've got an edge on him now that we've purchased all these new farmin' inventions and use the more affordable and efficient Chinese labor. We'll be able to get our grain to market faster and fetch a better price than his. The demand for our quality economic wheat may force him out of business unless he changes his ways. Come on, let me show you how these contraptions work." Jonathan instructed Sam on how to use and maintain the new inventions.

Afterward, Jonathan brought his son over to the widened corral and the old reconstructed barn that housed the mules and horses. "You see, son, all of this will one day be yours. My hope is for you to take the reins. For now, my desire is for you to become the second man in control of this operation." Jonathan's mindset changed from employer to employee, to a father speaking to his son.

"David plans to leave for college soon. I believe he is destined to be a minister of the gospel, and the Lord will call him somewhere. He'll be sowin' seeds all right. Seeds of the Word of God, and the world is his field. Ma and I are delighted with the direction in which God is takin' him.

"As for Sarah, she has her family to care for, although I plan on offerin' her husband a position here on the farm.

"Last but not least is Naomi. If you didn't return, she would've inherited the majority. She, without fail, has proven her desire to care for this business and has done a good job. My intention is for her to receive a portion. However, one day Naomi, too, will find a husband and raise a family. In light of this situation, I prefer to keep the property and business in the Sower name for generations to come.

"So, you see how grateful I am you returned, son, and pray you had a change of heart toward the ownership of this fine land. I hope we are seein' eye to eye on this. Your position on this matter is important to me." Jonathan sat down on a hay bale as he allowed Samuel to speak his mind.

His eyes followed his son as he paced, rubbing the back of his neck and shoulders, shaking his head. *Hmm, what might he be thinkin'? Maybe my proposition is too much for him to take in all at once. He looks a bit overwhelmed.*

"Pa, I hope I can measure up to you and meet your expectations," Samuel blurted out. "I realize how much work you poured into this farm. The responsibilities are great. I, I do not want to fail you and Ma."

Realizing his son's insecurities, Jonathan did his best to quiet Samuel's innermost fears. "Have a seat next to me, son." He pointed to another hay bale as Samuel sat, head lowered. "I understand your concerns. The honor and responsibility are indeed great to receive such an inheritance. When your Grandpa passed on, I inherited his farm in Kentucky. However, the bad memories and destruction of the Civil War outweighed your Grandpa's good intent. The decision to sell the property was difficult for me.

"My deepest fear was that I had failed my father's dreams of ownin' land and keepin' the property in the family. Staying in Kentucky doomed us to despair, and our family rejected that inheritance because of the entangled misery. I realized I must retain my father's dream even if it meant finding a different location. But where?

"We don't have the ability to foresee the future. Only God has that endowment. All we can do is trust Him to guide us in life. We have to anticipate the doors of opportunity He opens and the doors He shuts. His will is the right answer for me, which is California.

"The life scripture that I hold dear to my heart is Proverbs 16:9,

'A man's heart deviseth his way: but the LORD directeth his steps.'

"The Lord led you back home, and your inheritance is an open door for you, son. Your concern shouldn't be to please me, but rather to please the Father above. I do expect you to pray 'bout this opportunity and seek God's will in your life. From that point forward, He'll direct you. And when God is leadin' the way, who am I to advise or judge what He has asked you to do?" Jonathan patted his son's shoulder.

"Pa, I will, and I perceive God's guidance in sendin' me here. All I have to offer *is* my best to the Lord and to you, which is all that you see standin' before you. I love you and Ma and am so grateful."

Jonathan stood and embraced his son to reassure him.

The day came to an end, and the three Chinese superintendents, Yung, Sheng-Li, and Tu, entered the first barn. The majority of the farmhands took leave after the harvest and planned to return in March after the rainy season was over, then the plowing and planting cycle began again. Only the three superintendents remained to care for the grounds.

"Ah, good timin', men. Let me introduce you to my firstborn son, Samuel." Jonathan gestured, his chest inflated. "Sam, these are my trusted superintendents. You've met Head Supervisor Ah-Yung. And this is Superintendent Sheng-Li and Tu." The men shook hands. "Sam is the heir to my estate. I will be trainin' him to oversee the farm. I expect you men to receive him as your superior."

6

A Grand Celebration

"Everythin' looks absolutely magnificent, Huang-Fu and Sheng-Li. Your family and the superintendents did an outstandin' job settin' up and decoratin' for our Thanksgivin' celebration. Our guest will never know this is a farm," Jonathan said as he perused the ten tables and chairs arranged in his front yard as his staff followed. "My family and I have lived in Snelling for nine years, and not once have we entertained on this scale. We are expectin' family, friends, and some local farmers from our community. So as you might imagine, I am a bit nervous. This event must run without any hiccups so that we make a lastin' impression with our neighbors."

Huang-Fu wagged his finger. "Not to worry, Mr. Sower. Sheng-Li and I have everything under control."

"Yes, you relax and enjoy party. Mingle with neighbors. We take care of the rest," Sheng-Li's eyes danced with excitement. "You will not lose face. It is our chance also to show Snelling our Chinese abilities. They will see we are a noble people too." He bowed.

"Indeed, you are. And clever too." Jonathan inhaled deep to relax. Footsteps coming from the farmhouse caught his attention. "Aha! My lovely wife will be most pleased."

"Oh, my!" Mary gasped, holding her hand to her heart. She walked down the porch steps toward one of the tables and admired its autumn adornment. "Who created these masterpieces? How appropriate for the occasion. A basket of dried corn, small squash, red apples, wheat stalks, and sunflowers."

"Liang and Jia-Li did, madam." A wide grin crossed Huang-Fu's face as he turned to his wife and daughter.

"Your talents are remarkable and dually noted." Mary ran her fingers over one of the table settings. "Our church friends will appreciate their china and silverware, addin' to the finishin' touches of the table's décor."

"Oh, look yonder, darlin'. Here comes the Snellin' Band." Jonathan turned his sight toward the barn where the musicians were unloading their instruments. "I'll direct them to the porch." He walked over to their wagon, pointed them toward the farmhouse, and then returned. "Well, our guests will be arrivin' soon. Are we ready to receive them?"

"We are, sir." Huang-Fu, his spouse, daughter, and the three superintendents, dressed in embroidered silk shirts with frog buttons and linen trousers, bowed. They scurried to their stations.

"And I failed to mention how beautiful you look, my dear." Jonathan doted over his wife in a high-bustled russet taffeta skirt and bodice, flaunting layers of ruffles and cream-colored lace. "Your gown accentuates the auburn ringlets drapin' from beneath your feathered bonnet."

Mary opened her fan and began to wave it. "Why, thank you, my love. I do believe you're makin' me blush." She fluttered her eyelashes and then fancied his masculine physique. "And you are quite handsome yourself in your frock coat and top hat." She adjusted his thin cravat. "There you are. Perfect."

"Shall we go fetch our family?" He lifted his right hand toward her, and she placed her gloved hand over his as they glided into the farmhouse.

"*Oompa, oompa, boom, boom, boom.*" The quadrille band's tuba, trombone, clarinet, and bass drum blared out tunes. The fiddler played along and would later call out instructions during the contra dance. The guests poured in as Jonathan, Mary, Samuel, Naomi, and David greeted.

Amongst the arrivals were the McSwan family, Patrick and Ingrid Fay, Eustace and Marlena Kelly, Frederick Maxfield, church members and their families, and other prominent citizens of Snelling, totaling eighty people. The womenfolk promenaded in their finest bustled ball gowns and the gentlemen in their frock coats or sack suits, cravats, and top hats or derbies.

Jonathan near choked when Sarah and her family stepped in line to be greeted. Although he knew the Hamptons had been invited, he wasn't sure his emotions were ready for this moment. No words would come to his lips.

"Pa, this is my husband, Lad, and our children, Amanda, Billy," she removed the veil from her baby's face swaddled in her daddy's arms, "and this is Isabelle."

"My darlin', Sarah. I've missed you in a terrible way. Welcome home." Fighting the tears, he took hold of her right hand and planted a kiss. He knelt on one knee to get to Amanda's eye level. "My, aren't you the sweetest young thing. You are the spittin' image of your mama when she was your age. Would you mind givin' your papaw a hug?"

"Go on, Mandy. Give him a hug." Sarah nudged her, and they embraced. Meanwhile, Mary gathered Billy in her arms.

Jonathan stood and extended a handshake to Sarah's husband. "Finally, I have the pleasure to meet my son-in-law. Welcome to Sower Farms, Lad. This weekend sometime we shall get better acquainted." Turning to his family, he brought them forward. "You've met my wife, Mary. This is Sarah's siblin's, Samuel, Naomi, and David."

Lad's face flushed. "The favor is mine to meet the entire family after all these years. I do look forward to our time together this weekend." His eyes rested on Samuel. "I've heard much about Sarah's big brother. Welcome back, Sam."

"Glad to be home." Samuel chuckled. "I've been a bit of a riddle to my family the past few years as you have, Lad. The wandering son and unknown brother-in-law finally appears. The missing pieces of the puzzle are found. We can put our family's minds at ease now that the mystery is solved." He shook Lad's hand. "Yes, I look forward to gettin' to know you also."

"We've hired a nanny for this occasion, dear. She is indoors." Mary turned toward the farmhouse. "Come. Let's bring the children to her, then you both can take a seat at our family's table."

After the children were situated and the adults seated, Jonathan stood on the porch in front of the band to make his announcement. "Happy Thanksgivin', dear friends and family. My wife and I are thankful and honored to have you join us in celebratin' the return of our eldest son, Samuel." He pointed to Samuel, who sat at the head table with the family.

The guests applauded as Samuel humbly stood from his seat and bowed. His face turned pinkish due to the attention he received from the cheering crowd. Joy radiated through his beaming grin.

Oh, my son, I hope your roamin' days are over. There's much to look forward to here in your hometown.

Jonathan shifted his sight to observe Sarah and Lad squirming at the table. They held hands and stared at their plates. She fussed with her hair, and he tugged at his cravat. The young couple's distress was veiled by their awkward pretenses, faux chortles, and grins.

They must've wrestled with the idea of attendin' this celebration. Well, at some point, they had to amend their relationship with the family— what better time to do so than durin' Thanksgivin' and Sam's return.

In anticipation of Sarah and Lad's anxieties, Jonathan made it a point to forgive them and dismiss any ill sentiments. He even afforded them a room at the Snelling Hotel, should Lad feel uncomfortable around them. After all, this was his first time to introduce himself after four years of marriage to his eldest daughter and fathering his three grandchildren.

Scanning his family, Jonathan became aware of Naomi's intense gaze upon Samuel. Anger and jealousy reared their ugly head as she clenched her teeth behind a lucid smile and clapped with arduous effort. She gloated as her eldest brother received the attention she never had, despite her travail on the farm. He couldn't blame her for her heartache. Samuel made a mess of his life, yet he was receiving the honor.

After this event is over, I'm to expect an ear full from her. Ever since she was caught stealing for the Edgar siblings during grade school, years ago,

Naomi's never been one to conceal her feelings from me or her ma.

Then there was David, who sat quietly, observing the family members much like what he was doing.

He probably discerns the tension and is prayin' for each of us as I speak; for Samuel and his misguided life, for Sarah and Lad and their troubled marriage, for Naomi and her pent-up emotions, and for his mother and me and the drama we'll have to face the next few days.

Jonathan continued to welcome his guests, "As y'all know, we were worried for Samuel an' we thought we lost him to this impoverished world. We are grateful to all of you who have prayed with diligence for his safe return. The Lord is faithful, and we acknowledge His mighty hand of grace as He watched over Samuel, even durin' his darkest hour of need. I'd like y'all to join us in prayer as we thank our wonderful Father in heaven for His goodness and also ask for His blessins' upon the meal."

Jonathan and his guests bowed their heads and closed their eyes as he prayed. "Heavenly Father, we stand humbled before You. Your love and mercy abound to us who are undeservin' of Your grace. Great is Your faithfulness, despite our failures and our weaknesses.

"I thank You, Father, for the friends and family before me and for watchin' after my son, Samuel, and returnin' him home safely.

"Please bless all of our lives and continue to guide and protect us. Lord, we pray for Your blessin's for this bounty of food and upon this evenin' as we gather with a heart of thanksgivin' for what You have done to save us through Your precious Son, Jesus Christ. In His name, we pray. Amen."

The guests agreed. "Amen."

Jonathan joined his family at the table, and with immediacy, Huang-Fu, Liang, Jia-Li, and the three superintendents, Yung, Sheng-Li, and Tu, began to serve the turkey and all the fixings. Everyone was pleased and commented on the servant's fine work.

Unbeknownst to Fred Maxfield, Jonathan noticed him sneering at his employees as they received accolades from the guest. Before the staff reached his table, the disgruntled land baron dismissed himself. *Hmm, where is he goin'? To the outhouse? No.* Jonathan's gaze followed him as he snuck around the back of the barn, skedaddled to his carriage, and departed the grounds.

Throughout the town and known to all, Maxfield had prejudices toward the Chinese people and hired only white farmworkers, despite the wage differences and their lack of efficiency. So many yellow-skinned foreigners, as they were called by the town's people, migrated to California to seek the American dream. It caused Fred and those who worked for him to become resentful. Many of Jonathan's employees complained to him about Maxfield's ill-mannered practices toward them, from ostracizing to being lynched. Although the Chinese did the work other immigrants chose not to do, Fred still resented the fact they took the jobs, finished well, and found favor in the eyes of their employers.

If only Fred could overcome his prejudices, he'd discover that the answer to his financial difficulties to improve his business lies in hiring more affordable and reliable employees. The money he'd save might be used to upgrade his agin' farmin' equipment and livestock. I do believe hell would freeze over first before the likeliness of that would ever happen. A misfortune for him indeed.

"Enjoy your meal, Mr. Sower," Sheng-Li said as he set a prepared dish before him filled with a grand helping of roast beef, turkey, gravy, sweet potatoes, corn, green beans, and cranberry sauce.

Jonathan's eyes grew large, and his mouth watered. "Indeed, I shall. Y'all have outdone yourselves. The meal's presentation is superb and your service is excellent. I commend each of you."

"Thank you, sir. I shall inform the others of your gratefulness." Sheng-Li bowed and proceeded with serving the remaining guest.

The gaiety commenced after the guest consumed their meal. The employees cleared the tables and washed the dishes as the band continued to play music throughout the evening. The guest found themselves mingling and discussing each other's affairs as some kicked up their heels and waltzed on the front lawn.

Mary's taffeta skirt swished as Jonathan whisked her about to the song's tempo. Her palm in his she invoked praises. "Jonathan, I do believe this celebration is a success."

"I do hope so. If anything, I pray our neighbors' doubts and suspicions for the Chinese is alleviated through our staff's well-organized efforts for this event and their excellent mannerism."

After everyone had departed, Jonathan and his family retired for the night after they agreed to dismantle and clean-up the subsequent day. Sarah, Lad, and the children returned to the hotel and planned to return to the farm in the morning. All were pleasantly exhausted.

In bed, Jonathan kissed his wife. "And now, darlin', let's get some rest. We'll need it for what lies ahead the next few days."

7

Selfish and Jealous

Pa, the welcome home festivities for Samuel were sensational. How come you've never given me such a grand affair for all my hard work on the farm? "Yes. No. Ah, that won't do at all," Naomi spoke to herself in bed as she stared at the ceiling. The words went round and round in her head all night long, not allowing one ounce of sleep. The rooster crowed, and it was time for her to rise, milk the cow, and collect the eggs for breakfast.

Last night's gala made her blood boil. *Samuel this and Samuel that. Don't I count for anything around here?* She couldn't lay in bed any longer, so she sat up, stretched her arms above her head, and filled her lungs with air to jump-start her body for the never-ending farm chores.

A hint of dawn lightened her curtains, providing enough illumination for her to stumble in the morning shadows. Locating the matches on her nightstand, she lit the oil lamp. The frumpy day dress and apron hung from her beds post awaiting another day's dirt and grime as she traipsed the dusty grounds and handled the livestock. After dawning her earthy attire, she combed out her long locks and tucked it into a snood. With woolen socks, boots, and her winter cape on she caught her reflection in the long mirror, and her stomach turned. *It's no wonder you haven't caught a man's eye yet. Look at you, Naomi, soon to be an old maid before your time.*

"Oh, phooey," she said to her image. "Farmin' is all I have. Perhaps I need to find a life outside of this place. Maybe I should follow Sarah's footsteps, fetch me a lavish gown, and go cavortin' at the contra dance in town."

No. Don't you dare, Naomi. Where is your sense of decency? A voice within, other than her reasoning mind, startled her. *A good Christian lady wouldn't do such a thing. Be patient and wait on Me.*

"What? Who said that?" Her eyes swept the room. "Great, now I'm hearin' things."

Do you not recognize My voice? My sheep do. The inaudible utterance said.

Scripture from John 10:4 came to her remembrance, *When he putteth forth his own sheep, he goeth before them, and the sheep follow him: for they know his voice.* "Is that you, Lord Jesus speaking to me?" Naomi turned away from the mirror and turned her face toward the ceiling as if peering toward heaven.

Yes. It is I, the Great I Am. Be not afraid for I go before you. Cast your cares upon Me, for I care for you.

"1 Peter 5:7," she said. Her knees buckled, and she planted her face on the floor in shame. "Lord, please forgive me. I'm a wretch not worthy of recognition. My own father does not see me of value. Why should you?"

I am near to those who have a broken heart, and save such as have a contrite spirit.

"Psalm 34:18." A flood of warmth blanketed her, much like an eagle surrounding her hatchling beneath its wing. Abundant love followed causing her to lift her head and sit upright to speak face-to-face in the Holy Spirit's presence. "Lord, please help me speak my heart to my father. I pray that's the right thing to do."

Moreover, if thy brother shall trespass against thee, go and tell him his fault between thee and him alone: if he shall hear thee, thou hast gained thy brother.

"Matthew 18:15." She wept and shivered with humility.

Be careful for nothing; but in everything by prayer and supplication with thanksgiving let your requests be made known unto God. And the peace of God, which passeth all understanding, shall keep your hearts and minds through Christ Jesus.

"Philippians 4:6,7. Thank you, Lord. I put my trust in you. Amen."

Bewildered by the moment, she stood and saw her reflection in the mirror again. However, this time a glow radiate about her. Despite the drab attire, her face shined in a modest beauty. The Lord touched her in a way unexplainable that only she can describe.

A bolstered confidence energized her, so she marched downstairs, grabbed the milk bucket and egg basket from the kitchen, and then hustled to the barn to complete her daily chores. Her heart danced as the sun's tip kissed the horizon to begin a new day. Barn door in hand, she opened it wide to allow light inside while finding her way to her favorite cow's stall.

"Good mornin', Betsy." Naomi settled on her stool and placed the bucket beneath the cow's utters. "There is a song in my heart. I shall sing to you Savior, Like a Shepherd Lead Us." The melody flowed from her lips. Betsy's tail wagged, and the lactation streamed as Naomi tugged in rhythm.

"Savior, like a shepherd lead us, much we need thy tender care.
In Thy pleasant pastures feed us, for Thy use Thy folds prepare.
Blessed Jesus, blessed Jesus, Thou hast bought us, Thine we are.
Thou hast promised to receive us, poor and sinful though we be.
Thou hast mercy to relieve us, grace to cleanse and power to free.
Blessed Jesus, blessed Jesus, let us early turn to Thee.
Early let us seek Thy favor, early let us do Thy will.
Do Thou Lord our only Savior, with Thy love our bosoms fill.
Blessed Jesus, blessed Jesus, Thou hast loved us, love us still."

Chores completed, she returned to the farmhouse. The rising sun's breath had consumed the dawn's mist. Huang-Fu and the superintendents worked in the front yard dismantling the dew-laden tables and stacked the chairs. They placed them on the wagons to return them to their rightful owners, along with the china and silverware.

"A beautiful morning to you, Miss Naomi," Huang-Fu greeted as

Yung, Sheng-Li, and Tu stood with grins behind him.

"A fine mornin' indeed. Breakfast will be ready shortly."

"Yes. We will eat after we have finished here," Huang-Fu said.

Liang and Jia-Li labored in the kitchen, starting a fire on the stove and in the dual hearth. Naomi placed the milk bucket on the counter and brought the eggs to the sink to be rinsed.

"Good morning, Miss Naomi. Coffee almost ready," Liang said.

"Thank you, Liang. Has my father awaken yet?"

"No. Have not seen him. He must be very tired from last night's celebration. Maybe he still asleep."

"Yes. I think you're right. I'm glad someone can sleep. It seems like our chores are never done, are they?" The three ladies tee-heed as they prepared breakfast.

FOR DAVID, IT WAS A STRANGE YET FAMILIAR EMOTION to share the same room again with Samuel. It did not take long for them to adjust to each other. Boyhood pranks resurfaced once more. David lay in bed snickering as he recalled one occasion when he awoke to the stench of Samuel's dirty sock under his nose. Peering over at Samuel lying in his bed on his side facing the wall, David calculated his prank. With stealth, he placed the half-filled water pitcher on his brother's pillow. The plan was for the container to tilt and spill on Samuel's face when he turned to get out of bed.

Making no noise, David dressed and tiptoed downstairs to join Naomi for breakfast. "The top of the mornin' to y'all," he said with a bit of thrill in his voice. He sat at the table next to his sister.

"And to you too, brother dear," Naomi said, raising her cup then taking a sip.

"Coffee, Mr. David?" Jia-Li approached with a kettle in hand. As she served him, they ascertained an abrupt roar coming from upstairs.

"Ugh … David!"

Jia-Li stepped and turned her focus toward the cry. "Sounds like Mr. Samuel. He is calling for you." Her face displayed urgency.

Rolling with laughter, David held his abdomen. "No, no. He is quite all right. I'm the least of all company he desires right now."

Jia-Li's expression became confused.

"Oh, no, what did you do now?" Naomi laughed as she censored him, her eyes wide with curiosity.

"Who? Me? Nothin' out of the ordinary," he replied nonchalantly as he continued to consume his breakfast, all the while having a smirk on his face.

Samuel's holler must've awakened their parents. Soon enough, the three could be heard as they trotted down the stairs and headed for the kitchen. They sat down at the table as Jia-Li served them. Everyone stared at Samuel, whose hair was wet and slicked back.

"Hey, are we goin' somewhere today?" David asked, chortling.

His mother brought the hot cup of coffee to her lips. "No, I don't think so. Just stayin' home and relaxin'. Why?"

"Well, it appears like Sam's all washed up and ready to go out courtin' someone today. Did you meet some fair maiden last night at your debut?" David chuckled.

Samuel took his cloth napkin, wadded it up in a ball, and flung it at David across the table. David blocked himself, and the balled-up projectile ricocheted off his arm and brushed Jia-Li's cheek as she was walking behind him with the pot of hot coffee. It frightened her and caused the dark liquid to spill on her blouse.

"Aye-yah!" Jia-Li's wee voice cried as she jerked back. She steadied the pot in her hands and turned her sharp gaze at Samuel. His face exhibited the expression of a frightened child caught stealing goodies from the candy jar.

"Oh, my goodness. Jia-Li, I'm sorry." Samuel rose from his chair, ran over to Jia-Li, picked up the napkin, and began wiping her coffee-stained silk blouse.

"Here, let me take the pot from you." He fussed.

Every sort of Mandarin word disbursed from Jia-Li's lips, which no one in the family understood, as she tried to push Samuel's hands away from her. The family seemed to deduce from her blushed face and frantic body language that Samuel's attempt of recovery was not helping the situation.

His mother rose from the table and went to Jia-Li's aid. "Samuel, stop. You're embarrassing her."

Taking the napkin away from Samuel, his mother placed her arms around Jia-Li's shoulders in her motherly fashion and walked the shaken young lady to the sink.

"Are you all right, dear? Did you get scalded?"

"No, madam, just, as you say, embarr … embarr…"

"Embarrassed." His mother helped her complete the big English word.

"Ah, yes. Embarrassed," Jia-Li repeated in broken English. "I am okay. I go change my blouse and return to finish serving."

"All right, dear."

Jia-Li turned to confront Samuel first, then David, and smiled as she shook her head. "You brothers. Naughty boys this morning." She giggled and went out the back door to change in the cabin.

As his mother passed by, a loving pinch landed on him and her other guilty son, knowing she need not say more about their misbehavior. She returned to her seat, relaxed, and finished her breakfast. Next to her, his father sat glaring at him and Samuel as if they were still grade school children.

David bowed his head, hiding a smirk. He could picture a halo resting on horns above his brow. "Sorry, Pa. I'll try to behave." His ironic apology clashed with his good boy reputation. Soon the entire family hee-hawed beyond control.

Upon Jia-Li's return, the family, except for Samuel, finished their breakfast and headed for the sitting room. Samuel stayed behind to help Jia-Li in the kitchen to try to redeem himself.

He began to clear the table and bring the dirty dishes to the sink.

"Ah, no, Mr. Samuel. I do this." Jia-Li quickstepped to Samuel to keep him from assisting. They both wrestled for the plates in his hands.

"Please … I insist. It is the least I can do to repay you for my naughty behavior."

He turned to face Jia-Li, his towering five-feet-nine-inch physique overshadowing her petite frame. The pure scent of sandalwood soap emanated from her dark, ribbon straight hair and smooth, tan complexion. Her almond-colored eyes met his as they stood only inches apart. Jia-Li's angelic face aroused in him a mysterious and forbidden emotion. If he were the old Samuel who caused a ruckus around the railroads, he would have swept her into his arms and kissed her. Conscience told him her culture did not permit this kind of behavior. She was different in many ways.

They stood suspended in each other's aura, as their surroundings dissipated. The earth could quake right now, and he wouldn't notice while being captured in her essence. A moment of awkwardness crept in until she breathlessly interrupted the mutual silence. "Mr. Samuel, allow me."

The mention of his name coming from her lips stimulated his senses and caused his head to swim in illicit affection toward her. He tried his best to stop his heartstrings from reeling, but he wouldn't. He couldn't.

Jia-Li must have also sensed the revealing moment because she stepped back. "I will wash dishes now."

She turned away from him, placed the dishes in the sink, and leaned into it as if to steady her own emotions. With special care, she grabbed the kettle of warm water, filled the basin, and began washing the plates.

Samuel could not take his eyes off of her as he gathered the remaining platters and silverware. She was a different kind of beautiful … exotic, alluring, and innocent, bundled together into a petite and simple package.

He brought the items to her and tried to avoid eye contact, which would prolong the vacillating but pleasurable moment. As he stood next to her, a dangerous yet desperate desire to draw close to her reeled inside him and hoped she felt the same.

"I'm going to join the others unless there's something else I can help you with, Jia-Li," Samuel spoke low and deep as he placed the dishes in the sink.

Jia-Li stopped what she was doing, continued to peer down into the warm soapy water, and whispered, which caused him to lean toward her cheek. "Thank you, Mr. Samuel. You have done enough."

As Samuel inhaled, he placed his hand on the curve of her back, creating a stimulating communique between the two of them. She arched her back to his touch, closed her eyes, and her face glimmered with pleasure like the expression of one tasting a creamy, decadent chocolate confectionery for the first time. Upon removing his palm, he stepped away while gazing at her once more before he accompanied his family in the other room. He could hear her trembling sigh as she dipped her hands into the tepid water. He left the kitchen and tried his best not to dwell on what happened between them.

IN THE NEXT ROOM, Naomi and her mother were busy knitting, and David and her father were reading. Samuel came in and grabbed the *San Joaquin Argus* from the sofa and began to thumb through its pages.

As the yarn quickly passed along the wooden needles, Naomi ran the statement in her mind and built up the courage to speak to her father. She put her project down, walked over to him, and whispered, "Pa, may I have a moment with you in private?"

Her father placed his book on his lap and turned to face her. She must have had an expression that demanded an immediate response because he bolted to attention.

"Well, all right, darlin'. Let's go into my study."

After closing the office door behind them, they sat across from each other by the dual hearth.

"Pa, you know I love this farm as if it were my own and would do anythin' you asked me to do. I don't ever recall a time when I disobeyed you. For five years, I've been workin' hard, and never have you once thrown me a party or thanked me as you did with Samuel last night. Yet he comes home spent in lascivious livin', and you throw a lavish gala in his honor. And to top it off, you gave him Grandpa's ring." Naomi sat on her seat's edge as she revealed her heart's agony.

Her father appeared dumbfounded as he leaned back in his chair, crossed his right leg over his left knee, and rubbed his graying beard with his index finger and thumb.

She assisted him with almost every aspect of farm labor and had become his shadow. He even mentioned to her on several occasions she was like staring at his own reflection when he observed her as she worked. Yet, he never commended her, or himself, as a matter of fact. Her heart sank as she realized he might never offer her the property, and she would lose any chance of inheriting it now that Samuel was back. Silent seconds passed, which seemed like hours as he stared at his hands. Shifting in his seat, his compassionate gaze fell upon her.

"Oh, my darlin' daughter, I apologize if I hurt you in any way. I never intended to. Dear, you are always with me, an' I am ever so grateful the Lord gave me such a loyal, hard workin', and determined daughter. To me, you are as my own heart and soul. I can see myself in your eyes. Your tireless efforts haven't escaped me. As tradition dictates, the eldest son receives the inheritance and is expected to carry forward the family name. However, believe you me, I plan to give you a good portion, too. As for the celebration last night, it was the appropriate response to thank God for His preservin' hand to return Samuel, safe and sound. He was lost but was found again."

Naomi understood her father's position. His actions were correct toward Samuel. If this axiom was self-evident, then why was her entire being in despair? How selfish of her to behave this way. She ought to also be grateful for her brother's return. As for the family inheritance, her father had every right to choose whom he wills. It was wrong for her to assume she could trade her hard labor for the property. Rather than expecting her father owed her the family business, she should be thankful he considered offering her a portion of the inheritance. Heedless to her involuntary reaction, she began to weep in conviction.

"Pa, there is no need to apologize. You were right in what you did for Samuel. I was bein' selfish and a little jealous. Thank you for considerin' me as a recipient of the inheritance. Will you forgive me?"

"It's quite natural for you to react with those emotions, foremost because your contributions to the family business are many. I'm glad you shared your feelin's with me. Your thoughts and recommendations are important to me. Does your Papa still have your heart?"

"Oh, Papa, of course. Always." Naomi rose from her seat, sat on his lap, threw her arms around his neck, and laid her head on his shoulders as she had done when she was a child. "Thank you, Pa."

Her father embraced her and kissed her forehead. "That's my girl."

They both returned to the sitting room and continued their projects as they waited for Sarah, Lad, and their children to arrive.

8

Go to Him in Prayer

The Hamptons pulled up to the corral in their Conestoga around ten o'clock in the morning. The staff cleared most of the tables and chairs and the farmhouse appeared as Sarah remembered it when she left home four years earlier. Images of her and Joshua flitting about the farm while employed by her father filter through her mind. Only the pleasant memories remain and she buried and avoided the difficult ones. Amazed at herself, the rush of troubled emotions no longer surged from within. The time away, having a family of her own whom she adored helped to heal and forget those old wounds. Her new life exudes troubles of its own which require her attention.

Her appetite troubled her to be in Snelling again. Not so much because of the memories of Joshua, but because she knew she had to confront those that she abandoned and left hanging without closure when she eloped. The previous evening's affair left her stomach in knots to come face-to-face with those whom she hurt by her abrupt choices.

I'm so glad I survived the Thanksgivin' gatherin' last night. All I could do was hang my head in shame and avoid confrontation with my family and the McSwans until a better time. I do hope this weekend with my kin will find restoration—one step at a time. I shall meet with the McSwans on another occasion.

Lad's open palm reaching up to assist her off the wagon returned her to her senses. "Are you ready, darlin'?"

"Oh, yes, dear." Sarah handed the portable wicker basket to Lad first, then Isabelle. The two toddlers stood on the ground next to him as he placed their baby sister inside the basket and helped their mama climb down. Sarah lifted the basket with their infant while Lad carried Billy and held Amanda's hand as she waddled with her baby rag doll in her arms.

Sarah rapped on the door and adjusted Isabelle's swaddling clothes. Her mother's warm smile greeted them.

"There's my grandbabies!" Her mother reached for Amanda's hand as a little round face with rosy cheeks gazed upwards from her ruffled bonnet.

"Good mornin', Sarah, dear … Lad. Have y'all had breakfast yet?"

"Oh, yes, Mama. We ate at the hotel." Sarah put the bassinet down as she removed her cloak and hung it on the rod by the door.

"Well, how 'bout some coffee?"

"I wouldn't mind having a cup. Thank you, Mother." Lad allowed Billy to stand on his own, then carried the bassinet.

"Not for me, Ma. I'm still nursin'. I'll take a glass of apple or orange juice."

"All right, I'll ask Jia-Li to fetch some. Why don't y'all join the rest of the family in the sittin' room?" Her mother walked over to the kitchen to inform the staff then returned.

Naomi spread a quilt on the floor for the toddlers to play with their wooden toys and rag doll. Lad positioned the portable wicker bassinet with their frail baby next to the blanket. He joined Sarah, who sat next to David on the sofa.

Samuel went to the office to fetch a couple of chairs to bring to the sitting area. On the way back, he held open the parlor room door for Jia-Li, who carried a tray of refreshments. His eyes roamed her stature, and his entire body seemed to emanate charismatic energy. Sarah couldn't help but notice a subtle tête-à-tête between the two.

"Pardon me. Ladies first, and, this time, I won't spill the coffee on your blouse." Samuel teased as he allowed Jia-Li to pass through the doorway. He continued behind her with two chairs.

"Oh, Mr. Samuel, you are too kind and funny." Jia-Li's eyes glistened at him.

They walked into the sitting room with a radiant smile on their faces. Jia-Li set the tray on the serving table by the back window, served coffee, then left the room. Samuel's focus followed her as he placed the chairs by the fireplace and sat in one.

The family did not seem to notice, but Sarah did. She was familiar with that titillating, coquettish exchange. Flirtation was an art she mastered when she was a single woman. Memories flickered of her dalliance when she first met Lad at The Barn in Snelling, where many young adults gathered to dance and socialize.

Ah, young love. So daring and exciting. A chapter in life yet to unfold. How courageous of you, Sam, to be attracted to a gal of a different culture. You're going to stir commotion once again for this family. Oh my, when will this merry-go-round ever end?

Lad's coffee cup clinked as he sat beside her. She glanced at his strong, rugged cow-wrangling hands, gently handling the fine china with care. *The story of my life. Had I known what lay ahead of me and Lad's life together, would I have pursued our relationship? Halt at once, Sarah. Stop doubting your decisions. You love the man beside you and the beautiful children you've both created.*

"Well, isn't this wonderful to have the whole family together again?" Her mother, the peacemaker, started the conversation.

"Indeed, it is, Ma." Sarah hoped the tension in the atmosphere would relieve itself.

"I can't believe I'm an uncle three times over. I apologize for not keepin' in touch. Congratulations to you both," Samuel said, grinning.

"Lo, children are an heritage of the LORD: and the fruit of the womb is his reward." David recited Psalms chapter 127:3 to affirm Samuel's statement.

"We understand you are quite the preacher, David. What's this news we hear of you goin' to college in Indiana?" Sarah turned to her younger brother as she held the glass of apple juice on her lap.

"Well, Lord willin', I will attend next fall. I've submitted my application. Now it's a matter of patiently waitin' for the letter of acceptance from the dean. It's a private Christian university. I hope to receive a degree in theology."

"How about you, Sam? Are you done with railroadin' and pannin' for gold? Will you be workin' the farm with Naomi and Pa?" Sarah tried her best not to sound as if she were mocking Samuel, for she knew all too well she had nothing to boast about in her own life. She desired her family to be honest regarding their circumstances so that she could do the same.

"Yeah." Samuel shrugged his shoulders, proceeding to stare down at his boots. "I'm done with chasin' rainbows. I guess I had to find out the hard way that this type of gold doesn't exist. At least not for me. What I didn't realize was that the gold was always under my feet, if I would've only stood still long enough to notice it. It was here on the farm, but I was too stubborn to listen to Pa's advice."

Naomi chimed in from where she sat on the floor playing with her niece and nephew. "I could've told you that and spared you the heartache of going through all the rough times. But who am I to tell her eldest brother what to do? It seemed to me you had everythin' figured out." Her words were piercing and riddled with guilt-producing innuendos aimed at Samuel. "I'm thankful though. Because you left home opportunity availed itself to me to fully comprehend our family wheat business. I poured my heart and soul into this farm."

Samuel breathed deep, clenched his jaw, then turned to Naomi. "You've every right to kick me out of here, Naomi. The farm is operatin' fine without me. I don't mean to cause any trouble. I can leave after the holidays if need be." Lowering his head, he turned to their father. "Pa, thanks again for takin' me back and forgivin' me for bein' mule-headed."

Her father was quiet, listening to the family get past the formalities of reacquainting themselves. The tension in the room could not be avoided, and a hurdle his family must overcome. "Samuel, I'm doin' what every loving father would do for his children. You know my door is always open to y'all. There is plenty of room and work on this farm for everyone. So no one has to leave. I'd rather y'all stay and build this business together. I desire to offer my family all that I have. However, I'm not goin' to force myself upon you either.

"My hope is for all of you to make the right choices in your lives accordin' to God's will. The reality is we don't always do this. I speak from my own experiences. Sometimes learnin' from one's own mistakes is the best lesson learned."

Naomi's demeanor softened, Samuel's lightened, and the rest of the family relaxed into their chairs. Their father's forgiveness, mercy, compassion, and vision of unity set the boundaries they needed to hear.

Jonathan paused and turned to Sarah's husband. "Lad, there is rumor Mr. Montana will be havin' you boys bring a large herd of longhorn from Texas next spring."

Nearly choking on his coffee, Lad's face paled. "Yes, sir. My comrades and I are going to meet up with the cattle drive at the border of Arizona and New Mexico, where we'll make the exchange, then bring them home."

"That's a far distance to travel. How long do you suppose it'll take to get there an' back?" Her father asked as he shifted his gaze to her and the children.

Warmth rushed to her face. Her head jerked to face her husband, her brows knit together. The second-degree grilling from her father did not annoy her as much as her husband's secrecy. Jonathan had always disapproved of them eloping and Lad abandoning her when she needed him most.

She knew her father understood the beguiled life of a cattleman. Like Lad, as a young man, he once desired to be out in the mountain and desert ranges surrounded by nature. When she and her siblings were children, her father used to tell stories about his adventures while he navigated his horse about a stampede of longhorn and listened to cattle low at night as he and his comrades gathered for supper around the campfire, singing cowboy songs. By the end of the drive, he always appreciated the return home to be with his family for a home-cooked meal. Reluctantly, the itch to be out on the range would rear up after another month or two.

Lad's steely cobalt eyes squinted and glared at her then at her father. He was like one of the lassoed cattle, struggling to avoid the slaughterhouse.

It'll take upwards of six months. Are you really goin' to leave me and your children stranded for that long without any protection and help to run the farm? The thought made her seethe and pierce her lips.

His coffee cup rattling in his hands, Lad coughed. "Sir, I'm not sure how long this drive will take. I was hoping to make arrangements to have one of the Chinese servants stay with Sarah and the children durin' this time." He seemed to read her mind.

Her father's countenance displayed his disapproval through troubled eyes. He frowned at her as she clenched her teeth then stared at the glass of juice in her hands. The news caught her by surprise.

"So when were you goin' to tell me, Lad? When you were already halfway to Texas?" She slammed her glass on the coffee table and stormed out of the sitting room and into her father's office. She was angry and in tears. The sound of Lad's boots stomping the wood floors followed close behind her.

Soon after, she could hear the sobs of her children. The arguing was a familiar scene for them, yet they still were startled by it. Amanda's lower lip would quiver, proceeded by wailing cries. Billy would join shortly after he sensed his sister's fears, and Isabelle would not react at all, although her eyes would enlarge. However, this time, their wails stopped within minutes. She knew her mother and sister must be comforting them.

Lad shut the door behind him. "Look, I planned to tell you, Sarah, once I knew for sure Mr. Montana's decision."

"Why is it that I'm always the last to know? And by the time you tell me, I have no say-so in the matter anyway." She paced in front of the window, stomped her feet about her bustled skirt, and dug her fingernails into her palms. "Don't you have any concern for how me and the children manage alone without you? They're growin' up not knowin' their father."

Lad didn't move a step. He just folded his arms across his chest and tightened his lips.

"Ah!" Sarah threw her hands up, tears flowing, and peered out the window toward the harvested fields. There was nothing she could do about Lad's work situation. They needed the money, as much as she hated his absence. She felt numb, lost, trapped, and hopeless.

Just then, a gentle rap on the office door broke the silence. "May I come in and speak to you both?" Her father's voice filtered into the room.

Lad went to the door with his head hung low. He paused to take a deep breath as if ready to receive an ear full of chastisement from her father as he once did from his own grandfather. Lad had told her how his grandparents raised him after his parents abandoned him with the hope of finding gold in California. They had promised to return for him once they were settled. But the years went by without a word. He vowed to search for them once he was of age. However, his grandfather would scold him and smack him with a switch anytime he'd mention his plans.

Lad opened the door to find her father, forcing a smile and holding his Bible to his chest. "I'm sorry, Mr. Sower, for ruining the kinfolk reunion. Please come in. This is your office, after all."

Her father's eyes filled with compassion for them. His steps were slow and methodical as he moved into the room. "Let's have a seat by the hearth," he said. "No, son, you didn't ruin anythin'. Come on now, we're family. We hide nothin' from one another.

"I'm aware you've been strugglin' with this work schedule for some time. My intention for askin' you about the cattle drive is so I can offer a solution, not to start a family feud. I've always wanted to help but didn't know how to. After you had eloped, your ma and I assumed you didn't want us in your lives. I wished you both gave us the pleasure of enjoyin' your decision to marry and allowed us to get acquainted with you."

"Oh, Pa, that wasn't the reason why I agreed to elope with Lad. During that time, I was so overwhelmed with Joshua's death. I didn't have the heart to involve you and Ma in my relationship with Lad. The only escape was to be married and be carried far from here. Lad did this for me. I fell in love with him, and he swept me away," Sarah said, voice trembling.

She glanced at her husband. "But I realized this decision to elope was not fair to Lad, for I cheated him of a lovely weddin' and the opportunity of gettin' to know his wonderful in-laws. I'm so terribly sorry, darlin'."

Lad pierced his lips as she continued her explanation to Jonathan.

"I know I should've called on you, Pa, but my conscience kept telling me you were angry with my decision and you'd convince me to return home. I wasn't ready for that yet. Having Ma assist me with the children is all that I could handle for now."

Jonathan leaned back in his chair. "I see. I figured Joshua's death had somethin' to do with your choices. Well, I do pray that is behind you now. What was done is in the past. How can I hold a grudge against both of you when I gaze into the eyes of my grandchildren and embrace them in my arms?" He leaned forward to assert his proposal. "All is forgiven. May we start over and be a family? Will you allow your Pa the pleasure of helpin' out, if possible?"

Sarah turned to Lad, whose despair-filled eyes mimicked what her heart felt because they had no other solutions. Nodding at one another, they held hands and listened to what her father had to say.

"Well, first, I want you to pray about what I'm goin' to offer. Don't respond quite yet. Give yourselves time to seek God for an answer, all right?

"Lad, I understand you love workin' with cattle. I could use a good and reliable farmhand to work with my livestock on the farm. David will be leavin' for college next year, and I will need to have his position filled. So give it some thought. Give God a chance to help your marriage and go to Him in prayer. Please read 1 Corinthians 7:1-16 and Ephesians 5:22-33. Afterward, let me know your decision. The other details will work themselves out." Her father wrote the Bible references down on a piece of paper and gave them to Lad, along with his personal Bible.

Sarah examined Lad's eyes, now sparkling with hope and curiosity, but she needed answers before they could make a decision. However, those questions held no weight compared to what her father was asking them to do first … go to God. Sarah had drifted so far from God, and Lad had never been exposed to the truth of the Gospel. Even if God's plans were shared with him in the past, he never mentioned it, probably because he was not ready to receive salvation at the time. Humbled by her father's mercy and grace, they nodded at one another in agreement, for they had no other alternative.

"Thank you, Father. Yes, we'll pray and discuss your offer and let you know our decision." Lad gave her father a firm handshake. Calm and hope filled her heart, and they returned to the parlor.

The remainder of the weekend was splendid as the family continued to reacquaint themselves and share their past six years of experiences apart. The Hamptons returned to their small farm in Mariposa while the rest of their relatives prepared for Christmas.

9

A Dollar a Day

Jonathan sat behind his oak desk and scribbled on a piece of paper. *Let's see—2500 in acreage divided by 60 plowed and sowed acres a day. Then 20 working days per month into that number.* He calculated and dropped his jaw. *My Lord, just a little over two months! A savings of six months and labor cost. I'll save a fortune as well as increase my capital with the early-to-market grain. Mr. Nielson will be pleased indeed.*

An uncontrollable grin consumed his face as he pushed his chair aside. Jonathan leaped with excitement, kicked up his heels, and did a little jig as he neared the office window. He threw the shutters open wide and adored his property. With both hands to his lips, he blew a kiss toward the land and to the heavens.

"Thank you, Lord, for leading my family and me to California. I'm forever grateful for your foresight and guidance. Sower Farms is almost ten years in the makin'. We love this place, Father."

Toes tapping, he continued to dance before God when an image of his father appeared in his mind. A minute melancholy subdued his joy as he reflected upon his past and prayed aloud. "We'd be lost and miserable if we stayed in Kentucky on my pa's farm. If not for the Civil War, that location might've been an excellent abode."

He shook his head in dismay. "Atrocious calamities. Too many ghosts for any child to contend with. I pray that piece of land serves its new owners well. At least they did not witness first-hand the horrors we experienced. Well, what they don't know won't hurt them, I suppose. I do thank you, Lord, for your grace and mercy toward my family and me and findin' a new home for us where I can continue my father and grandfather's vision."

Jonathan peered out the window toward the clearing skies. Scattered clouds with silver trim from the late winter morning sun dotted the hemisphere surrounding his lands rich moistened soil. The barn doors flung open as Samuel and his three superintendents chattered and proceeded to the farmhouse.

Listening to the sound of the front door opening and the men's laughter as they paused in the foyer to remove their outerwear and hats, Jonathan seated himself behind his desk to await their report.

A rap sounded from his opened office door, and Samuel popped his head inside. "Pa, are you ready for us?"

"Yes. Please come in. Warm yourselves by the fire."

The three superintendents bowed by the entry. Huang-Fu followed with a tray of hot coffee, biscuits, and jam, placed the service on the center table, and left the others to their business.

"Good mornin', Mr. Sower. Thank you. Yes, still very cold outside," Sheng-Li, the head superintendent said rubbing his hands to generate warmth. "But no rain today. Good day to begin plowing and sowing."

Samuel and the employees shook the moisture off their clothes from the morning Tule fog and huddled by the hearth. The winter showers had slowed to two days a week, which left the rolling hills green, soft, and pliable, ready for a new harvest.

"Thank the Lord. Appears you men are of the right attitude today. Music to my ears when you boys are gettin' along well and enjoyin' yourselves without any complaint or troubles." Jonathan stood, moved closer to the roaring flames, and sat in his winged-back chair. "How are the horses and mules, Sam? Are they ready for another planting season?"

"You bet, Pa. They are strong and fit as a fiddle." Samuel chortled at his related musical pun. "Or should I say, as an ox."

"You are your father's son, indeed." Jonathan guffawed. "You fellas help yourselves to some of this hot brown gargle and warm dough-gods and jam." He pinched some tobacco from the tin on the side table, shoved the dried crumbled leaf into his clay pipe, lit it, and puffed till the aromatic smoke spewed from his lips. "Do you suppose one dozen farm workers will be enough to meet the day's quota of work, Sheng-Li?"

Queue swaying from his vigorous nod, the lead superintendent poured himself a cup. "Yes, sir. That should be enough to start. Depends on the skill of men. I will let you know if more needed as day progress."

"Fine. You, superintendents, get the farmin' equipment and mules ready while my son and I gather up some laborers."

Anguo grunted. "I caution you, Mr. Sower. Be careful when approaching Chinese camp. White farmworkers picketing, and they are very hostile. They throw stones at Chinaman waiting in line for work."

The troubling news stabbed the wheat baron's chest expelling short, jagged coughs. "Darn those Maxfield men. This grievous undertaking can only be them causing this ruckus. Boycott and rioting is the only hand Fred has to play to stop his competitors. His prejudice will be his downfall. The bank won't lend him any more money to purchase new equipment. So he's stuck between a rock and a hard place."

"Pa, I'll grab our shotguns should those feller's become a nuisance to us."

"Yep, you do that, son. Let's finish our Arkbuckle, and we'll fetch the wagon."

"Sure thing."

After having their fill, the crew retrieved their jackets and hats in the foyer and followed their boss to the barn where they hitched the horse to the wagon and the mules to the sulky plows. Shotguns hidden from sight, father and son travailed into town.

Jonathan snapped the wagon's reins, and they rode past dozens of Caucasian men loading into several wagons owned by other local farmers in the area. As the Sower men approached the Chinese camp on the west end of Lewis Street, a group of white men with crude signs picketed about a block away. *Go home, Coolies. Hire whites only. More pay, more work.* The signage read like flying musket balls targeting their opposing threat.

On the other side of the street, conical-shaped basket-weaved hats bustled about the edge of the dirt road, pointing toward them. Their only weapon of defense was their lunch pails to shield them from stone projectiles coming from the angry mob.

Hands near his shotgun, Samuel readied himself. "Pa, is there another route to take around this mess?"

"Well, we can go north a block to Green Street where the church is. They wouldn't dare picket in front of holy ground. From there we can take Montana Street and get to the Chinese camp from the west. It'll take a little longer, but we'll be safe from these buffoons."

"Sounds like a good plan to me." Samuel craned his neck to check for any perpetrators along the new direction. "The coast is clear. Let's go."

Jonathan clicked his jaw and turned the horses and wagon around then headed north and several blocks further west. Arriving at the Chinese Camp, the eager prospective Asian farmworkers scramble toward them.

"Looks like we've got a pick of the litter, Pa."

"I always do, son. It seems lately only a few farmers hire our able-bodied friends. Must be the social pressure forcin' them to change their business strategies. But I'm not afraid of these opposers because we have God on our side."

Samuel nod and quoted Romans 8:31. "If God *be* for us, who *can be* against us?"

"That's right, son. The Lord called us here for a reason and had opened the door to workin' with these people. To me, their work is equivalent to the white workers, if not better. And they require far fewer wages than the others, too. That labor savings afforded us new farmin' technology." Jonathan parked the wagon in front of the tanned faces surrounding them. He stood and held up a silver-seated liberty-and-eagle coin to show the men and said in simple Mandarin, "One dollar a day."

Several hands jutted forward, waving in the air. The determined farmer searched for sturdy frames amongst the eager grins. He selected one dozen of them. They jumped on board, and he turned the wagon around to head back to the farm by way of the diverted direction.

"Coolie lovers! Ching chang chong! Slope! Pan face!" The white farmers and workers hurled derogatory slurs from across the street along with stones. Jonathan, Samuel, and the men lowered their heads and kept quiet as they pushed forward.

Head shaking in disbelief, Jonathan said with restrained breath, "Yeah, and I'll go smilin' all the way to the bank while you boys are grindin' your teeth over your prejudices." He knew the Chinese laborers proved their worth on the railroads and in the farming industry by their agricultural and engineering abilities used in their homeland. After they completed the railroad, many of them had built the levees throughout the thirsty flatlands of Sacramento and the San Joaquin Valley, which provided irrigation to the vast crops including his farm. Fortunately for them, while the white employees strike for better income, he'll be the only employer in town to hire the Chinese to be strikebreakers, as they were consenting to labor for lower wages. *Never shall I go back to these white workers again, unless they are willing to humble themselves and work with others regardless of the color of their skin.*

At the farm, Sheng-Li, Yung, and Tu instructed the new group of laborers how to field plow and seed broadcast, using the new farm equipment as Jonathan and Samuel observed. At first, the innovations seemed daunting as each man stumbled about the contraptions. However, once mastered, their rhythm of guiding the horse- or mule-led machines from one row to the next seemed to move like a well-choreographed contra dance. Once established, Jonathan returned to his desk and Samuel to the barn.

Sheng-Li tapped on Jonathan's office door at nine o'clock to report on the plowing progress. "Mr. Sower, I believe we need to hire more men. We have fallen a little short of our schedule this morning because of training."

"All right. I'll gather another four men."

Jonathan returned to the Chinese camp to locate additional workers. He did the same as before, showing the men the one-dollar coin, and the men boarded the wagon. Sheng-Li continued to instruct them at the farm.

By noon, there still was a need for a few hands, then again at three in the afternoon, and finally at five o'clock in the evening.

At sunset, Sheng-Li returned to Jonathan's office. "The men have finished the work for today. They are gathered in the barn."

"Yes. I'll bring the men their wages." Jonathan opened the Mosler money safe behind his desk and removed a wooden box filled with coins. He counted twenty-eight dollars, placed them in a leather pouch, returned the rest into the small vault, and walked to the barn with Sheng-Li.

The superintendents gathered the last group of men, first to receive their wages, then the next, until the first lot was called. Each of them received one dollar for the workday.

Grumblings stirred from the laborers who started at dawn's early light and sweated in the sun the majority of the time. They shook their fists at the farmer and shouted in Mandarin.

Sheng-Li interpreted. "Mr. Sower, the first group of men you hired are angry because they expected to receive more pay than those who came in the afternoon and evening."

Jonathan paced and crossed his arms over his chest. He stopped and confronted the workers as Yung continued to interpret. "Why do you men question your wages? Did you not agree with the amount I showed to you when you started this morning? As the owner of this farm, do I not have the right to pay as I please? So why this act of insurgency upon my gracious benevolence as if I were evil? The salary is a dollar a day, and all of you are welcome to return tomorrow at sunrise."

The Chinese farmhands acknowledged the agreement and could say no more. They returned the following day as if the ordeal never occurred. They continued to dig rows in the earth with the innovated John Deere steel plow and sow the wheat seeds with the help of the new broadcast sower.

With this technology, California can surpass the Eastern prairie regions and become the number one supplier of grain. His grin lengthened as he leaned back into his chair and propped his feet up on his desk. He strategized the new planting season in his mind.

The next task would be to maintain the crop irrigation, weed, and reap the harvest come late summer, rather than the trailing autumn. *With Sam beside me, I can design a new plan to expand into the fruit and nut industry. All I need now is Lad's decision to join the family business.*

10

Papa Always Comes Home

The rooster crowed. February arrived, hastening Lad's departure for the six-month cattle drive, which Sarah dreaded. She lay in bed anchoring in her memory every line and contour of her husband's face silhouetted by the dim dawn light drifting in the window. Going on five years of marriage and she sensed she barely cracked the surface of his rough cowpoke exterior. She placed her hand on his chest, being careful not to wake him.

Is there a heart in there? She imagined an empty chest cavity. *If there were, then you wouldn't be so inclined to walk out on your family today. The guilt and compassion in your heart won't allow you to leave.*

His chest rose and fell beneath her palm.

We can pack all our belongings and move in with my parents right now if we must. I'm all right with that, but I don't think your manly pride will come to agreement. Otherwise, you would've given Pa an answer by now.

The rooster crowed twice, but she froze, hoping he wouldn't wake just yet. *A little while longer, please. Allow me to enjoy your presence while you lay peaceful here beside me.* They had little time to contemplate and discuss her father's proposal. Their usual arguments festered as this day fast approached.

Often she reasoned with herself regarding the next cattle drive and hoped it would be Lad's last. *He can't quit his job just yet. Mr. Montana relies on him. Or, let him have his last hurrah out in the prairie with his comrades. Six months to herd cattle and consume stale chuck wagon food should be enough to cause a cowboy to want to stay home. That length of sacrificial dedication is an excellent way to wind down his career.*

This time would be different. Sarah had some comfort in knowing she could turn to her parents since they had extended their grace and forgiveness. She could avoid lunacy with their company. The reconciliation allowed her the freedom to visit them and request financial assistance in hiring an elderly farmhand to tend to her small farm while she cared for the children.

Thrice the cock crowed. Lad's eyes fluttered, and he sat up in bed, not sensing her presence. He seemed as if he were already camped out on the prairie waking to another day's work. Head jerking about him, he stood and stubbed his toe on the nightstand.

"Ow! Dang, it." He found a lucifer and lit the oil lamp. The light illuminated the room with warm muted shades and gave heed to Sarah's allure poised upon her pillow. Her untied chemise fell below one shoulder and cascade low from above her bosoms. Golden unbrushed locks dangle between her cleavage.

The sudden recollection on his face and the rise in his long underwear would be her instrument of reason to sway him to stay.

"Are you surprised you're still home?" she said. "Or would you rather be with the cattle right now?"

"Ah woman, you're making it difficult for me." He left the light on, removed his clothing, threw the sheets off the bed, and lay next to her. Lips joined together to taste their love's bittersweet passion. His hands ran her body's smooth, gentle curves above her nightdress, causing her to squirm with excitement in anticipation of the pleasures to come. Pressed against her thigh, his maleness teased her. With his teeth, he yanked on her chemise exposing her suppleness. Kissing every inch of her body, Lad centered himself upon her and found his way inside. They lavished every last moment in each other's embrace until the morning sun dripped into the room drowning out the lamp's glow.

Alas, the moment arrived, and she had to let him go. Their love sessions would be his anchor to keep his heart tied to home, although his body will be miles away. At least that is her hope. Remembering their moments of bliss should keep him from wandering into another bed. She gave her all to Lad. *No other woman can love you as I do. I'll make sure of that.*

Face-to-face upon their pillow with arms and legs intertwined, to release her husband proved as difficult as peeling the delicate skin off a ripe peach with bare hands. He kissed her once more, gave her a gentle push, and they both inched their way off the bed. They dressed and began their day, she in the kitchen as he packed his saddlebags.

Silence dominated the home as the young family sat quietly at the table finishing their breakfast. The apprehension of another goodbye gnawed at Sarah's appetite. The lackluster countenance on her children's faces revealed their depth of understanding of this moment when their father would part from them again. Hearts heavy and the air's despair set thicker than molasses.

"Go on now, Amanda and Billy, give your papa a big hug before he leaves." Sarah encouraged her daughter and son as best she could. Lad pushed his chair away from the table, turned to his children with arms stretched open, and forced a smile.

Placing them on his knee, Amanda hugged her daddy's neck. Her lip quivered, and tears pooled her blue eyes. "Papa, don't go."

Billy's mouth started to pout, too, as he wrapped his chubby arms partly about his daddy's waist while staring at his face. He seemed to be trying to memorize every detail of his cropped beard, dark hair, and compassionate cobalt eyes.

LAD FOUND LEAVING HOME MORE DIFFICULT now that he realized he would miss his children's many first moments while he was away. Six months instead of the usual four. He did not have the heart to tell them that this journey was going to be longer. He embraced them and kissed their foreheads.

"Amanda, Billy, you know Papa always comes home. Be strong and help Mama while I'm away. I promise not to be gone too long. I love you very much. Tell you what, when I return, I'll bring a special toy for each of you. Okay?" He held his sobbing children in his arms for a moment then loosened his grip.

"Now let me give your mama a big hug, too." Lad stood and embraced Sarah, who seemed to be restraining her tears in front of the children. He knew she had to be strong for them and not display any fear or weakness.

Oh, my lovely wife, there's nothing I can do to assure you of my love and faithfulness. We can argue until the cows come home and you won't believe me. How is it that I can trust you to be chaste and not the other way around? After all, you were the flirtatious one when we first met at the Barn.

A cry came from Isabelle's cradle. Her broken silence allowed him to compare Sarah's daily influences to his piquant life on the road as he and his comrades roamed from town to town. *Well, I do suppose greater temptations surround me than do you.*

Isabelle's painful sorrowing called for him and his wife's attention again.

I realize my cow punching days are soon to come to an end. But it'll be on my terms. I don't want anyone to take the blame for my decision. Especially you, my love. This six-month journey will allow me plenty of time to think things through without any external persuasions. Leaving this work will be like abandoning the only family I've ever known until you came along and stole my heart. You and the children are my real kin now, and I don't want to lose you. So I hope you'll be patient with me.

To draw in his redolence, Sarah leaned into his neck. He pulled his head away so that he could look into her melancholy brown eyes. "Darlin', I'll be sure to send posts when I arrive in a town. I love you, and I'll be home as soon as I can."

Lad did not have anything additional to say, and he knew this heartbreak all too well. After they kissed, he walked over to Isabelle as she sat propped up in her crib. He lifted her frail body and caressed her wee hands. "My darling girl, you should be chasing your sister and brother when I return. Pa will always be thinking of you." He held her close then placed her back in her bed.

The rustic cedar closet beckoned him to claim its contents.

He removed his gun belt, wrapped it around his hip, and inserted his .44 caliber Colt revolver in its holster. Sarah fetched Lad's dark brown canvas duster from the wooden dowel by the front door. He slipped his arms into the long coat, and she properly squared the shoulders at his back. With the black coachman hat secure on his head, he took hold of his Winchester rifle in his left hand and his lariat in his right. His spurs clinked as he moved toward the cabin's doorway.

Amanda and Billy stood behind Sarah and clung to her skirt. They trembled as he pulled the handle of the door then turned around once more to look at his heavy-hearted family. However, the guilt weighed more this time, because he was leaving not only his wife but also three children who needed him, more so Isabelle.

He turned his gaze into the misty morning sunlight, pondered for a moment, and forced himself to take a step forward as the rugged cabin door closed behind him. The stifled whimpers of his family drifted from the window. *God, if you are real, watch over my family until I return.*

11

Obscure Streetwalker

"Leonard, I would appreciate Mr. Maxfield providin' me protection from the Chinaman who walks through our street ev'ry mornin'. I doubt he is up to any good, and he scares me somethin' fierce." Leonard Lambert's wife, Evelyn, gripped his hand at the breakfast table beside the kitchen window.

"What Chinaman?" Curtains pushed to the side, he narrowed his gaze on the fast-paced, darkly clad slumped figure crossing his front yard's dirt road. "Humph. The Boss pays good money to house his superintendents and their families in this town. I'm sure he won't have any qualms if I took this matter into my own hands." Leonard envisioned himself with his cohorts, Harold and Grier, assaulting this stranger at an inconspicuous location. *Hum.* Calculations flit about in his mind. *Some blood money will be necessary to get them to participate in this scheme with me. This dirty work may require a financial loan from boss Maxfield.*

Certainty ranked in Leonard's mind that this sneaky Chinaman would not bode well with his discriminating employer, Frederick Maxfield. Amongst his employer's prejudices are the foreigner-loving plebeians who aided the celestials, in particular, Jonathan Sower. He was positive the obscure streetwalker worked as the Sower Farm's butler and cook, which all the more gave him reason to turn to his employer for financial assistance to succeed with this assault.

"Well, we can't have any Coolies coming near our white women. So you say he comes by every mornin'?" He rubbed his scruffy goatee. "Let me see what I can do." Leonard began to formulate a plan in his hate-driven mind.

A FEW DAYS LATER while the sun sat below the horizon and the rooster had not yet crowed, the Suen family began their day at Sower Farms.

"Do you have your list ready for me today, Liang?" Huang-Fu, the middle-aged butler, shuffled into the lantern-lit kitchen. His graying queue whipped about as he moved.

Liang handed her husband the Mandarin-scribbled paper. Assisting him, she placed a sturdy bamboo staff horizontally behind his neck over his shoulders and hung two large, empty baskets on each end.

Huang-Fu and his family found themselves preparing menus on a grand scale when the Chinese farm workers returned to plow and seed the fields. The fresh vegetables needed for their cuisine were unknown to many Caucasian farmers, so they grew their own at the camps. He made a daily trip across town to purchase exotic ingredients such as bok choy, bitter melon, bamboo shoots, dried mushrooms, and silk squash.

"As usual, be alert and careful, husband." Liang placed his basket-weaved hat on his head.

"I will. Don't worry, wife." He kissed her cheek, turned, and headed to town on foot. The town people's anti-Chinese sentiment remains at the forefront of his mind. Those who claimed to be godly struggled with their Christian morals toward his invading far eastern people.

At least the men who lived in the Chinese camp walked together to Sower's farm when they crossed the growing town of Snelling and the long stretch of Merced Falls Road. Strength in numbers kept them safe from outlaws, thugs, and the derision from the town's people. The co-workers served as a diversion for the middle-aged butler from the resident's prying eyes.

Huang-Fu wished he had a companion to walk with him to town daily. To trouble his employer with such an absurd request was costly and unnecessary. So he took his chances. In his mind, he replayed his early morning strategic route and carried it out completely.

The wet, sandy pebbles crunched beneath Huang-Fu's black canvas slip-on shoes. As he approached the Snelling cemetery, he lifted his brim enough to glance down Emma Street. The Tule fog concealed him and others who may be outdoors. *Be utmost quiet.* His heart raced whenever he approached the residential areas of the still-waking town. *Must hurry through back streets. Keep head low and focus on ground.* His stealth-quickened steps avoided puddles and twigs. The empty baskets bounced on the staff's ends as his legs scuffled along. At the street's end, he lifted his sight to grasp his bearings. *Ah, camp ahead.*

Stovepipes spewed smoke from wood shacks and buildings lined along the camp's makeshift dirt roads. The male inhabitants prepared to leave for work, and the Asian Mercantile opened its doors for business. Tables laden with the early morning catch from Merced River of trout, wide-mouth bass, and salmon wreaked of freshwater fishiness. Above it on hooks dangled fresh plucked duck and chicken. Behind the counter lined against the wall, several distinguished teak cabinets displayed a multitude of drawers filled with Chinese apothecary medicine herbs. Bins of rice, dried noodles, and garden grown fruits and vegetables graced the store's center aisle.

The vast amount of produce Huang-Fu required allowed him vegetable picking rights to the mercantile garden. He filled the baskets and paid for his groceries. Balancing the basket-laden staff on his shoulders, Huang-Fu clenched his jaw and glanced at the rising sun behind the mist and the trees. *Please, God, help me get back to the farm unnoticed.*

THE EARLY MORNING FOG BLANKETED THE STIRRING TOWN of Snelling. A hint of gray light filtered through the darkened horizon and into Frederick Maxfield's kitchen, where he stood by his stove preparing a pot of strong coffee. His farm lay still on the town's southwestern outskirts. The livestock's muffled lowing and the rooster's call signified a start to another day for his life-consuming wheat business venture. In another hour, he expected to hear the sound of horse's hooves and wagon wheels as his farmhands arrived. Little did he expect a knock at his front door before he had a chance to have breakfast and change out of his long johns, night robe, and house slippers.

Who on earth would be starting work so early? Frederick tied his robe's belt, grabbed an oil lamp, ambled to the front door, and opened it. A familiar silhouette of one of his superintendents stood between him and the backlit fog. "Leonard, what brings you to my doorstep before the day's even begun?"

"Mr. Maxfield, boss, may I have a moment of your time to discuss an urgent matter concerning the safety of your employees and their families?"

"Oh." Frederick scoffed. "Does danger lurk to which I'm unaware? Please do come in and explain yourself. Join me for a cup of Arbuckle?"

"Don't mind if I do."

They sat at the kitchen table as Leonard began concocting half-truths about his wife's fearful predicament, and fabricated lies about the Chinaman, which were sure to ruffle his employer's vengeful feathers.

"Boss, I'm in a bit of a quandary. Just yesterday, my wife brought to my attention a stranger trespassing our property around six in the morning for the past month. I'm not sure how long he's been doing this. She's only noticed him of recent since she's been rising early to make cookies for the town bakery." He scratched his head and leaned forward to obtain Maxfield's full attention.

"I saw this stranger with my own eyes traveling in the early morning before the sun comes up. Appears to me he's a Chinaman. I can tell by his cone-shaped hat and the baskets hanging from his shoulders."

"Where do you suppose he came from, and what is his destination?" Maxfield's brows pinched together.

"He seems to be coming from the east. My guess is he is one of Sower's employees, possibly his cook going to the Chinese camp for their daily rations." Leonard shook his head in dismay with himself and his brilliant lie sure to cause anger. "Elizabeth tells me our hens are laying fewer eggs these days and suspects he may be stealing some from our chicken coup in the cloak of night. Who knows how many others he's been robbing."

"Those no-good, yellow belly thieves. The whole lot of them." Maxfield grit his teeth, and his eyes became fiery. "Well, how might I assist you, young man?"

Leonard's skin crawled with excitement since his employer's curiosity peaked in finding a solution. "I'm acquainted with two fellas who can assist me in ridding this streetwalker once and for good. They're for hire, and they aren't cheap." He loosened the bandana around his neck.

"Spare me the details, son. I don't want to know, nor do I want to be involved. Give me the bottom line. How much are they asking?"

Leonard coughed to bring clarity to his answer. "One hundred fifty dollars each, sir." He shivered at the thought of going through with this murderous plan. Before the two men could have another cup of coffee, Maxfield found himself cracking open his safe and expelling a purse loaded with coin and placing it in his superintendent's hands.

"You do what you must to keep your family safe. Just leave me out of it." He locked eyes with Leonard. "You have no idea where this ballast came from. You understand? And I expect you to pay back every last dime by the end of this year or I'll deduct it from your wages. Am I clear?"

Leonard shook Maxfield's hand. "Yes, sir, Boss. As clear as day." He took the bag and skedaddled out the door and to the barn where Harold and Grier waited.

HUDDLED BEHIND THE TALL WILD PINE and olive-colored black oak trees on Merced Falls Road, Leonard, Harold and Grier awaited Huang-Fu's arrival. To do major harm and leave him for dead with hope to arouse fear and send a warning to the Chinese farm workers is their intention.

"All right, men, cover your faces with your bandanas. We don't want anyone recognizing us. He should be comin' 'round the corner at any moment. Be real quiet now," Leonard snarled.

After Leonard discerned the Chinaman's footsteps, he signaled, and the thugs stepped out from where they hid. One before the streetwalker, one behind him, and Leonard stood to the side with a lasso in his hand.

"Where do ya think you're goin', Coolie?" sneered the thug in front. His eyes burned under his dusty, wide-brimmed hat. In his clutch, he weaponized a sturdy limb of driftwood he picked up at the Merced River crossing.

HUANG-FU FROZE as he stared at the masked assailant's eyes. He felt perspiration beads form on his brow and his heart pound adrenaline to his limbs. Next, what happened in seconds seemed like an eternity. The three thugs rushed at him. Having been taught some martial arts, Huang-Fu tilted the staff on his shoulders and dropped the produce-filled baskets on both ends to the ground.

The sturdy six-foot-long bamboo pole now became his defense weapon. He blocked several blows from the ruffians in front and behind him. *Clack, smack.* The pole and the driftwood collided. Whipping the staff around himself, Huang-Fu landed blows on one man's head and the other man's legs and sent them to the ground. However, the third roughneck on his side lassoed him, forced him to drop his staff, and rendered his arms useless. The thug wrapped the lasso tight around Huang-Fu's waist to his ankles, as if he were rustling steer. Once incapacitated, the other thugs regained their senses, rose, and beat him with the driftwood planks. Then they kicked his baskets, which scattered the produce about the ground.

Huang-Fu's blood oozed from his temples and saturated the dirt road. His body lay limp and broken, yet he forced himself to examine his assailants and listen for any clues as to who they were.

"Let's get out of here before someone sees us. Not one word to Maxfield unless you want the same fate as this Chinaman. Other than myself, he has no clue who my accomplices are," the thug who held the lasso warned in a low, raspy voice. He picked up Huang-Fu's staff and broke it over his knee. Their hateful, condescending laughter filled the air.

Another thug's spurs jangled as he walked by Huang-Fu's head. *Snakes.* These venomous creatures were engraved into his spur's heel bands.

Huang-Fu heard the thugs throw the makeshift weapons into the nearby trees, gather their horses, and ride away. The pain intensified, causing him to drift in and out of consciousness. He had just enough breath to keep himself alive. *Maxfield.* He did his best to memorize the name before darkness overcame him.

About an hour later, a clip-clop hoof sound intensified as it came nearer to Huang-Fu. He strained to open his bloodied eyes and saw one of the white workers from Kelly's ranch pass by, riding his spotted Mustang. *Please help me.* His failed attempts to push the words out from his phlebotomized lips only increased the painful pounding in his head. The rider spat on the ground and galloped past.

Almost another two hours later, one of the elders of a church in Forlorn Hope rode by in his buggy. He happened upon Huang-Fu's body and his familiar basket-weave hat laying a few feet from him. *Ah, I know this man. Surely he will stop to help.*

Huang-Fu's heart fell to despair as the man maneuvered his buggy clear to the road's opposite side and acted as though he had never seen him.

Ugh, the pain. I can't hold on any longer. The trees seemed to spin around, and soon darkness overcame him again.

12

From Tragedy Comes Love

Sower Farm's lunch hour fast approached, and Jia-Li and her mother raced about the kitchen to assemble a meal with what means availed them. Her father had not returned at his usual time between ten and ten-thirty in the morning.

"What shall we do, Mŭqīn? I am worried about Fùqīn," Jia-Li said when the grandfather clock chimed on the half-hour.

"Look down the path and check for your father. Yes, he is late, and I hope he is all right. If you do not see him, then find either Mr. Jonathan or Samuel and let them know. Fast now! I will ask Naomi to help me prepare lunch for the workers. I am sure they will understand," her worried mother said.

Jia-Li ran to the front porch steps and viewed the men in the distant wheat field as they set aside the farm equipment. They awaited Samuel to fetch them for lunch. However, the wagon did not arrive there yet. *He must still be in the barn.*

She glanced down the long wayside path that led to Merced Falls Road behind the schoolhouse. Not one soul roamed the road.

Scurrying to the large cedar-planked building that housed the horses and mules, she stood at the double doors and saw Samuel as he prepared to open one of the horse's stalls.

"Mr. Samuel," she cried into the dusty sun rays, which seeped through the barn wall's cracks. He put down the reins and rushed over to her.

"What's wrong, Jia-Li?" he said as if peering into her troubled mind.

"My father … he has not returned yet from town. He is almost two hours late. Mother and I are worried. This is not like him."

"Okay, let me get Fire, and I'll go look for him."

"Please, I come with you, Mr. Samuel."

"No, you must stay here. I have a bad feeling about this."

"Please, Mr. Samuel, please!"

SAMUEL COULD NOT REFUSE, for he knew she would follow somehow. Holding her shoulders square before him, he gave a stern warning. "All right. But if there is any trouble, I want you to stay on my horse and return to the farm."

"Yes, of course." She nod.

He pulled Fire from his stall and fixed the bit in his mouth. The matters urgency did not permit enough time to saddle him, so he transferred the reins into Jia-Li's hands while he ran in the house to appeal for David's help to fetch the workers in the wagon. He also located his father in the other barn and notified him of the situation.

"If you are not back in a few hours, I will come after you both," his father insisted. "Be sure to take your revolver with you, son."

"Yes, Pa, I will." Samuel quick-stepped to the house and retrieved his gun belt from his father's office. Upon his return to the barn, he helped Jia-Li up on Fire's bareback and climbed on behind her.

"Come on, Fire, let's go." He snapped at his reins and gave his horse a sharp kick on the side. The steed jolted forward and galloped through the wheat field's wayside path heading toward Merced Falls Road. The morning mist dissipated, but a slight chill still hung in the air.

Jia-Li clung to the horse's mane as they searched for her father's whereabouts. The tension in her body revealed she could not contain her emotions and anxiety. By wrapping his arms around her waist and tightening his grip, he hoped to provide a sense of security. Her long, silky, dark strands moved with the wind and brushed Samuel's cheek. The exotic oil fragrance emanating from her body danced in his senses with his every breath.

As Fire maneuvered toward the main thoroughfare, they noticed a cocooned body lying in the dirt about 200 yards in the distance. Samuel gave Fire another swift kick, which caused the horse to race to the site.

He hoped it was not so, but, soon, they recognized her father's belongings strewn about him.

"No … Fùqīn, no!"

Fire came to an abrupt halt near the fallen man, and Samuel quickly dismounted. He helped the frantic girl to the ground. Rushing to the body, they turned him over and examined his pale, blood-smeared face. She placed her ear to his chest.

"He is alive, Samuel."

With the hem of her silk shirt, Jia-Li tore it and wrapped her father's head wound while Samuel untied the mangled rope around his torso and legs.

"All right, I'm going to lift him on my horse's back. Hold Fire still for me."

Samuel gingerly picked up Huang-Fu's lifeless body and sat him on top, positioned his arms about the horse's mane, and propped his blood-drenched head on Fire's neck. He yanked on the horse's reins, and they sprinted beside him, keeping the injured man steady so that he would not fall. The doctor's clinic was another fifteen minutes away on foot.

The town's people gasped at the unusual sight of a white man with a Chinese girl and a near-dead Celestial on a horse's back. After Samuel tied Fire's reins to the hitching post, he pulled Huang-Fu's body into his arms. He hastened up the steps as Jia-Li rapped on the door.

"Lord … come in and lay him on my examining table." Dr. Cassidy directed Samuel inside.

Memories crossed his mind to early doctor visits as a young man. He recalled Dr. Cassidy's warm smile, kind eyes, and gentle hands, which had always calmed his fears. This gracious man performed as his family's physician for ten years now and demonstrated tremendous compassion for their unprejudiced views. Huang-Fu would be treated well by him.

"Why don't you both wait in the other room while I examine him?" the doctor said with utmost sensitivity.

"Don't worry about any expenses, Doctor. I'll cover everythin'. Huang-Fu is our butler and is dear to my family, and this is his daughter, Jia-Li. We found him beaten and lyin' on the side of Merced Falls Road."

"I will try to do my best, miss. Please, take a seat, and pray."

"Thank you, Dr. Cassidy." Jia-Li sobbed.

Samuel placed his arms around Jia-Li's shoulders as the doctor entered the examining room, washed his hands in the white metal basin, and used the toe of his boot to close the door. Without hesitation, Sam guided the shaken girl to the couch.

"I don't know what Mother and I will do without Father." Tears fell from her eyes.

Samuel pulled her next to him, embraced her, and she leaned her head into his chest as he prayed and offered compassion and support.

"Dear God, we thank you for your mercy upon Huang-Fu and for keeping him alive through this terrible ordeal. We pray for Your healin'. Sometimes we can't understand why things of this nature happen, but You do, and we hope You can use this awful circumstance for Your glory. Please give Dr. Cassidy wisdom and the skill to perform the necessary treatment. Father, provide comfort and strength for Jia-Li and her mother. Reveal Your awesome power to this precious family, to me, and to those that committed this heinous act. We pray that these men will sense conviction and be repentant for what they've done. Father, please forgive them for their trespasses and give us the ability to do the same. In our Savior's holy name. Amen."

About an hour later, the doctor emerged from the examination room, closing the door behind him, his apron covered with crimson stains.

"Miss, your father is stable for now. He lost a lot of blood, has a concussion, and fractured his collarbone and a couple of ribs. You must leave him here until he wakes and regains his strength. Then you may consider bringing him home. However, he will need to remain in bed for at least six weeks.

"He is in good care, so go home, get some rest, and put your minds at ease."

Jia-Li stood to her feet. "Can I see father before we go?"

"Of course you can, dear." The compassionate physician opened the examining room door and allowed the couple to enter.

The makeshift torn-silk-shirt bandage no longer wrapped Huang-Fu's head, and a linen blanket covered his body. The washbowl by the opposite wall overflowed with watered-down blood and several wash rags.

"I cleaned his head wound and stitched the lacerated area. The gauze covering his temple will need to be changed every so often." He gathered Huang-Fu's bloodied clothing from the table next to the bed and handed them to Jia-Li. "You may take his belongings home with you. For now, your father is wearing a patient's gown."

As she leaned over her father's pale face, Jia-Li muttered into his left ear. "Fùqīn, if you can hear me, know that I love you. You are safe here with Dr. Cassidy, and he will care for you. Please do not give up. You must fight for your life. Tomorrow, I will return with Mǔqīn and plan to visit you until you are strong enough to come home. Rest, Fùqīn. We are praying for you."

Afterward, Samuel whispered into his right ear. "Mr. Suen, it's me, Samuel. I think you can recognize my voice. You need not worry about Jia-Li and Liang. Just concentrate on returning to good health. Your family is appreciated … and I love Jia-Li very much."

Upon expressing his heart, he glanced at Jia-Li and locked his eyes with hers. He broke the unspoken cultural taboo that kept their hearts in bondage from one another. He reached to hold Jia-Li's trembling hand across her father's prone body.

"I love you, too, Samuel." Her poignant tears turned into joy-filled affection, which radiated her sweet face.

They peered down at her father. Although his eyelids remained closed, his facial expression seemed to acknowledge their disclosure, and his lips curled with approval.

"Mr. Suen, I hope you approve of my affection for your daughter. You rest now, and we will return in the morning with your wife." The love-struck couple released one another's hands, gave her father a gentle squeeze on his hand, and exited the examining room.

"Doctor, thank you again for everything." Samuel extended a handshake to the trustworthy friend.

"Thank you so much, Dr. Cassidy. We will see you tomorrow."

Jia-Li curtsied and smiled.

After they left the clinic, Samuel assisted Jia-Li on to Fire's back, and he sat behind her. The horse's mane still saturated with her father's blood, she leaned back against Samuel's chest. She relaxed while seated in his embrace, rested her head upon his neck, and immersed herself in every ounce of his affection. No words transpired between them as they rode home. Yet he knew they understood each other's silence.

They arrived at the barn and put Fire in his stall. Closing the gate behind him, Samuel once again embraced her, looked into her softened eyes, and kissed her.

"I love you, Jia-Li." Samuel's erratic heart raced as her dark ribbon locks fell away from her face when she peered back at him. The faint sandalwood scent from her body filled his senses like an aphrodisiac, which aroused in him an exotic and pleasurable awareness unlike he's experienced before. They held one another for a long moment, gazed into one another's eyes, and kissed once more.

On the way back to the farmhouse, Samuel shoved his fists into his pant pockets. He desired to hold her hand, but he couldn't. They must conceal their love until the appropriate time. An invisible aura surrounded them as they walked together, which seemed to announce their secret affections. Samuel hoped, for now, their love to be unnoticeable.

What is happening to me? Do I dare enter into this forbidden relationship? My heart is willing, wanting, yet my mind tells me, 'no.' If this is Your will, Lord, then nothing shall hinder Your plan.

"THAT CAN'T BE! Who would attack a defenseless old man?" The troubling news about his butler came as a shock to Jonathan. He pounded his desk and growled as Samuel and Jia-Li shared the day's events. "I feel horrible. This is my fault. As an employer and friend, my heart aches because I should have provided a more secure plan for my Chinese workers knowing the hate crimes perpetrated against them. Dear Lord, give me wisdom on how to handle the matter." He bowed his head for a moment to listen to God's inaudible voice. Not more than a few seconds later, Jonathan raised his chin and addressed his staff.

"Liang, is it possible for you to prepare your next day's grocery list before the men go home? If you can do that, then I will provide one of the superintendents with the funds to purchase the groceries and bring it back with him the following morning. Yung lives at the camp and walks through town with the other farmhands. This option may be our best solution for now. Will this suffice?" Jonathan exercised sensitivity toward Liang's fragile state of mind.

"Ah, yes, Mr. Jonathan. I suppose this will have to do until my husband is well enough again. I do not want to add more work to your men that you already require of them." Her voice trembled as she gripped her daughter's hand.

"No trouble for me, Lao Liang. Mr. Jonathan's suggestion is the most probable way of handling this, even if Zhǎnglǎo Huang-Fu has recovered. To travel alone anywhere is not safe for us. We cannot let him go by himself again," Yung responded according to their culture's tradition using proper titles. "I will wait for your grocery list before I go home."

"Shi, Xiao Yung. You and Mr. Jonathan are right. I will give it to you at the end of the day. Thank you very much, Mr. Jonathan."

"It is no trouble, Liang," Jonathan replied with a warm smile. "Yung, please see me after receiving the list from Liang, and I will provide you money for the groceries, all right?"

"Shi de, yes, Mr. Jonathan." Yung bowed.

Jonathan concluded the meeting, and they resumed their work. Yung returned to the farmhouse at the end of the day as instructed and returned the following morning and dropped off the groceries and change. The wisdom God provided would be the new standard of operation for the domestic help, and Jia-Li and Liang were grateful.

AFTER THREE DAYS OF VISITING her husband after lunch at the doctor's clinic, Liang held Huang-Fu's hand speaking soft, comforting words. Never had she considered her husband in this predicament. She always portrayed his demeanor with strength and honor. Here he lay helpless and violated. Anger burned inside her against his perpetrators, along with a deep sadness coming to terms that her beloved may not revive. *Oh, but you must, Huang-Fu. I cannot live without you.*

"I am here, Zhàngfū. Will you not wake for me? I miss you terribly," she said. "I brought your favorite wonton soup. You must wake and eat if you are to survive." Placing her cheek on his hand, she wept and prayed.

"Dear God, save my husband and heal his wounds. Mr. David tells us You are a great physician and nothing is impossible for You. Huang-Fu is still much needed at farm and by me and daughter, Jia-Li. Please, my Lord, bring him back to me."

A few minutes passed, and Huang-Fu's hand flinched beneath her face. At first, Liang thought she provoked the reaction, but again the movement. She lifted her head and peered down at his fingers twitching before her.

"Qīzi." *Wife*, Huang-Fu said with sputtered words. "Wǒ èle."

Shocked by her husband's awakening and his first words, *I am hungry*, Liang rolled with hysteria. "Thank you, Jesus! My husband is alive, and he is hungry!"

The examining room's door swung open, and Dr. Cassidy entered. "I heard some voices and laughter coming from this room. Are you celebrating without me?" The gleeful physician chuckled aloud. "Welcome back, Huang-Fu."

The ailing patient's face glowed despite his weariness. "Hello, doctor. Thank you for caring for me. How did I get here?"

"Samuel and Jia-Li found you fallen on Merced Falls Road. They brought you to my clinic in very bad condition."

"Oh, somehow I knew that. As if I can hear their voices whisper in my ear while I sleep." He smiled while his eyes ruminate the unfamiliar surroundings.

"Be still now. Your collarbone and some ribs are broken. You will need six weeks of bed rest and no heavy lifting." The doctor touched Huang-Fu's side.

"Āiyō," Huang-Fu cried.

Liang gasped. "Impossible for him to do. Husband is hard worker." She wagged her finger. "But I will make sure he stay in bed, and I will be the one to wait on him."

"Well done, Mrs. Suen. He'll need all the help he can get. Now that he is awake, he can let me know if I missed anything. If all goes well, he can go home by the end of this week."

Liang clapped her hands. "Thank you, Dr. Cassidy."

The doctor sniffed the air, "What is that delicious aroma I smell?"

"Oh, I brought husband's favorite wonton soup. Plenty here for all of us. Would you like a bowl?"

In unison, Huang-Fu and Dr. Cassidy said, "Yes!"

13

Waiting for an Answer

David took his mind off the dreadful anxiety of waiting to hear from Taylor University by tending to the young vegetable sprouts in the farmhouse's backyard next to his mother's fruit trees. To lessen their dependency upon the Chinese community garden, the Suens planted their own produce in their spare time, along with him, his sister, and his mother. Huang-Fu was well enough to begin his work in the kitchen, and Yung continued to purchase the items on the list Liang provided at the end of the day.

"Ma, did we receive any post today?" David asked as he did every day beginning in April. He was aware of the university's admission process, which began around the spring semester. Over a month passed and yet no response. The anticipation tested his patience.

A pout hinged beneath a smile, his mother's almost rehearsed daily answer would be, "No, son. Not yet."

Not a moment too soon, in mid-May, while he was gardening with his mother, sister, Liang, and Jia-Li, a knock came to the front door. He continued to plow as his mother removed her gloves and scurried into the home. A few moments later, he heard her quickened gait as she maneuvered through the kitchen, opened and slammed the back door, and trotted toward him with squeals of excitement.

"It's here, David. It's here!" His mother waved the awaited message about her as she ran to him and placed the travel-weary envelope in his hand.

After reading the name of the sender, *Taylor University*, David could only stare at it. He froze, frightened to reveal its contents. This insignificant small piece of paper held the key to his life's direction. *What path will you take me, Lord, if I'm not accepted? I'm not going to allow discouragement to get the best of me. I'll move on and seek another college until I've exhausted all avenues.* His mind and emotions sought reasoning to cushion him should the answer be negative.

Hands trembling, he handed the revelation back to his mother to disclose. God used her to mentor and guide his life's spiritual journey. The maternal support she provided matched no other, and he could not contain his gratitude.

"Ma, do me the honors and read it for me. Besides, my hands are dirty."

His mother's gentle smile and the touch of her hand on his sun-warmed cheek told him she understood his apprehension. Her intuition and Biblical fortitude always calmed his nerves and served as a pillar to uphold him during difficult times. As a farmer who tends to his garden daily, she deserved to taste the fruit of her labor. Four children are her young sprouts, which she nurtured to the best of her ability. David desired his mother to take part in this moment no matter what direction he traversed. To be accepted at a college would be her crowning achievement.

"All will be fine, David. The Lord has a plan for you, regardless of what this letter says. You are called to preach, son. No university can tell you that. That authority comes from God alone." She embraced him and proceeded to open the envelope and expel the contents.

"Dear Mr. Sower:

We are honored to inform you of your admission to Taylor University. On behalf of the faculty, we commend you on your personal and scholastic accomplishments.

To reserve your place among the graduates of Taylor University, please send a $25 non-refundable enrollment deposit as soon as possible if you have already determined this university is the best place for you.

Again, congratulations on your educational accomplishments and your admission to Taylor University. Best wishes for continued success. We look forward to seeing you here on campus this fall semester.

Sincerely,
Thaddeus Reade
Director of Admissions and Recruitment"

14

Internal Conflict

"Come on, baby girl. You need to eat." Sarah fretted as she tried to force Isabelle to consume a piece of flapjack with butter and honey, her favorite breakfast meal. For three days she would not chew or swallow. Too enervated to cry or respond, her eyes watered as she faded in and out of consciousness. Sarah knew her weak daughter was constipated and in pain.

"You're a little more than two years old, little one. You should be wantin' to walk, giggle, and play with your bub and sis," Sarah said under her breath. Instead, Isabelle's legs were feeble, her eyelids were always droopy, and her cry was languid. To avoid another expensive doctor's appointment, Sarah evaluated Amanda's and Billy's healthy appetite to Isabelle's as she sat slumped in her handcrafted oak highchair across from them at the kitchen table. Sarah hoped to remedy the situation herself, but nothing she did seemed to work.

I've done all that I know to do. That's it. I'm going to take you to see the physician in Mariposa. I'll sell one of our hogs if I must to pay for the medical care that you need, sweetheart. She removed the particles from her mouth, lifted the highchair tray over her head, cradled her frail body, and lay her down in her crib.

"Children, finish your breakfast, and then we'll go into town to drop-in on a few people." Sarah disguised her voice with a tinge of perkiness because she did not want to alarm Amanda and Billy. "Wait here while I tell Mr. Qiang to prepare the wagon for us."

Sarah ran outside to her small garden where the elderly Chinese farmhand was watering the vegetables.

"Qiang, the children and I will need to go to town today to see the doctor. Please ready the horse and wagon."

"Yes, madam, right away." He bowed, put down the pail, turned on his heels, and hustled to the modest corral. After placing a lasso around the draft horse's neck, he led him to the Conestoga.

Inside the cabin, the children finished their breakfast, and Sarah placed the dishes in the dishpan.

"Mama, are we going to see Mr. Bogart?" Amanda inquired, eyes glistening. He owned the mercantile store in Mariposa and always had a special treat for her children upon their arrival.

"Yes, sweetheart, but first we're gonna stopover at Mrs. Delina's home. Now hurry and put your boots on, the both of you, while I dress Isabelle." Perturbed by her failing promise, Sarah did her best to coax the youngsters to hasten themselves.

Sarah recalled her milk going dry when trying to feed two babies close in age. To remedy the problem, Delina Bergman, an acquaintance she met at the local doctor's clinic, was still lactating and offered her service since her two young children no longer needed to be breastfed. The robust mother became her children's wet nurse when Sarah wasn't able.

After Sarah laced Amanda's and Billy's boots and placed their hats on their heads, she gently gathered the listless Isabelle into her arms, carried her to the wagon, and placed her in the portable bassinet's feather mattress covered with a quilt. The gullible young siblings followed, and Qiang lifted them and sat them next to their baby sister.

Sarah grabbed hold of the reins, released the side handle brake, shouted to the draft horse, "Hee-yah," and made a clicking sound with her mouth. The sturdy animal pulled forward with a little jolt and was soon off on a steady pace into town about fifteen minutes away.

"While I take Isabelle to the clinic, you both can play with your best friends. Do you remember how much you loved to ride Ira's rocking horse, Billy? And do you recall the dollies and their pretty little dresses that Connie had, Amanda?"

Sarah was quick to change the subject rather than dwelling on the doctor's visit. This had always been a difficult ordeal for them as toddlers. They had been either dragged into the clinic, while they waited in boredom as she paced, or forced to stay home with their grandma or their wet nurse.

Blank stares rebounded to Sarah.

"How 'bout we sing the new song Mrs. Delina taught you both? Remember?

> "This old man, he plays one,
> He plays knick-knack on his thumb,
> With a knick-knack, paddy-whack, give a dog a bone,
> This old man came rolling home."
> She sang with glee. "Come on now, join me!
> This old man, he plays two,
> He plays knick-knack on his shoe,
> With a knick-knack, paddy-whack, give a dog a bone,
> This old man came rolling home."

Soon Amanda and Billy started singing along, and their blank stares turned into joy and laughter when they arrived at the Bergman's quaint country cottage on Bullion and Fifth Street in Mariposa.

WHILE DELINA PEERED OUT her window's white-crocheted curtains, she could see the half-covered Conestoga stopped in front of her white picket fence. From Sarah's frenetic actions gathering her two toddlers, Delina discerned the urgency in her step and realized something dreadful had occurred. She scurried to the foyer door to open it.

"Well, look who's come to pop-in on me," Delina bellowed, holding the door ajar. "If it isn't my Mandy-girl and Billy-boy."

The jolly and able-bodied mother of two young grade-school children opened her arms wide as she trotted down the porch steps. Her white linen apron was pinned to the bodice of her orange-printed day dress and tied around her thickened waistline. The cream-colored hair net filled with her long auburn hair bounced as she approached.

While kneeling to scoop the young children into her embrace, Delina looked up at Sarah, whose widened eyes, furrowed brows, and frown expressed her panic-stricken state of mind.

"Good mornin' Mrs. Delina. Isabelle and I are going to visit Dr. Cavanaugh. May Amanda and Billy play with Ira and Connie for a while?" Sarah's smile was tense as she mouthed to Delina without vocally making a sound so the children would not hear, "VERY SICK."

Delina nodded her head in agreement and returned a wink. She released her grasp on the youngsters, stood, and turned on the balls of her feet to call out to her young ones. "Ira, Connie! Mandy and Billy are here!"

The *pitter-patter* of footsteps resounded as Ira and Constance ran on the hardwood floors of the ranch-style home toward the front door. The youngsters exchanged giggles and laughter as they darted back inside the house and into their rooms to play.

With the children indoors, Sarah explained her frantic disposition. "Oh, Delina. Isabelle is extremely ill and hasn't eaten for three days. I'm not sure how long I'll be at the doctor's office. Would you mind watchin' the children until I know more of her condition? Afterward, I plan to telegraph my mother for her help. I've never seen her so melancholy."

"Of course, dear. Don't you worry none. You know I love your babies as if they were my own."

"Oh, Delina, I greatly appreciate your friendship. How will I ever repay you?"

"No, no … don't even think about doin' such a thing. The pleasure is mine. Best be on your way then. Not a moment to lose."

SARAH CLIMBED BACK IN THE WAGON and cracked the reins as the horse pulled forward into town to the clinic on Sixth and Bullion Street.

Inside the clinic, Dr. Cavanaugh shook his head in dismay at Isabelle's lethargic condition. Without hesitation, he placed her in a child-size bed and asked several questions of Sarah as he examined the child's feeble body.

"When was the last time she ate anything, Mrs. Hampton?"

"It was about three days ago, Doctor."

"Do you recall what you fed her?"

"Well, the things we usually eat," Sarah said, trying to remember the meals she prepared earlier that week. "For breakfast, I made biscuits, or flapjacks with some honey, and eggs. For lunch, we had cold meat and bread, and for dinner, I made them stew. The children love fresh milk at every meal.

"Isabelle has always had a lack of appetite since she was born. Sweetening the lactation with sugar or honey to entice her helped a little, yet she only seemed to become more lethargic. I tried my best to get her to eat, Doctor, but I'm plum out of ideas and fearful for her life." Sarah held her tears back while caressing her baby's dainty fingers.

Putting down his stethoscope after listening to Isabelle's faint heartbeat, he turned to place a hand on Sarah's shoulder and encourage her. "Now, now, Mrs. Hampton. Don't you despair about how you raised Isabelle or your other two children. You've done what any mother would do.

"The fact is, I do believe your child has contracted a rare case of infant botulism. It's not uncommon in these parts where food can easily become contaminated with spores of Clostridium Botulinum. Some infants' immune systems are not strong enough to defend their body, and so the spores germinate and remain in the baby's intestinal tract." The doctor explained the best he could in nontechnical terms.

"I don't understand. Isabelle eats the same foods as the rest of the family, and her siblings do not seem to be affected by it." She defended herself.

"Children over the age of one normally build up a defense system in their bodies. However, in Isabelle's case, it appears she was born with weak immunity.

"I heard you mention honey as your method of encouraging her to eat. For most infants, this is not a problem, but for Isabelle, it is. This delectable treat contains a large amount of these spores. Also, improper canning of foods can do this, too. So, if you are preparing canned goods, Mrs. Hampton, I suggest the proper sterilization methods be strictly observed."

"Oh, dear. That is why Isabelle did not improve but only seemed to worsen as I added honey to her food. I had no idea." Sarah felt her heart sink to the pit of her stomach.

"Now, Mrs. Hampton, again, do not receive my counsel as being judgmental. You are innocent and intended to do well, as any other mother would have. You've done nothing wrong in caring for your children. It's rather quite normal. You didn't know Isabelle had an immune deficiency.

"No matter, your child is very ill. I suggest you allow her to stay in the clinic for a while until she becomes stable. This disease can be crippling and fatal. We're not out of the woods yet, and the next few days will determine her outcome.

"Isabelle will be on a treatment of botulinum antitoxin and be fed by tube. I'll also perform an enema to clear her intestines from the spores. The procedure can be difficult for her, and you must trust the Lord and me for His healing strength for your daughter." The physician's eyes were soft and filled with compassion as he delivered his prognosis.

"I would like to have a moment with her, Doctor." Sarah began to weep as conflict stirred in her heart. *The Lord's healing strength? Where was He when Joshua was ill? Why would God want to answer me after I abandoned Him for not listening to my prayers before?*

"Of course, Mrs. Hampton. I have to give her a mild sedative so she can sleep and allow her body to repair its self. She may not be awake much. Although she will be asleep, I believe she can hear your comforting voice and sense the touch of your hand. This should speed up the process of her healing. I'll administer the botulinum antitoxin and sedative now. As I prepare it, you can spend time with her. Afterward, I suggest you go home, get some rest, and care for your other children."

"Thank you for your kindness and service, Doctor."

Caressing her despondent daughter's hand as she lay helpless on the child-size bed, Sarah wept and whispered, "Mama loves you, Isabelle, and I'm right here for you. Dr. Cavanaugh is going to make you well…" She paused as the recollection of her father's words from their Thanksgiving reunion came to her mind. *Give God a chance to help your marriage and go to Him in prayer.*

Twice now, she had been instructed to pray and trust God. Her jaw tightened as she clenched her teeth. This time, it was her daughter's life that depended on it. How could she not do this for her? She would not be able to live with herself if something were to happen to Isabelle, and she did not take all measures to help her. *All right, God. You win. I'll pray to You even though You probably won't listen to me anyway, and You're going to do what You want regardless.*

She continued to speak to her child, "…and so is God. You just rest and get better, and Mama will be praying for you and holdin' your hand. Mama's goin' to pray for you right now.

"Dear God. We need you desperately. Please, Lord, touch my daughter's body and heal her from this terrible illness. I have nowhere to turn but to plead with You for Isabelle. You hold power to all life. Also, give Dr. Cavanaugh wisdom and divine skill to minister to Isabelle's needs. Thank You, Jesus. Amen."

Sarah opened her eyes, viewing her helpless child, and could not stop from feeling responsible for her condition. She turned away and walked to the window, began to weep, and prayed some more.

"Lord, please do not take Isabelle from me so soon. Forgive me for being bitter toward You about Joshua's death. He was Yours first before he was mine.

"Lord, if You spare Isabelle's life, I promise to return to You and raise my family, so they know You. I plead with You. Do not place my punishment for my iniquities upon them. I would rather have You take me instead and give me what I deserve than to allow my children to suffer on account of my rebelliousness against You. Oh, Father, please have mercy on me. I beg of You."

Dr. Cavanaugh returned to the examination room with the medication. "Are you all right, Mrs. Hampton?"

Wiping away her tears with a laced linen handkerchief, she turned to face him. "Yes, Doctor, I'm fine. Thank you so much. I'll return tomorrow." Sarah shook his hand and left the clinic with a heavy heart filled with uncertainty. *Will my daughter live? Have I been a terrible mother? Have I caused my child's illness? Will God answer my prayers?*

15

Finding True Peace

The Mariposa post office's convenient location one block away from the clinic on Main Street, in between Fifth and Sixth Street, required a minimal stroll. The walking distance provided enough time for Sarah to gather her thoughts and determine the right words to send to her mother via telegram. Inside the one-story brick and mortar building, she joined other residents and stood in line to send their post, purchase stamps, collect their mail, and place a telegram order.

Click, click, click the telegraph machine rang as the postal clerk sent a message on the latest technology to sweep the nation. This mechanical contraption attached to miles of electrical wiring connected the East Coast to the West Coast. This method deemed far more efficient and cost-effective than the pony express and became her lifeline to her family.

"Next, please," the clerk said.

She approached the counter to make her request. "Excuse me, sir, I would like to send a telegraph to Mr. and Mrs. Jonathan Sawyer on La Grange Road in Snelling."

"Yes, ma'am. Please write down your message on this form." The tall, lean clerk dressed in a postal uniform similar to a military officer's high collared frock coat and flat-top kepi handed her a piece of paper the size of a postcard.

He continued. "Allow me to explain the charges so you'll not be alarmed. The Western Union telegraphic messages are costly and charged by the word after twenty-five words. So you may want to abbreviate your sentences as much as possible without compromising your message."

"Oh my, quite pricey indeed," she said, checking her coin. She stepped aside, fumbled with her short but defined sentences, and wrote them down. *Isabelle very ill and staying in doctor's clinic. I need your help. Please come soon, Ma. With love, Sarah Hampton.*

"Here you are, sir," she said while returning the form.

The clerk read and counted. He peered up at her with a compassionate glance doing his best to be professional and not allow his emotions to dictate his duty.

Perhaps he's feeling guilty charging an exorbitant amount to a grieving mother with extensive medical bills. No matter. I must not spare the expense for Isabelle's sake.

"That's twenty words, ma'am. This message falls under our flat fee of one dollar and nine cents."

"Thank you kindly, sir." Sarah opened her satchel and handed the clerk her payment.

With immediacy, he tapped the Morse code on the telegraph machine, and sent it to the Snelling Ranch post office within seconds. Sarah could imagine the clerk on the receiving end who would translate and deliver the message on horseback to her parents at the farm the very same day.

THE CHILDREN PLAYED INDOORS when Sarah arrived to retrieve them from Delina's home. She knocked on the door, pulled on the strap of her bonnet, fussed with her frazzled hair, and took a deep breath to try and calm her distraught emotions.

Delina greeted her and peered down at Sarah's arms, perhaps hoping Isabelle would be with her. "Come in, dear, and sit down and relax. I'm makin' us some supper. One less thing you need to worry about now. Would you care for a cup of tea?"

"Oh, Delina, you are the most precious friend I ever had. Yes, please, I'll take a cup, and thank you so much for havin' us for supper."

Sarah hung her straw bonnet on a chair and sat down. Discouraged, she propped her elbows up, cupped her face in her hands, and inhaled. "Delina, God must hate me. My circumstances are unbearable. I don't know how much more I can handle. The doctor says Isabelle has a rare case of infant botulism and may be prone to be crippled if she survives at all the next few days. My life is one bad misfortune after another."

Delina poured boiled water from the kettle into a teapot sprinkled with spiced sassafras to steep and set two teacups on the table for Sarah and her. She pulled out the wood slat chair, sat down across from the grieving mother, and stretched out her hand toward her.

"Darlin', God doesn't hate you. He is a God of love and cares for His children. The Bible tells us He loved us yet while we were sinners. Do not lose hope, Sarah, dear. Here, would you mind if I read to you a promise God gave to us?"

Without hesitation or waiting for an answer from Sarah, Delina grabbed her small, hardcover, leather-bound Bible from the mantle above the hearth and returned to the table. She flipped through the pages, turned to Jeremiah 29:11-13, and began reading. "'For I know the thoughts that I think toward you, saith the LORD, thoughts of peace, and not of evil, to give you an expected end. Then shall ye call upon me, and ye shall go and pray unto me, and I will hearken unto you. And ye shall seek me, and find me, when ye shall search for me with all your heart.'

"Sarah, our rebellious human nature causes us to think about ourselves first before asking God His will for our life like the Israelites did time and again. In the beginning, they worshiped and trusted in God alone to lead them. Then, as time passed, other things became more important to them like idol worship, marriage to foreigners, the belief of pagan ideologies, and obeying their laws instead of God's. Therefore, God allowed them to suffer the consequences of their own choices in hopes they would realize their wrongdoing, repent, and return to Him trusting in His righteous ways to save them."

Straightening herself from a slumped position, Sarah bent her ear to listen with more intent as she teetered between hope and loving chastisement. *All right, Delina, you have my attention. Seems like the Israelites are revealin' the story of my life.*

Delina poured the tea into the cups and took a sip. "*We* can tend to fall prey to our desires, whether that be fame, fortune, and, yes, love for another person or some thing. Our passions become greater than our desire for the Lord. Despite our failures, God still loves us and longs for us to return and make Him the priority in our lives."

Sarah squirmed in her chair. *Love for another person. Could Delina be referring to my former love for Joshua? My love for Lad and my children? I suppose I do put them first before God.*

"Sometimes, the trials in our lives are a result of our own choices. God can use our bad decisions to help us with our spiritual growth. However, we can avoid difficult outcomes if we would follow God's prescribed instructions instead of doing what we think is right in our own eyes. All you need to do is be obedient and continue to trust Him, and your faith will grow as God proves His principals to be true.

"And other times, God allows the enemy to take away our blessings to reveal what our heart truly loves. Job experienced this. His entire family perished in a fire, and he almost lost his life to an illness. Boils consumed his body, and his friends blamed him for his predicament, which he had no fault at all. He proved the devil wrong as he persevered in his faith in God despite his circumstances. In the end, because of his faithfulness, God restored everything, and then some, in Job's life."

Opening the Bible, Delina read. "Romans 8:28 tells us, 'And we know that all things work together for good to them that love God, to them who are the called according to his purpose.'"

Delina shifted in her seat and held Sarah's hand. "From my viewpoint, the Lord seems to be trying to get your attention, Sarah." Her warm smile reflected genuine concern. "Our first love ought to be for the Lord Jesus and to follow His desire for our lives. Next, we are to love others, and last, our self. As we learn to trust and obey Him, we can begin to experience peace despite our difficulties because we are acting according to His will. He would never give us more than we can handle."

Throat dry and tight from sensing conviction, Sarah sipped her tea and allowed the warmth to soothe her. "Oh, Delina, you read me like an opened book. I believe you're referrin' to the love I had for Joshua and how I put him first in my life rather than God. I realize now the only reason I attended church is because I was attracted to him, although I heard the gospel and believed. After Joshua's death, I lost what little faith I had in God.

"In fact, my marriage to Lad is of my doin' also. I never asked God if he were the right husband for me. Is this why I have no peace? How can God bring me peace with all the horrible consequences He's allowed in my life?" Sarah gnawed on her lower lip.

"Oh, dear girl." Delina's countenance expressed pity. "God is not the creator of evil. The devil *is,* and he is the prince of this world. The choice is ours to either follow him or God. When we choose to follow the direction of the world, God gives us over to our choices, which according to Proverbs 14:12 states, 'There is a way which seemeth right unto a man, but the end thereof are the ways of death.'

"Tragic circumstances will always occur because we live in a sin-cursed and fallen world. James 1 tells us God allows these trials to test our faith to teach us patience. In the end, what is important is that we do not lose our faith and hope in Him. We must persevere and get back on the right path with God."

"Just like Job?" Sarah asked.

"Yes, not only for yourself but for those you love also. You must entrust you and your daughter's life into the Master's hands just as Job did, and Joshua McSwan. We can obtain peace when we know the Almighty Father desires the very best for us, whether he chooses to prolong our years on earth, or He calls us up to heaven to be with Him where there is no more death and suffering. Life here on earth is but a vapor compared to an eternity spent with Him.

"Trust in the Lord with all your heart, Sarah, and lean not on your understanding through this difficult moment. Acknowledge Him, and He will direct your path." Delina paraphrased Proverbs 3:5, 6. "If God is calling Isabelle home, find comfort in knowing she'll be with the Lord, and you'll one day be with one another again … but only if you believe in what Jesus has done to save us. If not now, God can heal her. Either way, He will heal her of her infirmities.

"I know this is hard to receive when your child suffers. Nonetheless, you must entrust all that that is yours, including your children, into the Father's hands."

Tears streamed as Sarah envisioned life without her youngest, yet in the arms of God and no longer in pain. *No, Lord. Please don't take her from me so soon. Grant her mercy and some time of sweetness in this world as a normal and healthy child.*

Delina continued. "Now you know how the Father felt to give up His only Son to suffer and die for us, rebellious sinners that we are, who are not worthy of one drop of His blood. Jesus did this to take the penalty for our sins, so we, who believe in Him, may obtain hope beyond this sin-cursed world we live in. There is something far better for us, and I look forward to the day when we shall behold God's glory and His land of promise … heaven!" She peered upwards as if angels flew overhead. "Hope in Him gives me peace, joy, and strength to endure the temporary struggles of this fallen world.

"A true believer can look beyond tragedies and difficulties when Jesus's promises are ahead of them. Let me ask you, Sarah, do you genuinely understand and believe in Jesus' promise of peace and eternal life through His death and resurrection?"

The words flowed out of Delina's mouth like streams of water, not only to refresh Sarah but to reveal to herself the true nature of her heart and to correct her of her misguided perspective. All the difficult circumstances made sense to her now, and she could understand their purpose. God allowed these things to happen to test her faith in Him and to show to herself what she loved most. All the people she put first in her life, God permitted the enemy to take away from her; Joshua, the first boy she fell in love with, her husband on long cattle drives, and now her baby to this terrible illness. He did this to test the depth of her belief, faith, and trust in Him and His promises.

"Apparently not, Delina. That's why my life is such a mess." Sarah realized she might choose to become more resentful and bitter toward God, or obtain peace by trusting Him like Job, and yes, also like Joshua, who knew God's plan is to provide a better place for those who love Him.

Joshua's words about his trust in God returned to her. *My father and I believe our lives are in God's hands. If it's our time to depart to heaven, then we have the peace of knowing that it shall be while we are doing God's work, and we will go to be with the Lord forever.* Now, she understood the peace Joshua had despite the hardships of servitude with his father's itinerant ministry. His mind and heart focused on heaven and God's promises of eternal glory. *I need to do the same. This is what Delina is trying to explain.*

Repentance consumed Sarah. Within seconds, a renewed strength bolster from within like the sense of cleanliness after a warm bath. Without hesitation, she sought to find Jesus's answer to her problems. "Many of the disappointments in my life are consequences of the choices *I've* made. Rather than trustin' God to guide me through these difficult circumstances, I shunned and blamed Him."

Sarah's mind spun with revelation. "Peace could be mine if I trust in the Lord's decision to take Joshua to heaven through illness. Relinquishin' control to God while Lad is out on cattle drives can give me peace from suspicion and doubt. Through belief in God's selfless and charitable plan for Isabelle, peace can overtake me instead of worry and sorrow. I could be assured peace if only I believe in the Lord Jesus Christ and His promises."

Sarah's riveted countenance dropped. "However, no accord exists in my misplaced life. I realize now how much I need God's peace that surpasses all understandin', and I need Him more than ever."

Although riddled with guilt, an unfamiliar calm and relief soothed her disquieted soul. "I'm the fool for blamin' God when I am to blame for my misfortunes. I guess I never understood the fullness of Jesus' love for me through His death and resurrection to save me from this wretched life. Not only has He cleansed me from sins, but His graciousness gave me the hope of eternity with Him that I do not deserve. I should be fixin' my mind and heart upon this promise rather than the troubles of the world.

"Yes, Joshua is in the better place, and so shall Isabelle be if that is the Lord's will to take her home now. But still, Delina, my heart breaks for them." Sarah wept.

"Oh, my dear, this is natural for you to feel this way. You'd be heartless if you didn't. When God created humankind, He designed us to live forever, and death had no meaning. Because of Adam and Eve's choice to sin, justice had to be served, and all humanity and creation were cursed.

"God understands our pain and grief and knows firsthand what that feels like to die and to lose a loved one. That is why God found a way for us to return to His original plan when He created humankind without sin resulting in eternal life with Him in the Garden of Eden. He did this through the death of His only Son to take the punishment for our sins. He died for us so we can live in eternity with Him once again!

"Jesus kept His eyes on the prize to live in eternal glory with the Father and with those who love Him. You need to do the same, sweet girl. Christians are just passing through this world and should be living in anticipation of the day when we will be home with the Lord." Passion flowed from Delina's speech.

"You are correct, Delina, and I thank you for takin' the time to minister those words to me and care for my family. Havin' this heaven-bound perspective makes all the difference and changes the way I view my circumstances. Instead of doom, hope now comforts me because of your explanation. You're an angel sent by the Lord."

"'Either what woman having ten pieces of silver, if she lose one piece, doth not light a candle, and sweep the house, and seek diligently till she find it?'" Delina quoted Luke 15:8. "Sarah, you are my lost piece of silver. I couldn't rest until I found you and brought you back to the Lord. Would you like to pray?"

"Yes, let's do so."

The two women prayed and trusted in the Lord's will for Isabelle. The encouragement strengthened Sarah's faith and renewed her spirit with the hope which brings stability in this difficult season in her life full of peaks, valleys, and joy-filled moments intertwined with tragedy. Sarah had real peace in her heart as she understood why God allowed these trials to take place. The spiritual accomplishment defies human explanation. Also, she knew without a shadow of a doubt that her circumstances were going to work together for good, and God would receive glory for the incredible results.

The clock on the hearth mantle chimed five times. "Oh, my, time does fly when we are talking about the good Lord. Darrel will be home soon from his tax office. I best be gettin' supper finished for all of us. Just relax now and pull your thoughts together. I'll be done in no time." Delina hummed as she prepared the evening meal.

Sarah, Amanda, and Billy spent the remainder of the day in the comfort of the Bergman's friendship and counsel. The Hamptons returned home and would come and visit Delina for the next few days while Sarah checked on Isabelle at the clinic until her mother arrived.

16

Mother's Support

While sweeping the front porch steps, Mary drew her attention to the stranger who rode his horse with an urgent gait along the main wayside path, which leads to the farmhouse. The young man dismounted the breathless pony and tied its reins to the corral's post. He strutted up the steps and on the porch, direct to her.

"Mrs. Sower?" he asked.

"Yes."

"I have a telegraph for you from Mrs. Sarah Hampton."

Mary paused and glanced at the Western Union envelope in his hand.

"Oh, yes, one moment, please, while I fetch some change." Mary put the broom down, walked into the house, and into Jonathan's office. Rummaging through the secretary's desk, she located her crocheted reticule and a dime, then returned to the anxious courier.

"Here you are. Thank you." Mary handed the courier the tip in exchange for the telegram as he jaunted away.

Hum. Most unusual for Sarah to send a telegram. Anxiety pulsed through Mary's veins. Already anticipating bad news, she sat down on the porch chair then proceeded to tear open the envelope and read its contents.

"Oh, dear Lord." She prayed to herself. "Please heal my granddaughter and strengthen my daughter until I get there."

I must pack and leave first thing tomorrow. The family must manage without me again. She tucked the telegram in her day skirt pocket and quickstepped to her room and began to toss clothes into her carpetbag.

Countless images of her eldest daughter's struggles since her adolescence trampled her mind. *Oh, my darlin' daughter. Now that you're a mother fearin' for the well bein' of your own children, you will realize the heartache and helplessness your father and I felt when you were growin' up with troubles and isolated yourself from us. I pray you can set aside your bitterness and reach out to those who love you.*

At suppertime, she informed Jonathan of their daughter and grandbaby's dire situation. They both agreed she should go first to Sarah's aid, and he would follow after he settled things on the farm.

WHEN DAWN BROKE THE NEXT DAY, Jonathan took his wife to the new stagecoach line in Snelling, where Mr. Stilman drove his team of four horses as far as Yosemite. The public transportation deemed a valuable service to travelers headed toward the Sierra foothill towns. A far better experience than Mary's prior visits to Sarah's home, which involved a two day grueling and precarious ride with Patrick Fay while hauling cargo in his oxen driven wagon. Their overnight stay happened upon a customer's home or pitched tent under the stars. Had Patrick not been acquainted with the family, Jonathan would not have allowed Mary to travel with him.

Jonathan studied his wife's appearance and burned it in his memory in preparation for their temporary separation. Mary appeared smart and attractive in her comfortable travel attire, which consisted of a dark cotton twill walking skirt, a white Gibson blouse, a silver-notched vest, and a lady's black Coachmen hat. A far cry from the frumpy rugged travel dress she wore when traveling with Patrick.

As he helped his wife on board the stagecoach, the driver placed her carpetbag in the luggage hold. Already seated was a young mining family with an infant, and three miners. The auspicious couple positioned themselves in the rear bench cradling their baby. Two of the miners offered to sit on the center bench, and Mary ensconced herself on the forward bench with the third miner.

"All right, folks, this'll be a two-day drive. We'll be stoppin' at Hornitos for an overnight stay. I know of a reputable Mexican hotel where we can each get a room and get plenty of rest," said Stilman as he shut the stagecoach door. Fidgeting, he pulled on his watch-chain in his leather vest's lower left pocket and glanced at the time. He readjusted his Gus hat and lifted the dark bandana around his neck to his nose to keep from inhaling the rugged trail's dust.

"Mr. Stilman, will ya guarantee my wife's safety to Mariposa?" Jonathan shook his hand as he passed him ten dollars, in addition to her paid fare.

"Yes, sir, Mr. Sower. My partner and I'll be sure she arrives safe and sound. Rest your mind at ease." Winking, he placed both hands on his colt peacemaker pistols in its double-gun holster on his hips. "Isn't that right, Rufus?" He waved to his partner, who sat in the driver's outside bench.

The rugged stagecoach driver, Rufus, had a dark, waxed mustache that pointed out from under his nostrils and simulated cattle longhorns. His long beard, of the same color, flowed to a point on his chest. The early morning sun cast a slight shadow over his forehead and eyes from the wide brim, six-inch crown of his black Gus hat.

Rufus assured Jonathan by lifting his Sharps rifle and Colt revolver above his head as he puffed on a short cigar stub which hung from the corner of his lip.

Jonathan responded with a shaky grin and peered into the cramped compartment. "I'll be waitin' for your telegraph, darlin'. Give my love to Sarah and our grandchildren."

Stilman jumped on board next to his partner. With the crack of Rufus's whip, the four-team stagecoach barreled out of town, and Jonathan returned to the farm.

MARY DID HER BEST TO CONCENTRATE on her knitting as the coach rocked, swayed, and bumped along the rugged trail. She decided to lean close to the open window for fresh air should she become nauseous from the perspiration which emanated from the dusty miner's clothing.

The sun rested low on the horizon when they arrived at what seemed like a small, run-down, sleepy Mexican village called Hornitos. Mary peered out the window, disgusted at the abandoned Fandangos and bars, which now littered the once-bustling street filled with undesirable gold miners. All who remained after the gold ran out were the Spanish-speaking inhabitants who rambled through the town's sad economic state.

Stilman carried Mary's carpetbag and escorted his customers into the small Murieta Hotel.

"*Buenas tardes, Señora* Murieta. Rooms for my passengers, *por favor.*" Stilman greeted the middle-aged hotel owner dressed in a simple Mexican frock and requested her service.

"*Si, por favor sígueme, señora.*" She motioned to Mary first to follow her up the flight of stairs to a room facing the main street. There, the hostess placed Mary's luggage on the bed.

"*¿Te gustaría cenar en su habitación?*"

Mary shook her head. "Uh, I don't understand."

The woman chortled and demonstrated with her hands and brought them to her lips as if eating, then pointed to the wooden table and chair in the room.

Mary understood the universal motions. Her tired, hungry body agreed. "Ah, *si, por favor. Gracias, Señora* Murieta." She thanked her hostess.

"*De nada.*" No problem. The cheerful hostess closed the door behind her.

No sooner had Mary changed into her nightgown and combed out her long, brunette locks a soft rapping on the door broke the moment of solitude. "Please come in," Mary said.

"*La cena, la Señora* Sower." *Señora* Murieta placed the dinner-laden tray on the rustic wood table. Mary handed the woman a tip, and she exited the room and bid her guest a good evening. "*Gracias. Buenas noches.*"

The aroma of the grilled chicken breast, warm corn tortillas, Mexican rice, and refried beans filled the air. Mary devoured the delectable cuisine.

In Kentucky, she would not have experienced the distinctive flavors of ethnic gastronomy. First Chinese culinary, now Mexican. Both were unique and delicious.

With a full belly and fatigued body, Mary prayed for her family before climbing into the inviting bed covered with a colorful *serape* blanket. Although her mind raced with anxiety for her granddaughter, it submitted without resistance to her energy-drained core, which resulted in a peaceful slumber.

EIGHT O'CLOCK THE NEXT DAY, the travelers met in the minuscule dining room to eat breakfast before they boarded the stagecoach.

"Did you sleep well, Mrs. Sower?" Stilman asked as he pulled the chair out for Mary.

"Yes, I did indeed. For a small hotel, the hospitality ranks high in my book."

"I do agree, ma'am. Only the best for my passengers." Stilman cleared his throat. "Did I fail to mention that the owners of this establishment are blood relatives to the once infamous and sought-after Mexican bandit, Joaquin Murieta?" He paused as Mary and the other passenger's gasped. "He was almost caught in 1850 in search of refuge with his cousins here in Hornitos. But he escaped."

"Yes, you did fail to mention that vital piece of information," Mary snapped.

"Well, ma'am, had I told you, you would've had me scramblin' to find another hotel. And, to be frank, there are no other hotels within miles from here, and I wasn't 'bout ready to sleep under the stars with y'all. And I don't think you would've wanted that either." Mary and the others guffawed and nodded their heads in agreement.

After the rousing *ranchería* breakfast of scrambled eggs, sausage links, *tortas*, fresh salsa, and guacamole, the travelers boarded the stagecoach and headed toward Mariposa. They traveled fertile grazing valleys, then climbed steep mountainsides through dense black oak and Ponderosa pine till they arrived at the bustling foothill town filled with miners and vendors who catered to their needs.

As the stagecoach came to a stop in front of the Schlager Hotel on Main and Fifth Street, Mary recognized Sarah, Amanda, and Billy waiting for her in the shade beneath the hotel's veranda.

"Grandma!" The young children rushed into Mary's arms and extended long-overdue embraces, followed by Sarah.

"Oh, dear ones, it's good to be with y'all again!"

"Ma, I'm so glad you are here. Pa sent a telegram to tell me you were on your way." Sarah hugged her, as tears welled up in her eyes. "Do ya have enough strength to visit Isabelle before goin' to my home? The doctor's clinic is just around the corner."

"Why, sure, I do. I need to stretch my legs a little after sittin' cooped up in that stagecoach for so many hours."

"Wonderful. Let me put your carpetbag in the Conestoga, and we'll take a stroll to his clinic."

After Sarah placed her mother's carpetbag into the wagon, they walked to Dr. Cavanaugh's clinic, where the ill-fated child was beginning to come around from her terrible ordeal.

SARAH MADE THE INTRODUCTIONS. "Dr. Cavanaugh, let me introduce you to my mother, Mrs. Sower. Ma, this is Dr. Cavanaugh. He has been carin' for Isabelle for the last few days, and, thank the good Lord she is respondin' to the medication and the treatment he prescribed."

"Pleased to meet you." Her mother extended her graceful yet firm handshake.

"The pleasure is mine, as well. Now would you like to visit your granddaughter?" The doctor returned the greeting and motioned the family toward the back room where Isabelle lay in bed, determined to keep her eyes open.

Still weak but alert, Isabelle focused her glassy blue eyes upon her family. A meager whimper transcended from her lips, which filled Sarah's heart with a rush of jubilation. Her daughter's response was a wonderful sound to Sarah's ears. For up to this time, Isabelle was not able to make any sounds because of her weakened condition. The elated young mother rushed to the bed and gingerly cradled her daughter as her mother held Amanda and Billy's hands.

"Oh, my precious little girl. Mama is here." Sarah massaged her palms and feet. Isabelle's whimpers simmered down as Sarah rocked her, and soon, she was fast asleep again. *Still no movement in her arms or legs, Lord. I pray for your mercy and complete her healing.*

Sarah passed the sleeping child to her mother, who kissed her on her pale cheeks, then placed her granddaughter back in the bed with care.

"Mama, Izzy go home?" Billy pointed at his younger sister, trying his best to form a sentence between sobs.

Sarah picked up her toddler and held him. "Very soon, Billy, very soon."

Upon hearing the young child's question, Dr. Cavanaugh reviewed Isabelle's progress with the women. "Isabelle can go home maybe in a week when she is able to eat on her own and after she makes a complete bowel movement. She may not have any mobility in her extremities for a while. Only time will tell as she becomes stronger."

Sarah's heart leaped. "Thank you so much, Dr. Cavanaugh. The Lord has indeed blessed you with a healin' gift. Although Isabelle is not altogether well, she has made obvious improvements because of your excellent care and knowledge.

"I heard her cry for the first time in a long time, and she was also able to recognize me and respond to my voice. I believe that the Lord will answer our prayers." Hope-filled, Sarah's focus shifted to her mother, whose jaw had dropped after hearing Sarah's Christ-centered statement.

Sarah turned to walk out the clinic door, chin held high, and brushed past her. "Yes, Ma. My faith is rekindled." With staunch acquiescence, she assured her mother. She couldn't help but regard the bedazzled grin of approval on her mother's rosy face.

"Thank you, Lord," Mary said as she grabbed Amanda's hand and followed behind Sarah and Billy. Singing joyful hymns, they walked back to the Conestoga and returned to the small farmhouse.

SARAH VISITED ISABEL AT THE DOCTOR'S CLINIC for five days straight while her mother cared for Amanda and Billy at the farm. This day would be momentous for Sarah as Izzy displayed remarkable signs of recovery. She cooed, smiled, and her eyes sparkled.

"You may take her home this Friday." Dr. Cavanaugh's words rang clear like musical notes to Sarah's ears.

Although Isabelle still had no ambulatory movement at that time, she was able to sit up, hold her head high, be spoon-fed, and swallow. The abdominal discomfort she had experienced had subsided, and she was able to pass normal bowel movements.

"The best medicine now is for Isabelle to be with her family and familiar surroundings," Dr. Cavanaugh said.

Sarah cradled Isabelle and rocked her as if dancing to a merry tune. "You'll be goin' home soon, dear girl. Home sweet home. Thanks to your amazin' doctor."

The exciting news urged Sarah to send a telegram to her father, requesting his visit. She did not expect Lad to arrive until the end of the month, so she offered her bedroom to her parents and planned to sleep on a feather mattress near her children.

FOURTH OF JULY WILL BE MEMORABLE since the doctor liberated Isabelle from his care and, Lord willing, from her infirmity, too. Like fireworks, joy burst within her. She pulled on the reins to maneuver the Conestoga around the town toward Dr. Cavanaugh's clinic. The Mariposa citizens were euphoric that Friday afternoon as they finished their preparations for the celebration scheduled for the next day. Red, white, and blue streamers draped the homes' fences up and down Boullion Street. The doctor's clinic displayed ribbon banners on the front door.

"Ah … Mrs. Hampton. Are you ready to take Isabelle home today?" Dr. Cavanaugh cheered.

"Oh, dear doctor, as much as your gracious benevolence continues to bless me, I'm more than eager to restore my family's life to normalcy as soon as possible."

"Well, Isabelle is a wonderful patient, and my wife and I welcome her to stay with us anytime she needs to. Now, allow me to show you a few exercises you must maintain daily so that Isabelle's muscles will be strengthened and not become atrophied."

Sarah stood at attention next to the physician by Isabelle's bedside as he demonstrated several arm and leg movements upon her unresponsive body. Without hesitation, Sarah applied the techniques to her daughter as the doctor provided poignant instruction.

"As an extra incentive, I suggest you make exercise enjoyable for Isabelle by creating a game of it, perhaps sing, or even have the other children play along, as well," he suggested. "Now, as for her diet, please avoid honey or corn syrup for now. You may want to mash her food so she may chew and swallow easier until more jaw movement becomes apparent. Fresh, well-cooked foods, instead of canned, would be preferable."

"Thank you again for your sacrifice and effort on Isabelle's behalf. I'm forever in your debt."

"No debt owed to me. Your dear mother settled all costs." The doctor winked. "Well, let's continue to pray for Isabelle's complete healing. I've done as much as I know how to do. Her life is in God's hands now. But I would like you to bring her back for examination in two weeks so I can ascertain her progress."

"I'll be sure to be here, Doctor." Sarah picked up her daughter. "Now, baby girl, are you ready to go home?" She kissed Isabelle's hands. The warm caress prompted a rewarding smile that enveloped the glow-filled face of the health-stricken child.

Isabelle cooed, and her soft, blue eyes twinkled. Sarah wrapped Isabelle in a quilt and carried her to the wagon. Dr. Cavanaugh and his wife, Mildred, followed behind her.

"We will miss your lovely daughter." Mildred peered at the child's angelic face. "Please let us know of her progress."

"I shall." Sarah transferred Isabelle to Mildred to hold as she climbed into the Conestoga. After kissing Isabelle's forehead, Mildred returned her to Sarah, who placed her in the portable wicker bassinet in the wagon. Sarah gave a final wave, then jerked the reigns, and headed for her home.

17

Father's Help

Jonathan spent the last two weeks delegating duties to his superintendents Yung, Sheng-Li, and Tu, in preparation for his one-month absence while he visited his daughter and grandchildren. Midsummer was a critical time for him to be away for the harvest was about to begin. Gathered in his office, he assigned the superintendents a measure of the wheat fields and farmhands, per their management abilities.

"Yung, I will give you the greater portion of the fields to harvest as well as employees to assist you since you are the most experienced of the superintendents," Jonathan instructed. "Sheng-Li, you shall receive a medium section, and Tu the smallest. After you've harvested your portions of wheat, you are to sell the grain to Nielsen's flour mill in Merced Falls and complete all transactions. Is this understood?"

"*Shi*, Mr. Sower." They bowed.

"Now, if you don't mind Yung, will you fetch Samuel, Naomi, and David? I need to tidy up matters with them as well."

The siblings piled into Jonathan's office and sat around their father's desk.

"I received a telegram from your sister informin' me of your niece's condition. She is well enough to return home but far from bein' back to normal. She still has no muscular control of her limbs. So as expected, I'm leavin' tomorrow to spend time with them and help where I can." Jonathan leaned forward and crossed his hands on his desk. "Business will continue, as usual. Naomi handlin' the financial matters and Samuel the livestock. The superintendents have their work assignments, as well. And David will be busy preparin' to leave for college."

"Pa, I pray you and Ma return before I leave." David straightened his posture.

"Son, I'll make sure Ma and I will be back by the end of July, whether or not Lad makes it home by then. I guarantee your Ma would not miss seein' you before you leave. I can make other arrangements for Sarah in case this is necessary. If Lad were correct in his calculations, the cattle drive should be completed well near the last week of July."

"All right, Pa. Please let Sarah know I'm prayin' for Isabelle's health and Lad's safe return," David said with calm assurance.

"Will you do the same for me?" Naomi chimed in. "I do pray Isabelle is well. I'd gladly help care for my nieces and nephew if only they lived closer to home. Pa, you'll have to convince them of this."

"I'll do my best. I already offered Lad a position to work on the farm. I'm just waitin' for his decision."

JIA-LI BROUGHT A PITCHER OF LEMONADE and placed it on Jonathan's desk. She filled some glasses and distributed one to each of them. When she gave Samuel his refreshment, he tugged on her available hand to whisper in her ear. "Thank you, my love. I'll see you tonight?"

"Yes, of course," she whispered in return. She cherished the freedom to communicate her feelings and enjoy Samuel's embraces when they met secretly in the backyard garden after their families had gone to bed.

It became more difficult to conceal their love. Their brief and modest innuendoes, such as touching each other's hands or the way they stared into each other's eyes, were sure to speak louder than their private whispers to each other.

On many occasions, she could sense her father observing them, yet he never vocalized his suspicions. *He must have forgotten since he was in a coma when we announced our love for each other.*

She suspected that both sides of the family were aware of their relationship, yet no one said a word. *They seem cheerful and happy around us. Maybe they feel awkward and aren't sure how to react to our mixed relationship. Or maybe they are concerned with how others will accept us. No matter. I love Samuel, and there is no stopping our love for each other.*

"SAM, ARE YOU EQUIPPED WITH ALL YOU NEED to care for the livestock?" Jonathan's eyes fixated on Samuel and Jia-Li's hands clutched together.

Jia- Li pulled her hand away as Samuel coughed to speak clearly. "Yes, Pa. A sufficient amount of feed is stocked in the barns, the horses and mules are shoed, and the farm equipment is oiled and ready to operate. You can rest assured everythin' is under control. Pa, just enjoy this time away and relax."

Confident of the superintendents, servants, and his children's abilities, Jonathan was relieved and packed his carpetbag. He booked passage with Stilman's stagecoach to Mariposa the next morning and arrived in Mariposa on Wednesday, greeted by Sarah at the Schlager Hotel.

THE MONTH OF JULY PASSED LIKE A WARM SUMMER BREEZE wafting through the wheat field as Jonathan and Mary enjoyed their grandchildren and assisted Sarah as much as possible. A buggy ride to Mr. Bogart's Sweet Shop to purchase the latest toys and sample treats with Amanda and Billy became their once a week visit.

"Hello, folks. What can I do for you today?" Mr. Bogart inquired of Jonathan, who held Billy in his arms, and Mary, who held Amanda's hand.

"Good day to you, sir. My wife and I would like to spoil our grandchildren rotten." Jonathan chuckled. "What do you have that is sweet and memorable?"

"Well, funny you should ask." The proprietor snapped his fingers. "The latest rave invented in Philadelphia this year is the ice cream soda. It's a mixture of soda water over one scoop of vanilla ice cream with your choice of flavored syrup. I plan to make this refreshing dessert daily. Would you like a tall frosty glass?"

"Why, indeed." Jonathan licked his lips.

"What flavor do you want to try?"

"Well, I think Billy and I would like to try chocolate. How about you, ladies?" Jonathan asked of Mary and Amanda.

"Oh, I believe we'll try strawberry, please," Mary said.

Mr. Bogart took four tall glasses and set a scoop of vanilla ice cream in each. He added the flavored syrup, placed one glass under the soda fountain, and filled them to the rim. Adding the soda made the frozen cream fizz and froth to the top of the glass. Jonathan, Mary, and their grandchildren sat on the tall wooden stools at the counter as Mr. Bogart handed them their ice cream sodas, each with a long straw.

"Ummm." They hummed with wide-eyed wonder.

"I believe your little shop will be the talk of the town," Jonathan said.

IT WAS THE LAST FRIDAY IN JULY, and Sarah found herself peering out the cabin window almost every hour as she awaited Lad's appearance at her front doorstep. Isabelle was growing stronger but was still not able to use her limbs. Although Dr. Cavanaugh remarked on Isabelle's improved health, Sarah struggled with how she might approach Lad about her condition. She was so grateful to have her parents with her for support when that time came.

"Ma and Pa, I don't know what I would've done if you weren't here watching after Amanda and Billy. The last few months without contact with Lad proved unbearable. He's still unaware of Isabelle's illness. I can't live like this with him away.

"I pray to God Isabelle will be able to walk one day, but what happens if she can't and remains crippled for the rest of her life? I don't expect you to come help me every time Lad is away." Sarah shared her heart with her parents as they sat by the hearth that evening.

"Now, Sarah, my offer still stands for Lad to work on the farm so you can be close to us. It may not pay as well to start but should be enough to rent a home in town eventually. You both can save money by living with us for a while. Lad can be home and tend to the livestock as he always enjoys doing."

"Pa, I would be content with that. However, Lad might think differently. I'll do my best to convince him when he gets here. He should arrive any day."

"Jon, do you suppose we ought to stay at Schlager Hotel for now until he returns?" Mary suggested.

"Yes. Let's plan on checkin' in tomorrow."

"Oh, Pa and Ma, you don't have to. Not yet," Sarah pleaded.

"Dear, when a man comes back from a long journey, the first thing he'll want to do is rest in the quiet and comfort of his own home. Not to worry. The hotel is only a place for us to lay down our heads. We plan on spendin' our time with you all day long," her father said. The next morning, her parents checked into the Schlager Hotel.

ANOTHER FOUR DAYS HAD PASSED. The lone rider and fatigued mare sauntered along the horizon and up the dirt path lined with olive-colored oak trees and tall cedar pine. In the distance, Lad recognized Qiang tending to the small vegetable garden as he viewed his humble farm. *Wait. Who is that man shoeing the draft horse?*

As he approached, the figure became more apparent. *Hmmm, why is my father-in-law here?* Puzzled to see him engaged in chores, Lad tipped his hat when Jonathan peered up while holding the horse's foot between his knees.

Jonathan lowered the hoof, stood, arched his back to stretch, and greeted him. "Welcome home, son."

"Howdy, Pa. Pardon my asking, but shouldn't Qiang be doing that?"

The dusty and tired cow puncher inquired as he dismounted his mare.

His father-in-law walked over to him to help remove the saddlebags and signaled Qiang to place Lad's horse in the corral. "Oh, I don't mind so much. Besides, it's one less thing for you to do after your long journey. You're probably wonderin' why I'm here, aren't you?" Jonathan handed Lad his accouterments.

Lad shrugged his shoulders, nodded, and carried his saddlebags into the house while he trailed Jonathan. Exhausted, he figured the answer to his father-in-law's question would soon reveal itself.

Upon entering the home, Lad placed his items by the front door as the women stopped what they were doing, and Sarah froze, mouth agape. Her eyes lit up once the moment registered in her mind. Her body followed suit, and he soon found her engulfed in his arms and smothered by her kisses.

"Oh, Lad, you're home. You are finally home," she said as he returned her kisses.

Amanda and Billy also ran into his clutches as his in-laws stood watching the joyful family reunion. Afterward, they, too, welcomed him home.

"We pray you had a safe journey, dear. So glad to have you back home." Mary encouraged Lad with a graceful smile.

"I'm glad to be home." He took in the aroma of the home-cooked meal, reeled in the arms of his wife and children around him, and even felt gratified with his in-laws' assistance to his family in his absence, which brought him much peace and consolation.

"Pa, to answer your question earlier, the thought did cross my mind. However, I figure that six months is a long time, and Sarah must've become moonstruck not having another adult to talk to. So, I figured she called on you both to keep her company." Lad kissed his mother-in-law on her cheek.

"Well, I thought this day would never come. That was a long stretch of land to cover. It was too long of a time to be away. As much as I love the wilderness, it still doesn't compare to being home with the ones I love." He hugged his children again.

"Come on now, children, give your father some time to relax and maybe take a hot bath. Afterward, we'll sit down for supper together and celebrate his return." Sarah chortled as she helped Lad remove his worn-out duster and hat and hang them on the post by the front door.

"I'll have Qiang fetch water for the tub." Jonathan winked and moseyed outside.

"Hold on now. Don't rush away so quickly, Amanda and Billy, I promised you that I'd bring something back for you from my journey." Lad grabbed his saddlebag, reached inside, and pulled out a hand-carved pony he made for Billy and a doll-size porcelain tea set for Amanda. The children's eyes grew wide as they reached for their gifts.

"Thank you, Papa," they both exclaimed.

"How about some sweet tea, Lad?" Mary asked.

"Yep, that sounds wonderful. I'm parched." He reached into the saddlebag and grabbed a hand-sewn cloth doll for Isabelle and walked over to the cradle to greet his youngest child. She peered up at her father, cooed, and smiled. Lad picked her up and noticed right away her lack of muscular response.

"How is my angel?" Lad asked with tenderness as he sat at the kitchen table, cradling her in his arms. He held her hand to kiss it, but when he released it, her arm fell to her waist like a carcass. He had hoped to see her walking by now.

"Sarah?" Lad turned to his wife for an answer. Under his rough cowboy exterior, he had a tender heart for his family. She brought the sweet tea to the kitchen table, knelt by his side, held Isabelle's hand, and placed her right arm on his shoulder.

"There is much that I need to share with you, Lad. The last six months were horrendous for us, too. Isabelle is holdin' her own right now. Isn't she beautiful?" Sarah was always quick to change the subject to a more pleasant conversation until the time was right to discuss matters further.

"She is beautiful like her mama," Lad responded as he kissed Sarah's forehead. He then rose from his seat and placed Isabelle back in her cradle. Reaching into his saddlebags once more, he retrieved a flat box.

"This is for you, my love."

Inside the box was a black velvet ribbon with a gold ring charm that had four colored gems dangling from it. These were the birthstones for each family member to wear around her slender neck. He was told that this was in high fashion amongst the Victorian women of the day.

Sarah gasped. "Oh, my, darlin' … this is absolutely precious." She tied the velvet ribbon behind her neck then glanced at the choker from her hand mirror.

"Well, I think I better take that bath now. I smell like one of those cattle myself. And for now, I don't even want to see another longhorn for a long while." Lad excused himself as he entered his bedroom and began removing his gun belt and clothes. Qiang filled the bath with water and then fetched the hot kettle from the stove and poured it in. Lad soaked in the hot bath for an extended time until the women called everyone for supper.

AFTER SUPPER, THE ADULTS GATHERED AROUND THE FIREPLACE as the children took their baths.

"So, tell me, sweetheart, what is ailin' Isabelle?" Lad gazed into Sarah's eyes, waiting for her answer.

"Lad, I don't know what I would have done without Pa and Ma here to help me. Darlin', we almost lost Isabelle while you were away. I thank God that Dr. Cavanaugh diagnosed her early enough to save her life. She has a weak immune system. Only time will tell if she will remain in this state. God will have to perform a miracle for her to walk again and use her arms and hands. I do realize that I cannot bear another six months of you bein' away, let alone three months. It tore me apart not to be able to contact you or know where you might be on the trail." Tears fell from her eyes.

The few seconds of silence in the room felt like an eternity. Lad could feel his countenance taking on a frown of conviction.

"I still have the position I offered you on the farm, son. Just let us know your decision." Jonathan smiled, then backed away. "Speakin' of the farm, Mary, I think it's time we head back home. We have some work to do of our own. We don't want to miss seein' David before he leaves for the university. How about we leave tomorrow mornin'?"

The conviction lay heavy on Lad's heart. He knew that the time had arrived for him to hang up his cow punching ways and settle down to be a family man. The last grueling six months in the desert wastelands and lonesome prairies caused him to long for his family and the embrace of his lovely wife. He had many restless nights as he struggled with the offer his father-in-law had proposed before he left home. Now, to hear the news that his family really needed him, but he failed to be there for them, caused him much grief. The decision came easy, but the transition, he knew, would require some level of difficulty. Driving cattle was all he knew from the time he left his grandparents' farm as a young man. Nevertheless, he would take this direction.

Lad reached over to hold Sarah's hand then turned his focus upon his in-laws. "The last six months gave me time to think and sort things out in my mind. Cattle drives aren't the same now that I'm a married man with a family. All I could think of was being home with them and in the arms of my beautiful wife." Lad glanced at Sarah and patted her hand.

"Pa … I'm ready to take your offer," Lad said, chin held high.

"Oh, really, Lad?" Sarah's smile beamed from ear to ear.

"Yes, darlin'. I truly mean it. When would you like to do this?"

"As soon as we can." Sarah placed her hand over her heart.

"All right." Jonathan's eyes sparkled. "We can reconfigure the sittin' room into your family bedroom until you can find a place to settle down."

"Thank you, Pa, for your generosity to offer your home. I promise it'll only be a short while until we can build a home of our own. Once we sell this property, we can purchase a small portion of land and build our home in Snelling. We can use the money we've saved to do this," Lad replied.

"It's settled then. Just let us know when you're ready."

His father-in-law turned to his mother-in-law, who fidgeted with her apron due to the rapid decisions that just occurred. *She must be pinching herself, wondering if she were in a dream. We can finally move forward.*

"Oh, my! You cannot even begin to understand how happy you have made me … us." Mary raised her hands toward the heavens. "We best be gettin' on our way to the hotel before it gets too dark out, Jon, and let this family get some rest." A wide grin appeared on her face.

Lad and his family exchanged fond farewells with Jonathan

and Mary. Lad's mind filled with hopeful expectations for the upcoming relocation plans to Snelling.

18

Unprofitable and Unproductive

"We're almost home, darlin'. I can see our wheat fields on the horizon." Jonathan craned his neck out the stagecoach window as they passed Nielson's Flour Mill. Several wagons from neighboring farms lined one after another to drop off their season's harvest.

Jonathan snickered at the sight as he read the insignia's on the wagons as they rolled along. "Maxfield Farms. Kelly Ranch. Good, very good. If all went well, Sower Farm wagons should be nowhere in sight. My men should have delivered our harvest almost two months earlier than our competitors."

Inhaling deep and closing his eyes, Jonathan allowed the autumn warmth to caress his face as the stagecoach crossed the Merced Falls Bridge. The sun's rays glistened like brilliant diamonds upon the surface of the moving Merced River. The smell of harvested fields permeated the air.

Mary put her knitting on her lap. "Two months is a long time to be away from home. I can't wait to get back into my old routine."

The coach wheels bumped along as the road transitioned from the bridge to the other side of the river bank to the furthermost east end of his wheat fields. When Jonathan opened his eyes, what he saw troubled him. Several hundreds of acres of wheat still stood cresting in the breeze like a gentle ocean wave. "What in tarnation?" His jaw dropped.

"What's the matter, Jon?"

"Why hasn't this section of wheat been harvested? This situation is not good. Not good at all, Mary. I hope the time to harvest this field is still at hand. The first thing I'm going to do is call an urgent meeting with the superintendents once we arrive home. I believe I assigned the furthest acres to superintendent Tu. He better provide a good explanation." He shook his head, distraught.

Upon returning to his farm, Jonathan met with his superintendents in his office to discuss their business operations. The three men sat across from him at his desk, ready to give their report.

Yung placed a handwritten note signed by Harold Nielsen in front of him, equal the value of the greater portion of the field he harvested.

"Mr. Nielsen was delighted with our timely harvest this year, Mr. Sower. The new harvester increased our productivity. We were the first to provide grain well ahead of schedule. Our prompt timing pleased him to be at the forefront of the market," Yung said with a fragmented Chinese accent.

After Jonathan viewed the sizable check, his brows raised, and his eyes widened. "Well done, Yung. I also am pleased." Jonathan calculated ten percent of the amount as Yung's bonus for his exceptional trustworthiness and cunningness to handle business on his own. Jonathan then opened the safe behind his desk and paid Yung in cash. "Here is your reward for your excellent work, Yung."

Yung puffed out his chest, beaming with pride. "Thank you, Mr. Sower. You are most gracious."

Enthralled by his co-worker's bonus, Sheng-Li presented his accomplishment. He pulled the note from his dusty shirt pocket, waved it like a banner, and placed it in Jonathan's hand. The written amount was also sizeable, equal to the proportion of field given to him. Sheng-Li grinned. "Mr. Nielsen most happy, Mr. Sower."

"Ah, well done, Sheng-Li ... well done." Again, Jonathan reached into the safe and handed Sheng-Li his ten percent bonus.

Beads of sweat formed on Tu's forehead as he fidgeted in his seat and peered down at his hands folded on his lap. "Mr. Sower, I know you are shrewd businessman. I was afraid to destroy crop, so I waited for your return. Look, you still have what is yours."

"Afraid to destroy my crops?" Jonathan tried to contain his anger. "Your slothfulness will be the cause of my crops' destruction. For your sake, I hope the wheat is not spoiled and can still be harvested. Your actions are not acceptable, Tu. What were you doing all this time?" Jonathan asked, disgruntled.

Tu could not answer. Instead, he stared at his trembling hands and nodded as if in agreement.

"Mr. Sower, may I speak to you privately in the parlor?" Yung's lips tightened as he glanced at Tu.

Jonathan huffed in disappointment. Responding to Yung, he snarled. "Yes, of course." They walked over to the other room.

Sheng-Li's tense voice carried through the office as he scolded Tu in Mandarin.

"Mr. Sower, I am sorry to report Tu's lack of discipline in your absence. Sheng-Li and I tried our best to warn him of his laziness, but he only ignored us. We found him away from his duties visiting the gambling halls in camp. We used his share of farmhands because they desired to work. I hope this meets your approval."

"Indeed, Yung. Your management skills please me. However, I'm disheartened by Tu's indecision. With much regret, I must make some changes. All right, let me handle this situation, Yung." Jonathan rubbed the tightened muscles in the back of his neck, and they both returned to his office.

"Tu, I am disturbed by your lack of leadership in handling my affairs. Your undisciplined action will cost me a considerable amount of money. I pray that the crop is not spoiled. You could've given your portion of the field to Yung or Sheng-Li to reap since you did not hold confidence in yourself.

"You are correct that I'm a resourceful businessman, but I do so with fairness. I've decided to dismiss you and give your position to another.

"That'll be all for today, gentlemen. Thank you."

"Thank you, Mr. Sower." They bowed with respect. Yung and Sheng-Li returned to work. Tu, in disgrace, sulked, shoulders and head lowered, and returned to his home at the Chinese camp.

MARY, NAOMI, DAVID, AND THE SUEN FAMILY tended to the garden and orchard every day and enjoyed its bountiful variety. The vegetables and fruits flourished in the backyard of the farmhouse and cabin, except for one tree. Amongst the fruit trees were an apple, pear, plum, peach, lemon, and an unproductive orange tree.

After she harvested the rewards of her labor and placed them in several fruit baskets, Mary inspected the slow-growing, barren citrus tree.

"After three years, this orange tree has not produced one fruit yet, Huang-Fu. This unproductive plant is good for nothin'! All it's doin' is suckin' the nutrients from the soil. I'll have David cut down this poor specimen before he leaves for the university. I'm afraid it'll start affecting the other fruit trees."

Huang-Fu also examined the malnourished orange tree dwarfed by the other well-producing fruit trees. "A ya! No, Mrs. Sower. Do not cut down. Allow me to fertilize. If no fruit by next year, then cut down."

"All right, one year. I was about to give up on this tree, but you spared its life for one more opportunity to prove itself." Mary shook her head in disappointment at the little tree.

19

Golden Horizon

A thick woolen coat, gloves, and scarves packed snug into David's carpet bags seemed rather odd when the warmth of the California sun exceeded high ninety degree temperatures in the San Joaquin Valley. Freezing temperatures in California are scarce except for in the Sierra Mountains' upper elevations. The family's good friend and business associate, Patrick Fay, did the honors of purchasing the heavy outerwear while making deliveries in Yosemite after he became aware of David's acceptance at a college located in the northeastern United States.

David closed his two carpetbags on his bed, buckled the straps, and placed them by his bedroom door, ready to leave for college in Upland, Indiana. *Well, I hope I brought enough warm clothes. I do recall the bone-cold winters back east.* Eleven years had passed since he and his family moved away from their Civil-War stricken home in Perryville, Kentucky, to begin their new life at Snelling. Returning to an area that held macabre memories for his family sent shivers to his soul. He hoped Indiana's landscape display less Civil War carnage than his place of birth.

A stint of ambivalence crept into his anxious spirit as he awaited the moment to begin his four-year seminary course. Although the dormitory provided meals, the thought of leaving home's comforts unsettled him, yet stirred excitement for other reasons. No longer would he tolerate the position of being the family's baby as he received directives from his parents or his older brother and sisters. He could be his own man, who makes his own decisions. Being treated like an adult appealed to David. He looked forward to the challenges ahead of him.

At three o'clock in the afternoon, his parents accompanied him to the Wells Fargo stagecoach in town to extend their ecstatic farewells. On many occasions, they expressed to him their delight. *Son, we are so proud one of our children is college-bound and desires to obtain a prestigious degree.* They were doubly proud of him to aspire for the noble career as a clergyman. Yet, the thought of the four-year separation tore at his mother's emotions.

"Now, David, you be sure to write to us often and let us know if you need anythin'." His mother's eyes began to water as she brushed the lint from his tan-colored frock coat lapel. "Also, make sure you mind your health, eat regular meals, and get plenty of rest so that you can think with a clear conscience."

Sensing his mother's anxiety, David grasped her shoulders and pulled her into his warm embrace. "Oh, Ma, don't you worry about me. You know I'm in God's good and capable hands. Of course I'll write." He kissed her on the cheek then turned to his father, who also gave him a warm embrace and patted his back.

"Son, you are embarkin' on a path far more courageous than anyone in this family has ever attempted. 'The fear of the LORD is the beginnin' of wisdom: and the knowledge of the Holy is understandin'.'" His father quoted Proverbs 9:10.

"Thank you, Pa." David took a deep breath and glanced at the rugged seasoned drivers postured on the shotgun seat of the stagecoach, ready to lead the fresh team of horses. Bandanas drawn to their faces, one checked their guns and ammunition supply for the two-day, non-stop journey to Stockton, and the other studied the travelers' manifest.

"Bowers from Mariposa," the lead driver called.

"Here." A scruffy voice arched from behind David.

"Shearson from Merced Falls."

"Present." Another voice bellowed.

"Sower from Snelling."

"That's me, sir." David raised his hand and had a brief remembrance of his grade school days during roll call.

"Hop on board, folks." The driver growled at David and the other passengers. "We don't want this to become a three-day ride. "I hope y'all took care of your personal business because we're only gonna stop every twelve miles at the swing stations to water or make an exchange for a fresh team. The only significant stop we'll make is in Ceres. You can purchase a hot meal at the local hotel and attend to personal matters like an outhouse break, or even replenish your baskets with more palatable food. Inside the coach is a basket with beef jerky, biscuits, and coffee. I can't promise the coffee won't spill on your travelin' clothes with the rocking and all. I'll do my best to avoid the potholes.

"Oh. And let's hope we don't run into any outlaws. I just polished my revolver and shotgun." He guffawed and rubbed his shotgun with a rag.

David cringed at the driver's tactless sense of humor then proceeded to board the shiny, berry-red stagecoach with gold trim. *Lord, please extend your traveling mercies. Protect us from outlaws.*

The driver cracked the whip, and the team of horses kicked up their hooves. The stagecoach jerked into motion toward the golden horizon. David watched his parents as they waved good-bye and until they were no longer in his sight before he leaned back into the coach's cushioned bench seat.

"So, where's a young whippersnapper like you headin' to?" the middle-aged man dressed in a wrinkled linen shirt and worn-out frock coat sneered. His raspy voice matched Bowers' response earlier. His hands were calloused from what appeared to be from swinging a miner's pick. Many of the Sower farmworkers who once mined had similar callouses. Ninety percent of men that came from Mariposa were miners. He inhaled one more long drag of his hand-rolled tobacco then flicked it out the stagecoach's open window. No women were present, so no doubt this passenger took advantage of the moment as he measured David's well-groomed appearance.

David sat on the opposite bench facing the back of the coach and placed a small basket with food prepared by his mother between his feet. He coughed as he took mindful note of the two passengers with him. "Yes, sir, my name is David Sower." He extended a handshake to the Mariposa man across from him and to the Merced Falls man sitting beside him. Most men who came from Merced Falls worked at either Nielsen's flour or lumber mills. This fellow wreaked of cedar, and his hands were sap stained. "My travel takes me, Lord willin', to Indiana. I'll be attendin' seminary."

The roughneck miner snorted. "Does that mean I must mind my tongue throughout this entire ride since a preacher is on board?" He glanced at the lumberman, who moved to the left window to allow David some elbow room.

The lumberman leaned back in a slouched position with his left leg crossed over his right knee, and fists shoved into his pant pockets. He sat upright and nodded his head toward David. "Jack Shearson." He smiled and addressed both men. "I was workin' at the lumber mill in Merced Falls when I received word about my brother in Sacramento who took ill. I'm a laborin' man myself and not much for attendin' church as I should. However, I do believe in the good Lord above and have respect for those who preach the gospel to this ungodly and law-deprived territory."

The miner readjusted himself on his seat, rubbed his fists together, and cracked his knuckles. He seemed to understand who the sturdy lumberman eluded. Forcing a smile and trying to be pleasant, the miner introduced himself. "Clyde Bowers." He sputtered at David. "I'm headed to San Francisco. Minin' has dried out for me. Heard cargo vessels are lookin' to hire a few good men. I figure I can find some work in the city and a new way of life, while I still have spare change in my pocket."

He slid over on the bench seat to be across from Jack. "Speakin' of spare change, how 'bout a game of cards to whittle the time away?"

"Now you're talkin', man," Jack said as he shifted a sideward glance at David.

"Thanks, but I think I'll pass. I have some reading I must attend before I arrive at the university." He reached down, pulled out a book from the basket between his feet, and perused the text as the two men laid out their cards on the middle bench in-between them.

The time was almost 10 p.m. when they arrived in Ceres. The way station and the town were quiet except for some distant laughter and tinkering piano notes, which came from the saloon a couple of blocks away. At the hotel, the men could eat a hot meal and replenish goods while laying over for about two hours before boarding the midnight stagecoach destined for Stockton. Although the wall clock rang late, the hotel staff anticipated the stagecoach's arrival and kept the stoves warm for their hungry guests.

"Good evening, gentlemen." The hotel clerk with slicked-back hair and a thick mustache stood from behind the reservation desk as he removed his timepiece from his vest and took note of the time. "Right on schedule. I can always count on the timeliness of the Wells Fargo stagecoach. You men must be ravenous by now."

"You reckon?" Clyde bellowed.

"The parlor is to your right, the saloon is to your left, and the outhouse is around the back. We also have a bath on the second floor at the end of the hall."

As Clyde and Jack turned toward the parlor, David excused himself. "I'll meet y'all at the dining table. I need to visit the outhouse and washroom." He noticed a chalkboard at the front entrance with the scribbling *Prime rib dinner for one dollar*. "Would you mind ordering the prime rib for me, Jack?"

"No problem, son," Jack replied as he and Clyde rolled up their sleeves and sat themselves down at a parlor table.

David figured he could use the wash time to refresh himself and allow the two ruffians a moment to speak to one another without any inhibitions.

Upon David's arrival at the parlor table, the waiter placed the hot food before them. The table became quiet as the men plowed into their dinner.

"Ah, this meal is the best eatin's I've had for days." Jack leaned back and rubbed his belly. "How much time is left before we have to return to the station, young man?"

David pulled out his pocket timepiece from his vest. "It's 10:45. We have another hour. We best be back fifteen minutes early to check-in."

"Well, what do ya say about a round of poker in the saloon, Jack?" Clyde chimed in.

"How can it be we've only known each other for less than a day, and we already think alike?" Jack retorted.

David responded with a chuckle. "Great minds think alike, and fools never differ."

"I guess we must be the fools then." Clyde laughed as he scooted his chair behind him and winked at David. "Be sure to come fetch us when the time comes."

"Will do, Clyde. I'm just goin' to enjoy another cup of coffee and study a little more."

Fifteen minutes had passed as David relaxed and continued to read Albert Barnes' released book *The Way to Salvation* when a woman in her late twenties entered the parlor. Dressed in a hip-length tailored dark cerulean coat trimmed with black braiding, worn over a storm cloud-grey ruffled bustled skirt with a train, she appeared quite refined. Atop her brunette ringlets masterfully arranged on her head crowned a decorative hat of the same grey color with streaming ribbons of midnight blue.

"Right this way, Miss Foster." The waiter seated her at a table kitty-corner to David. "What may I serve you this evening?"

"I'll have a cup of tea, please, and perhaps a small pastry. I'm due to be at the Wells Fargo station in forty-five minutes."

"Very well, madam."

David peered up to listen to the conversation and felt inclined to introduce himself. He put his book down and walked over to where she sat.

"Pardon me for the intrusion, but I overheard you mention to the waiter you'll be boardin' the Wells Fargo stagecoach in a few minutes. I, too, will be travelin' on a stagecoach destined for Stockton at the same time. Are you boardin' the same?" David asked, using his best mannerisms.

"Why, yes." Pausing for a moment, she noted his politeness and perhaps concluded with accepting to converse with him. "It's a pleasure to meet your acquaintance. My name is Adele Foster. I'm to be the new schoolteacher in Sacramento. Would you care to join me for tea?"

"The pleasure is mine, madam, and an honor to share tea with you. Allow me to get my belongings." David fetched his basket and book and placed them on the empty chair next to him at her table. He introduced himself, and they discussed both of their plans in education.

Forty-five minutes passed without notice, and David peered at his pocket watch. "Well, I do believe the time has come for us to return to the station. May I escort you there?"

"Well, indeed, young Mr. Sower. I, too, would be honored."

"First, I'll notify our co-travelers. Afterward, I shall gather you."

Notifying the others only took a few minutes. The four passengers returned to the station and boarded the stagecoach headed for Stockton. After brief introductions, they found a comfortable position as they rested their body and head against the rocking carriage's side walls. They did their best to sleep despite the dirt trail bumps, the noise of the horse's fast-moving hooves, and the creaking of the carriage.

By dawn's first light, the stagecoach arrived in Stockton where David, Jack, and Adele boarded the Western Pacific Railroad's steam train to Sacramento. They said farewell to Clyde, who took the train to San Francisco.

This journey would be David's first train ride, and the fascinating invention enthralled him. From Sacramento, he alone transferred to the Central Pacific Railroad to take the eight-day journey to Chicago, Illinois. He said good-bye to his traveling companions only to meet new friends headed east.

The blend of white steam and dark gray smoke billowed from the smokestack as the engine roared up the grades of the Sierra mountain range. David relaxed as he peered through the window of the Pullman railcar, admiring the tall pines and the steep cliffs as the railcar hugged the edge of the mountain. An image crossed his mind of his brother, Samuel, along with a Chinese railroad gang hanging from the cliff edge and setting off nitrogen blasts. *And Pa said my path is courageous.* Amazed, he shook his head.

Several passengers sat next to David in the railcar, parlor car, and bunked next to him in the sleeping car. The first-class passengers had the freedom to move from one car to another. The dining car menu boasts exquisite fare served on platters engraved with the Pullman insignia on each dish.

After the rugged Sierras came the wastelands of the high desert. The majestic purple mountain range of the Rockies dazzled David as he beheld the panoramic window view. The stark scenery which followed contrast of the rolling prairie lands of Nebraska.

David did his best to recognize certain landmarks along the way, which he might have seen during his family's wagon train travel eleven years earlier. However, the landscape appeared different while traveling on the steady-moving steel transportation. He recalled the Conestoga parked by rivers to water the animals and at Union forts to resupply. Now, this iron horse stopped at new bantam towns to refuel and pick up more passengers. It took six months to travel by Conestoga wagon from coast to coast. Today, it only required eight days by train.

"Magnificent," David said aloud as he made himself comfortable in the parlor car's lounge chair while staring out the window.

"Is this your first train ride, young chap?" inquired a portly gentleman dressed in a dark frock coat and black satin vest with silver thread inlay. He sat in the parlor chair next to David, mesmerized by the scenery, as well.

"Yes, sir. It is."

"I've been traveling on this train now for three years, at least twice a year for business. There hasn't been a day where I haven't seen something new on the horizon every time I travel, whether that be new territory or town. I'm astonished at how this country is growing because of the locomotive." The gentleman grinned as he defined his train experience.

"The last time I traveled these parts was eleven years ago. Nothin' seems as I remember. I'm amazed at what man can accomplish through providence. This country is indeed a nation under God," David remarked as pride swelled up in his heart for his country.

"Hear, hear. Well spoken." The gentleman toasted David's statement and took a sip of the bourbon in his hand then continued gazing out the window.

At Omaha, Nebraska, David boarded the Union Pacific Railroad steam train bound for Chicago, Illinois. From there, he rode on another Wells Fargo stagecoach for a two-day trek to Upland, Indiana, arriving at Taylor University. He settled into his room at the dormitory then school commenced a week later.

20

Faith Rekindled

"**S**am is awful kind to lend us his bedroom until we find a home," Sarah said as she rested her back after she piled the clothing-filled canvas bags into the Conestoga for the two-day relocation to Snelling. She glanced once more at the small farm, sold to a miner's family two weeks earlier just after the harvest.

"Yep, but where will he sleep?" A rope secured the bedding, table, and chairs as Lad fastened a knot to the wagon's cleat.

"Well, accordin' to Ma's letter, he'll set up a cot in Pa's office for now. Amanda and Billy can share my old bed in Naomi's room. We can push together Sam and David's beds and place Izzy's crib next to us."

"Do they have room in the barn to store our furnishings for now?"

"Oh, no worry. There is plenty of room in the barn. Pa will make sure of it."

Lad scanned the grounds as if capturing a tintype in his mind of the small farmhouse and two acres land which housed him most of his adult life. "I'll sure miss this place." He glanced at Sarah.

"I don't blame you, dear. This home is your first purchase with your hard-earned wages." Eyes widened and stomach turned, concern immersed her as she studied her husband. *Are we making the right decision to move to Snelling and begin anew? Do I have the right to require my husband to change his career for me and the children's sake?*

"But I'm looking forward to our new chapter in life." Lad's grin widened. "Having family to surround me has been my boyhood dream."

"All right, darlin'. You had me worried there for a second. Thought maybe you were havin' regrets."

Lad snickered and shook his head. "No, not at all. I'm fixed and ready to leave this all behind me. Everything is packed. I'm ready to go. Last thing to load is the children." His feet hustled to the cabin, and Sarah followed close behind to gather their brood and place them in the Conestoga. Everyone on board, Lad commanded the horses, and the family began their journey to Snelling.

THE HAMPTONS ARRIVED at Sarah's parents' farm in early October. After a few days of settling in, Sarah and her mother brought Isabelle to Dr. Cassidy's clinic as Jonathan trained Lad and acquainted him with his new responsibilities with the livestock. The travel and the new surroundings exasperated Isabelle. Once again, she lost her appetite and became lackadaisical.

"Isabelle is such a frail little child with a weak immune system." Pale and listless, her daughter lay on the physician's examining table as Sarah massaged her feeble legs.

"This move was a risk you had to take, Mrs. Hampton. Give her time to adjust to her new home. Please do your best to force her to eat. As it is, her weight is below normal."

With a spoon, he dropped some milk on her tongue. "Her gag reflex is functioning, and she does not seem to have any abdominal pain. Stress is the cause of her lack of appetite."

Gentle hands scooped up the child and placed her in Sarah's arms. "Please return in a week if you do not notice any improvement."

"Thank you, Dr. Cassidy. I'll do my best." Sarah kissed Isabelle's cheek and followed her mother to the buggy.

BUMPY ROCKING MOTIONS IN THE BUGGY RIDE home kept the conversation lively between Sarah and Mary as Isabelle slept in her mother's arms.

"Have you and Lad given any thought about attending church with us?" Mary cracked the whip, and the horse neighed. "Perhaps we should ask Pastor McSwan to pray for Isabelle."

"Oh, Ma, please give us time. I haven't seen the McSwans since Joshua's death. For me to visit them again under these circumstances might put us in a most awkward position. Besides, I'm not sure Lad is ready yet either—one step at a time, Ma. Please don't give up on him … on us. You know I love the Lord and desire to worship him again."

"Well, the Bible instructs us to go and reconcile face-to-face with our brother or sister in Christ first before we offer our gifts to Him. Would it help if you came alone to church so you can reestablish your relationship with the McSwans before bringin' your family?"

Sarah thought about her mother's suggestion as they rolled into the barn. "Yes, Ma. I'll take your advice to heart."

LAD LISTENED TO SARAH REITERATE THE DOCTOR'S PROGNOSIS to the family at supper that evening, and his heart sank a notch.

"Thank you, Pa and Ma, for allowin' us to stay with you and helpin' us to relocate to Snelling. I believe this is God's plan for us to be here and to heal our little girl. Wouldn't you agree, Lad?" His wife's searching fawn eyes demanded his compliance.

How could you ask me that question, Sarah? You know I gave up on God a long time ago when He failed to answer my prayers.

Painful suppressed thoughts bombarded his mind. Spring of 1849 was the last time he laid eyes on his parents when they took him to his grandparents' home in Virginia. He remembered his mother's tearful embrace and the echo of his father's whispers to his grandpa. *We'll be back to fetch Lad after we get settled in California. Word has it, the rivers are overflowin' with gold. I'm sure it won't take long. Maybe a year or two.*

He inhaled and held his breath as if drowning in murky waters. *Laddy, Laddy, orphan boy!* The hurtful words of his grade school peers stabbed his heart.

A year passed, then two, then five, then fifteen. After Lad became nineteen, his grandfather passed, and then his grandmother a few months later. After he laid them to rest, Lad set out for California with hopes of finding his kin. The wagon train master hired him as a drover for the cattle belonging to the westbound travelers. Once there, Jackson Montana, one of San Joaquin Valley's wealthiest cattlemen, employed him to drive his herd.

To this day, not one clue of his parent's whereabouts had emerged from California's depleted gold-mining towns or the citizens who remained.

With a rugged façade and keeping his distance from people, he hid his pain of abandonment. Yet he missed the close relationship he once had through the unconditional love he received from his grandparents. His parent's decision to leave him only confused his understanding of love's vast emotions. He felt unworthy to receive love because the ones who were supposed to be his prime source abandoned him. *Did I do something wrong for my parents to leave me behind? Am I not good enough to be their son?* The unanswered questions returned to him. Perhaps this reason is why he enjoyed the company of cattle instead of interacting with humans.

Although his grandparents brought him to church, he had difficulty comprehending the *love of the Father*, to which the parson spoke with passion. Paternal love was a concept he could not relate to, so he never had a need for God in his life. Faith and hope in God were something he abnegated when his biological parents failed to return for him. He perceived God did not love him because He did not answer his prayers to locate his parents.

"I do appreciate all you have done for us, Mr. and Mrs. Sower." He cleared his throat after he realized his mistake. "Father and mother." *Ugh. I've never had parents to address. Strange to be saying this now.* "Please excuse me. I think I need some air." Lad placed his crumpled napkin next to his plate, pushed away, and retreated to the front porch. His throat became tight as the wave of emotional pain consumed him. The news about Isabelle only stimulated the repressed memories and caused him more guilt. *I can't abandon my family as my parents did me.*

"OH MY. MUST'VE BEEN SOMETHIN' I SAID. I best tend to my husband. Please pardon me also," Sarah said, sensing his anguish. She dismissed herself, then tiptoed and stood next to him at the front porch rail. They cast their sight over the harvested wheat field, which glowed in the moonlight.

Careful to avoid eye contact, Sarah did not want to intrude into the troubled room in Lad's soul. Her husband never expounded about the hurt he experienced from his past. This was the only area in his life he kept to himself. By placing her right hand at his elbow, she made him aware of her consoling presence.

"I'm sorry, darlin' for my insensitivity. I should've spoken to you in private first about Isabelle before blurtin' it out at the dinner table. Will ya forgive me?"

"Oh, my love, your timing doesn't bother me. I'm the only one to blame for Isabelle's condition, and I let you down. If I had stayed home, then perhaps I could've taken better care of you, and she might've been born in good health. I wouldn't be able to forgive myself if something were to happen to Izzy."

"Now, Lad, darlin', don't you start blamin' yourself for her condition. No one is to blame. Our other two children are healthy. I did everythin' the same while carryin' Isabelle as with them. Only God knows why Isabelle was born with this illness. God's ways are higher than ours.

"The scriptures tell us in Psalm 139:13-14, 'For Thou hast possessed my reins: thou hast covered me in my mother's womb. I will praise Thee; for I am fearfully and wonderfully made: marvelous are Thy works; and that my soul knoweth right well.'" Sarah justified her daughter's condition. "God determined a plan for Isabelle while He formed her in my womb. He purposed a design for everything He does."

"Well, I do blame myself because I'm not a Christian. How can I believe in God when I lost faith in my parents, who promised to come back for me? According to my grandparents, they attended church like clockwork and read their Bible. If that were true, then how could they disobey their God-given responsibilities to their child?"

"I can't answer your questions, Lad. Perhaps no one witnessed their misfortune during the gold rush. Those founding days proved as an uneasy and unstable time for California. There were a lot of thieveries and killin' over this precious metal. It wasn't safe for men, let alone women and children.

"The Bible tells us to esteem others better than himself. You must try to respect your parent's decision to move to California as a risk they had to take for a brighter chance at life for all of you. I'm sure as Christians, they loved you with all their heart and had every intention of returnin' for you once safety became prevalent. Bein' parents ourselves, we understand that a child's love is more precious than all the gold the world can offer. Therefore, they must have regarded the same for you.

"As much as it hurts, you need to let go of your past and forgive them for separatin' their family. I'm sure they made the best with what life had to offer them, and difficulty influenced their decision, much like the choices we made for our family with the options which avail us. If you don't do this, then the hurt shall never be resolved, and you'll forever be left wantin' and be unfulfilled. This bitterness toward them may be your doom. Try to see from their perspective as an act of love and good intent. You must move forward. We're your family now, and we need you."

The spiritual wisdom flowed from within her.

Pausing for a moment, Lad turned to her, his cobalt pupils surrounded by thin red veins, immersed in a salty pool of tears.

"You're right, Sarah. Some unfortunate circumstances must've taken my parents' lives. The possibility has crossed my mind, and I didn't want to accept it. They were looking for a better way of life than what the hills of Virginia offered. Who can blame them for having that desire? This mystery continues to leave an enormous, empty hole in my soul. But then why would God allow them to die?"

"Darlin', God will not only fill the void but heal it, too. Please, give

God a chance. Death is familiar to Him, and He never planned it for humankind. Our lives were to be eternal like His. He even created a paradise for us to abode where no evil abounds. But because of Adam and Eve's disobedience, sin and its curse affected everythin' includin' the earth. So whether your parents died from another person's hand or of natural causes, death is not God's desire. He loves you so much and sacrificed His life to save yours so you can have a better future at a much better place. Hmm. Your parents acted in a similar fashion, and so did mine comin' to California.

"If your parents are Christians and they passed on, then they are with the Lord. Through Jesus, Christians have the hope of eternal life. He promises we will one day reunite with our loved ones, who also believe in Him, in heaven where there is no sin or sorrow. This is the bigger picture, and it is our hope. Without it, life is miserable and has no meanin'.

"This can be yours, too, Lad, if you accept Jesus Christ as your Lord and Savior. There is rest and peace for your soul. Think about it, my love."

Sarah kissed her husband's cheek and allowed him to ponder her statement as she returned to the house to tuck the children into bed and pray. *Lord, soften my husband's heart toward You. He needs to know You never abandoned him and that You love him. Reveal to him why you've allowed those difficult circumstances in his life. Thank You, Father.*

21

Kinfolk in Christ

Give God a chance. Sarah's words from a few days ago prod Lad, much like his cow poking days when he used to herd stubborn cattle to point them in the right direction. His wife desired to speak to pastor Daniel and Ruth McSwan in private, so Lad chose to stay home with their children this Sunday morning. However, his heart yearned to go to church to learn more about this resounding faith.

In the sitting room, Amanda and Billy were busy playing with their toys as Lad cradled Isabelle in the chair by the hearth. His lips quivered as she struggled to smile at him. A heavy, guilty yoke oppressed him as he kissed her wee hand. "I am so sorry my sweet angel. Your pa never wished this illness upon you. Will you forgive me? I will do my best for now on to be by your side when you need me."

Isabelle cooed as if she understood him.

"Please, God, I ask Your forgiveness for neglecting my family, for my sins, and my lack of faith in You. I want to believe in You, but I don't know where to begin. My faith is the size of a mustard seed. Will you help it to grow and become stronger? I need You, Lord. My daughter foremost needs You. Please extend Your mercy toward us."

With this simple and heartfelt prayer, Lad sensed a tremendous burden lift from his shoulder, and a spiritual blanket of love surround him. The physical manifestation of Jesus did not appear before Lad, but God's Spirit, without doubt, moved in and around him like a warm breeze caressing his body. A gentle consoling flooded through him, and his body relaxed in the serenity. *Everything will be all right, and God will, in due time, heal Isabelle.* This assurance is what Sarah spoke of while at the dinner table with the family the previous Thursday evening.

Lad had never experienced this manner of faith and hope before. The understanding birthed itself from deep within. *Did I just accept Jesus as my Lord and Savior? Am I now a Believer?* At first, he chuckled at himself. *Huh, imagine that. Me a Christian.* Joy then filled his heart, and an irrepressible smile enveloped his face. "Thank you, Lord, for your mercy."

The clock on the hearth mantel chimed twelve strokes. *The family should be home soon. Wait till they hear the good news.*

THE THREE-YEAR-OLD RED BRICK CHURCH on Green Street still wreaked of the pews' fresh lacquer. Sarah sat beside her mother to gather the unspoken maternal moral support needed to reconcile with the minister after the service. Lacking church discipline Sarah's mind wandered and visualized David at the altar as a deacon reading a sermon where Pastor McSwan stood. *My little brother will make a fine minister one day.* She smiled at the thought, not realizing the pastor responding to her actions.

"Rejoice with me; for I have found my sheep which was lost," Pastor McSwan said as he returned a nod to acknowledge her attendance. The minister's voice reverberated between the solid walls but softened with the room full of parishioners. His directed words required no amplification, and all heard him loud and clear.

Startled by his astuteness, the awkward attention embarrassed her. A flush of warmth washed over her face as heads turned her way. Oh, how she wished she could be a turtle at that moment and crawl into a shell to hide. Nowhere to run, she forced a smile and turned her sights to her hands on her lap, hoping to break the connection from the onlookers. The pastor continued with his sermon as her mind reviewed her confrontational strategy.

The service concluded, and the congregation disbursed. Sarah approached the minister and his wife as her family waited outside. The middle-aged couple froze as if they had seen a ghost.

"Pastor and Mrs. McSwan, it's me, Sarah." She curtsied and hung her head low.

"Sarah? Sarah Sower? Oh, my dear, I thought I recognized you smiling back at me. We are so glad to see you again!" Pastor McSwan reached out to embrace her. "A special place in our hearts remains for you and has been void since you moved away."

"My dear, words cannot express how happy I am to know you've returned home." Ruth wrapped her arms around Sarah's shoulders. Tears began to flow as the women embraced.

"I'm so sorry for my lack of communication with you for the past eight years. Joshua's death was the beginning of my life's struggles and has caused me to realize this life holds no value compared to what Jesus promises in heaven. The peace Joshua felt to be surrendered to Christ, even if it meant death, was difficult for me to grasp in my tender years. Joshua is in the better place where there is no more sufferin' or sorrow as we have here on our sin-cursed Earth. I was wrong for blamin' God for takin' Joshua so early because I didn't understand the ultimate glory of bein' in God's presence." Tears streamed her cheek.

"Sarah … you don't need to explain." Ruth squeezed her hands.

"No, please, Mrs. McSwan, allow me to share my life. My marriage to Lad is goin' on six years, and the Lord has blessed us with three children. God is usin' the sufferin' of our third child's illness to cause me to realize these earthly bodies are imperfect, cursed from sin, and in need of a Savior to rescue it from corruption.

"I've learned that God is not to blame for our degenerate condition because his original plan intended the human race to have eternal, sinless bodies like His. Adam and Eve's disobedience allowed sin and its penalty of death to enter God's perfect world, causin' spiritual separation between Him and us. God's mercy and grace provided a solution to redeem us back to Himself through His Son, Jesus, who received the punishment for our sins.

"Through all my hardships and failures, I finally realized and understood this truth and rededicated my life to Christ. God never intended for us to live with so much pain and sickness. I look forward to the day He promises in heaven, where there will no longer be death, sorrow, crying, and pain." She hugged her Bible close to her heart.

"Glory be to God for His faithfulness. Despite the difficult circumstances this has been for all of us, God used Joshua's tragic death for good and had graced you with spiritual insight, Sarah." The hopeful minister raised his hands toward heaven. "Now, you say your child is ill? James 5:14-15 instructs us, 'Is any sick among? Let him call for the elders of the church; and let them pray over him, anointing him with oil in the name of the Lord. And the prayer of faith shall save the sick, and the Lord shall raise him up; and if he have committed sins, they shall be forgiven him.' Would you like me to do this for you?"

"Yes, Pastor. Lord willin', I shall bring my family next Sunday. I had the opportunity to share the gospel with Lad, and I believe God is workin' on his heart. Thank you so much for not losin' hope in me."

Sarah sensed relief and overwhelming joy upon reconciliation with the precious family who was now a part of her life again. She feared that the reconnection would be like reopening old wounds for her and them as well. The result, however, had the opposite effect: the reuniting brought closure and emotional healing. Moving forward became her aim instead of running away and hiding from her pain. They parted with intentions to visit one another again.

The ride home with her parents, Samuel, and Naomi stirred in her emotions of bygone days from her youth as the family returned to the farm singing joyful hymns from the morning service.

During lunch, Lad and the children listened with intent to Sarah as she shared the momentous occurrence from church earlier that day. "All is well now between the McSwans and me. They request the entire family's attendance next Sunday. The pastor also suggested he lay his hands on Isabelle and pray for God's healing grace."

"Terrific news indeed, darlin'." Lad smiled and passed the bread to her. "Whew. These feet have not attended church in a long while. But I do look forward to going." He addressed Amanda and Billy. "What do you say, children? Shall we join your ma next Sunday and go to church?"

"Yes, Pa!" The children clap their hands, and their faces shone with brightness.

Lad's joyful emotions regarding his spiritual conquest during the morning wanted to explode within him. Yet he withheld his tongue so as not to rain on Sarah's parade.

Later in the evening, upon his first opportunity after his father-in-law blessed supper, Lad made his announcement. "I want all of you to be the first to know, as of this morning, I, too, am a believer in Jesus Christ. So not only are we kinfolk by law, but we are now kinfolk through the family of God."

Jaw dropped, Sarah threw her arms around his neck. "What? You did? You are? Oh, Lad. Congratulations, darlin'."

"I can now answer your question from last Thursday evening, Sarah. You had asked if I believe this was God's divine plan for us to be here and that He would heal our little girl. My response is *yes* on both accounts."

The family raised their glasses to Lad's salvation, and he sensed the bond of Christian love, which seemed closer to him than his biological family. This vicissitude is what he had longed for as a child.

THE FOLLOWING SUNDAY, the pastor anointed Isabelle's head with oil, and he placed his hand upon her torso and prayed as Sarah clung to every word, hoping for a miracle. "Lord Jesus, You are the great Physician, the one who can heal our diseases. What is impossible for men is possible with You. Lord, I present to You this young child, Isabelle, whom doctors diagnosed with infant botulism. If it's Your will, Lord, we pray for Your mercy upon her and grant her healing. We ask this in Jesus' name. Amen."

Sarah opened her eyes, peered up at her husband standing next to her, and then studied her languid child in her arms. *Oh, dear Lord, show us a sign, any sign, that You are healing Izzy.*

Nothing. Not one movement came from Sarah's sleeping child.

22

A Twist of Fate

Harold squirmed in his chair, sensing his boss's agitation as he paced behind his dark-polished teak desk. The Maxfield farmhouse office's crepuscular ambiance and cigar infused furnishings accelerate the fearful dread of confronting the shrewd and conniving wheat baron. Frederick Maxfield's unusual call for an urgent meeting after the harvest season concluded had the lead superintendent baffled. *The abundance of grain this year fetched a pretty penny, so why is the Big Bug troubled?* Harold pushed his straw hat back and scratched his head.

Arms crossed about his chest, Frederick pounced, making known his disgruntled nature. His reddened face and bulging eyes seemed to detach from his body from its inner pressure, like the propulsion of a cannonball. Instead, hardened words fire in succession from his mouth like bullets of a Gatling gun.

"What the heck were you and your men doing out in the fields the last few months, Harold? Were you lollygagging on my expense? I'm quite concerned to learn Jonathan Sower received a more profitable margin for his grain this year because his coolies delivered well ahead of the market. Your performances are not acceptable. Your men better not be shirking me." He wagged his finger. "Push them hard next season and do whatever it takes to bring our produce to the mill before Sower does, or else they can find themselves begging on the streets for their next meal." Frederick slammed his fist on his desk, hacked a mouthful of spit into the spittoon, and gnawed on the chewing tobacco shoved to the right side of his cheek.

Evil schemes formed in Harold Jensen's mind as his body jerked backward into his seat while his employer's fire-filled eyes stabbed him. "I'll be sure the men start ahead of schedule, and they aren't dragging their feet on the job, sir." He boasted, hoping to regain his employer's confidence.

Harold stood and pushed the wooden chair away with the back of his knees, ready to dart out of the office to avoid further reprimand.

"Ah," Frederick yelled and collapsed over his desk while clasping his head. Writhed in pain, he fell into his seat and tumbled onto the floor with a loud thud.

"Mr. Maxfield!" Heart racing, Harold rushed over to where his employer lay. He rolled the corpulent wheat baron over on his back and recognized the sloping paralysis on his face and body's right side. The lack of facial control caused Frederick's snuff-stained spit to drool from his mouth.

"Wha...wha...what?" Frederick slurred.

"Be still now, boss. I'm going to ask someone to retrieve the doc."

With quick thinking, Harold loosened the cravat around Frederick's neck, unbuttoned his shirt, and grabbed a small pillow from the settee to place under his head. Like a dirt devil whisking through a field, Harold sprung into action and hastened to the barn to locate the other superintendents.

"You look like you've seen a ghost." Leonard cracked a crooked grin as he shoveled the mule's dung into a wheelbarrow.

"Drop what you're doing and find the pill in town, Leonard. The boss is down. I think he had a stroke. Leave now and be fast."

"Yeah, sure, Harold." Leonard saddled his horse and stormed out, and another farmhand scurried to Harold's side after hearing the commotion.

"Grier, you must help me carry Maxfield to his bed."

"All right, hoss."

The two men bolted into the farmhouse and scrambled to the office where their employer lay unconscious. After carrying the paralyzed man upstairs to his bedchambers, they awaited the doctor's arrival.

THE SUPERINTENDENTS RETREATED TO THE OFFICE downstairs as Dr. Cassidy began his examination, wasting no time.

"Can you hear me, Fred? I want you to squeeze my fingers with your hands as hard as you can." The skillful doctor dangled his index fingers in the palm of the ailing man's hands and felt the uneven pressure as the patient tried to tighten his grip. Frederick's left fist grasped the doctor's right finger while his right hand clung to the doctor's left.

"Good, Fred. You're doing swell." The doctor removed his stethoscope from his black leather bag.

"All right. The first step is to remove this fid of tobacco from your mouth so you won't choke. There'll be no more of this disgusting habit. Do you understand me, Fred?" As on many occasions, the physician recalled warning Frederick of his unhealthy obsession while he scooped the drool-soaked chew from his cheek.

"Now I'm going to touch certain areas of your head. What I want you to do is squeeze my finger when I place my hand on the area you experience discomfort." Again, the doctor placed his right pointer in Fredericks's left palm and moved his other hand about his skull. His hand hovering over his right temple, the faint tightening occurred once more.

"Now Fred, rate the pain on a scale of one to three, three squeezes being the strongest."

Frederick gave two weak, but distinct, constrictions. The doctor waited a few seconds before confirming.

"So you rate the pain as two? Squeeze once for yes."

Again, he squeezed.

"All right, Fred, let me give you my prognosis. I am certain you encountered a stroke. The probability is that there is an aneurysm developing in your right frontal lobe and has not ruptured yet. If that happened, you wouldn't be able to respond nor understand what I'm saying to you. In fact, you'd be cold as a wagon tire. Only time will determine if you're to regain the use of your right arm and leg. From my observations of other cases, the damage is usually permanent.

"Fred, I'm sorry to tell you this, but this may be the end of your business career. The aneurysm must not herniate if you want to live. Stabilizing your blood pressure is my first countermeasure. For now, you must remain in bed until I observe what happens with the paralysis. Also, I'll hire a full-time nurse to care for you."

A tear trickled from Fredericks's left eye.

"This is difficult news for you, I realize. However, my God, man, you stared death in the face today. If you desire to live to enjoy tomorrow, you must lower your blood pressure and stress. There are no other options. For now, my recommendation is for you to rest and not worry about anything. After your strength returns, I'll arrange a meeting between you and your attorney. Let's allow a few weeks, all right?"

The doctor moved about and reached into his black leather case for a syringe and medication vial. "This is pain and seizure medicine." He clicked the needle, let out some air, and injected into Fred's left arm. Completing this task, he put away his paraphernalia and tidied the area.

"The butler will be instructed to tend to you until I can hire a nurse. We need to keep a close eye on your progress, so expect to enjoy my company every day.

"Now, let's change you out of this suit and into your long underwear." The doctor stripped off Frederick's outer layer of clothes, leaving his undergarments on, and tucked his bedsheets around him. "Please try to rest, and when you wake, I'll evaluate whether you can eat and help you with other personal needs. A pan will be at the foot of your bed."

The physician grabbed his medical bag and trod downstairs to inform the superintendents, who paced in Frederick's office.

"Well, gentlemen, your suspicions are correct. Your employer experienced a hemorrhagic stroke."

"Speak layman's terms, doc. What do you mean?" Chest distended, Harold stood and spoke for the group in his ruffian manner.

"What I'm trying to say is you men may be out of a job. The right side of Mr. Maxfield's body is paralyzed, and he won't be able to function as normal. Harold, if not for your quick response, he'd be dead. The stress of competition finally took its toll on the poor fellow.

To speak his name will be difficult enough, let alone run a business.

"My advice is for you boys to contact his lawyer straight away since he has no kin to assist him. In the meantime, I'll do my best to keep him comfortable and locate a full-time nurse to tend to him. The house butler will need to attend to him until she arrives. Unless something changes, you'll be seeing me often in the next few weeks."

"THE VIABILITY OF RECEIVING PROFIT within the first harvest should make selling your business more palatable to the buyer, Mr. Maxfield." The accountant grimaced as he closed the Maxfield Farms' financial ledger on his lap and handed the portfolio to the attorney seated next to him to the left of Frederick's bedside. "I'll be frank with you, sir. The proceeds from the sale will be sufficient for your medical expenses, and the land rent barely enough to cover your mortgage. You may have to liquidate other assets to put food on your table." He stood and walked to the bedroom window to view the property. "Maxfield Farms finances struggled before this tragic turn of events occurred. All the more now, the consequences may find you in the poor house. I'm afraid the bank will not extend you their benevolence any further, sir. Frugality must be your main concern."

Propped on pillows and reclining in his bed, Frederick turned his attention to the lawyer as he pulled out a contract from his attaché case. "I'll be sure to place an ad in the *San Joaquin Argus* for the sale of your business and the lease of your land. Your men must be patient and await the outcome of the sale."

Frederick glanced at Harold, who sat wide-eyed in a chair to the right of his bed. His chest ached beneath his nightshirt, and he could do nothing nor say a word in response. *A heart attack would suit me well at this moment, but that resolve is too easy. No, fate will make sure I suffer judgment, take all that I hold dear to me, and bring me to ruins.*

"We must work with expediency. The next wheat season is fast approaching. Only a few months remain to make a smooth and profitable transaction for the new buyer." The legal advisor leaned over Frederick and placed the contract under his left hand.

After dipping a steelhead pen into a small inkwell, the lawyer placed the writing utensil in Frederick's left hand. "Please, sign this contract so that I can begin the process. An X will do fine. As the witness, Harold will sign below your mark."

Frederick's hand shook as he scribbled an *X* on the sheet. The lawyer handed the form and pen to Harold, who also signed and dated the contract.

"All right. I'll start right away. Let's hope a buyer comes around real soon."

23

A Growing Business

"I can't believe my eyes!" With the *San Joaquin Argus* propped up to his face, Jonathan gasped while relaxing on the front porch as the warm scent of harvested fields filled his lungs.

"What's wrong, Jon?" Mary put down her knitting.

"The Maxfield Wheat Company is up for sale, and Fred is leasing his land … all 3,500 acres of it." Eyes enlarged, he reached for his clay pipe, took a long drag, and shook his head in disbelief.

"No. You don't say."

His wife jaunted over to him and peered over his shoulder to glimpse at the business section.

Stunned, Jonathan put the paper on the table and walked over to the porch rail to gaze at his harvested 2,500 acres of wheat. He envisioned fruit and nut trees added to his thriving agriculture land, now on the other side of Snelling.

"Jon, are you thinkin' what I'm thinkin'?" Mary asked as she stood beside him.

Nodding, Jonathan nibbled on his pipe he held to his lips. "This could be the answer we've been prayin' for, darlin'."

She tugged at his elbow and stared into his eyes. "Well, what are you waitin' for? Ya better get a jump on it before someone else does."

After several days of pouring over the financial ledgers with his wife and sending a formal offer to the Maxfield attorney, Jonathan announced his intentions to his family, who gathered in his office.

"As y'all heard by now, Frederick Maxfield has been met with a most unfortunate health situation and is no longer able to maintain his estate. He is forced to sell his business and lease his lands.

"After much prayer, your ma and I believe this opportunity is meant for us. We sent our proposal to his attorney yesterday. Lord willing, if they agree to the terms, Sower Farm will more than double in size. When it does, we'll need our family's cooperation and support more than ever." Jonathan paced by the hearth, his gaze locked on the wide-eyed faces around him.

"His property is enormous, Pa. How do you expect us to handle both farms?" asked Naomi.

"Not only that, the fact is Mr. Maxfield despises you and all our Chinese employees. I don't think he's going to want the Sowers takin' over his business." Brows furrowed, Sam grit his teeth.

"Now hold on. For some time your ma and I've been thinkin' how we might expand." Jonathan gazed at his wife, who sat calm and seemed to glow with inspiration. "My vision is to tap into the fruit and nut industry and still maintain the wheat. But because we're land-locked in Snelling, we didn't know how to accomplish this. It meant dividin' the different crops between the existin' parcels, which would lower our grain production and profits. This is not an option for us."

Eyes locked with Naomi, Jonathan threw his hands in the air. "Don't you see God's hands are all over this? By takin' over Maxfield's business, we can gradually convert his crop to fruit and nut orchards without touchin' our existin' wheat plantation. Not only will Sower Farm be the leader in the wheat industry, but we'll also be the top producers among the peach and almond growers, too! In due time, if the Lord wills, we can purchase his land as the business gains profit."

"Your plan sounds good and well only if your offer is accepted. I still think your chances are slim with Maxfield's hatred of all we stand for." Sam shook his head.

"Well, there is one thing I know about him. He is all about obtainin' top dollar. Now he has no choice but to sell the business and lease the land in his condition. Besides, he can't in no way pass up our proposal of ten percent more than their highest bid. Not only do we guarantee the maximum offer, but it also provides employment security for his existin' staff." A grin stretched across Jonathan's face.

"His existin' staff? Those mongrels! How could you employ them after what they did to Huang-Fu?" Clench fisted, Sam stomped his way to the window.

Jonathan stood by his son and placed his hand on his shoulder. "Now, there is no proof they committed the crime, Sam. If these men sinned, the Bible tells us their sin will find them out. Come on back and take a seat.

"I'll answer your question, Naomi. Let's face it, we're goin' to need the experienced workforce for a smooth transition. I plan to operate two separate businesses; Sower Farm One, and the new Sower and Sons Farm Two. The head supervisor for the Chinese staff at farm one will be Ah Yung, and Samuel over the former Maxfield staff at farm two. Ah Sheng-Li and a former Maxfield employee will be the assistant supervisors, and Ah Anguo and Lad will be the caporals with a former Maxfield employee as Lad's assistant."

"Do you think those men will listen to us?" Lad scratched his head.

Hands on his hips and feet planted firm on the ground, Jonathan said, "Well, if they want to remain employed, they will. Just because I've offered to keep them as employees don't mean they are permanent." He resumed pacing. "I'll give them a chance to prove themselves, as I do with all my workers. Plenty other men out there are eager for a good job for fewer wages, if their performance isn't up to par."

"Ugh. I'm not lookin' forward to this." Sam forced a smile and shook his head. "But if expandin' the business is goin' to make life better for us, I'm all for the change. I'll support you, Pa and Ma."

"That's what I want to hear." Jonathan patted Sam's back and bounced a stern gaze at the others.

"All right, I'll notify y'all the moment there is word. Once our offer is accepted, I'll plan a meetin' with the new staff."

"WELCOME, GENTLEMEN." Jonathan allowed Harold, Leonard, Grier, and Nevil into the farmhouse foyer. "This is a Christian home. Leave your gun belts on the table and follow me into my office."

The men's eyes enlarged with curiosity as they removed their weapons. Jingling spurs reverberated off the foyer's wood floors as they followed him. They sat in the open seats opposite the Sower superintendents as Jonathan stood by the hearth with arms crossed.

"I want to welcome y'all to Sower Farm One and the beginning of Sower and Sons Farm Two. I am the sole proprietor, Jonathan Sower.

"The men to my right are farm one's head supervisor Ah Yung, his assistant, Ah Sheng-Li, and caporal Ah Anguo. For farm two, my eldest son Samuel will be the head supervisor and my son-in-law Lad Hampton, head caporal.

"Since farm two is still utilizing manually operated equipment, staff requirements are greater, so additional assistance will be needed. Harold Jensen and Leonard Lambert will be Samuel's assistant, and Nevil Pierce and Grier Thomas Lad's assistant.

Jaw clenched Jonathan paced about the room amongst his expanded staff as the former Maxfield workers squirmed in their seats and riveted daggered stares at Sam, Lad, and the nationals they detested most. The air's intensity rose as thick as leavened dough.

Jonathan realized his offer placed the former Maxfield employees in a precarious situation. The indispensable positions dangled before them like a carrot before a hard-headed mule pulling a laden cart. *Despite their personal inhibitions, they must cooperate with the driver if they want to put food on their table.*

These men withdrawing now would only permit me to hire more Chinese nationals, which would defeat their labor protest and destroy their life's accomplishments at Maxfield Farms. I don't think their pride will allow them to quit.

Heaven forbid they figure out that I need their help for this fast-approaching planting season as much as they need their jobs. Should they understand my dilemma, they may hold this card against me and make life miserable. I must play a careful hand.

"It's no secret you men are not in favor of the way I run my business." After he had slowed his gait, Jonathan glanced at the disgruntled new employees. Both sides sat uneasily with their arms crossed and eyes glaring at one another.

"I'm a fair and gracious man and hold no prejudices to anyone. All I care about is gettin' the job done right. My desire is for y'all to remain under my employ, laborin' hard for an honest day's wage, and doin' what you are trained to do. The difference is you'll be workin' with the men I choose to manage Sower and Sons Farm, and I expect you to take their command. I run a business here on my farms, not some social club.

"You men are expected to get along and work with one another no matter what y'alls color of skin. To ease the tensions, I've chosen to keep things runnin' as they are. The Chinese workers at farm one, and the white workers at farm two. Are there any objections or suggestions regardin' this arrangement?" Jonathan held a stern composure. For a moment, he examined each man's brow-cocked expressions and sensed they had a myriad of disgruntled complaints. *They're doin' well not to contend with me.*

"All right, let's proceed as scheduled. An inspection of both grounds is to be completed and a report from the head supervisors on my desk by the end of November. I expect you men to give Ah Yung, Sam, and Lad your full cooperation. Please inform me of the equipment and livestock's condition at farm two. We need to be prepared to run both locations simultaneously without any hiccups or surprises.

"Thank you for your undivided attention, men. That'll be all for today." Jonathan ended the meeting, and the staff stood from their seats, ready to leave the room.

In an attempt to warm the ice-cold atmosphere, Sam scuffed over to Harold and extended his hand. "Lookin' forward to workin' with you men."

Like a trapped animal, Harold glared at Sam's rugged palm, sent stinging arrows with his eyes, and returned an agitated handshake. "I hope we'll meet your expectations." He proceeded to shake Jonathan's hand. "Thank you, sir, for the opportunity." Harold moved to Lad and, with immense hesitation, extended the gesture to Yung, Sheng-Li, and Anguo, not saying a word.

The former Maxfield team followed suit, shook hands with the Sower men, and tried their best to appear in agreement in the presence of their new boss. Jonathan's discernment warned him trouble lurked.

24

Monkeyed With

"**I**s it me, or did that ride through town seem longer than usual?" Lad asked as his horse trotted next to Samuel's past the Chinese camp on the west end of Snelling.

"No. You're right. Both Pa and I forked a hoss through this place a hundred times to fetch workers at the camp. In all my born days I never thought I'd be crossin' town to conduct business on Maxfield's farm. I think we're both dreadin' this new venture." Sam yanked on Fire's reins to turn south onto Snelling Road toward the new Sower and Sons Farm, formerly Maxfield Farm. "This daily routine is goin' to take some gettin' used to."

A few miles after they crossed the Merced Falls River, a dusty path diverted to the right, and a massive iron arch that bore steel-plated letters came into view. *Maxfield Farms.* "Tearin' down this gate will be the first item on my agenda." Sam scoffed as they passed under the arch.

"Well, good thing your father owns the business and can do as he pleases with the land. But with Maxfield as the landlord and still living in his farmhouse, he'll no doubt be keepin' his eyes on all we do. Even though he has a disability, I think his power and presence will still have a bad influence on his old staff. There'll be a bit of acreocracy going on between them if you ask me. I'm a bit uneasy about this, Sam.

My gut tells me we're in for a rough ride workin' with these addle-headed alfalfa desperados."

"Yeah. The feeling is mutual, brother. Workin' at farm two will be all-overish. We'll need to watch each other's backs around this bunch."

The expansive farmhouse came into view as Sam and Lad approached, dismounted, and tied their horses to a nearby watering trough.

"Maxfield's diggin's sure is a lot for one man." Lad spat on the ground.

Samuel inhaled deep to relax, adjusted his Stetson, and loosened his collar. "All right. You ready to make bricks without straw?"

"Yep. Let's get it over with."

Sam and Lad spent most of the day reviewing the inventory of the newly acquired assets with the assistance of Harold, Leonard, Grier, and Nevil. Although the new assistant superintendents had smiles on their faces as they demonstrated their willingness to cooperate, Samuel discerned their unhappiness and contention. The men whispered and snickered as they huddled around each other and sent squinty-eyed glances his and Lad's way. An eerie uneasiness about these men caused Sam's neck hairs to stand on end, making him alert and cautious.

"It's our bad luck that we have to work for the Sowers'. Now we're forced to listen to these young whippersnappers. Don't know if I can take this, Harold." Nevil voiced his grievance as he ate lunch in the barn with the other assistant superintendents.

"Don't you worry none, Nevil. Just because we work for them doesn't mean we must put up with them. Monkey with them is what we must do. You know what I mean?" He winked. "A couple of chuckleheads is what they'll be after we're done with them. We've got to be real sly about it, so we don't get caught. Our jobs are on the line, and we don't wanna lose them, do we?" Harold huddled the three superintendents together and spoke in a low voice. "Here's what we'll do..."

A WEEK LATER, inside one of farm two's barns, Sam, Lad, and the superintendents discussed the equipment and livestock. Crouched, Sam inspected the plows as Lad examined the mules.

"I'm amazed y'all are still usin' the sulkies. Bein' the largest wheat producers in our county, I thought for sure this farm would be up on technology," Sam said as Harold and Leonard dawdled along behind him whispering and chortling.

"Uh, well, sir, technology is expensive. I think Maxfield would rather put food in our bellies than steam in them engines." Harold guffawed, then stopped and stood to attention when Sam turned to face him.

A glimpse of Harold's abrupt actions caught Samuel's attention as he eyeballed each character and their quivered smiles. *What are these buffoons up to?*

Sam tried to ignore the warning signs in his head and continued. "Well, the steam-powered plow and harvester have cut our costs and reduced the time to produce the wheat by more than half. We've been able to go to market earlier and more often, increasing our profits because of these inventions. Expect big changes next season." *That should put some fear into their bellies.* The men's smiles soon turned to sour grimaces.

"Besides, these plows look as if they've seen the last of their days," Samuel said.

"Yep, and these mules are 'bout ready to kick the bucket, too." Lad returned to the group with Nevil and Grier trailing behind, downcast from the report.

Imaginary invisible padlocks upon the mouths of the four assistant superintendents' shut them up and quieted their mocking.

"All right. I want the plows and harvesters primed and ready for their last season. You'll see to it, Harold." Sam removed his leather work gloves and shoved them in his dungaree's back pocket and began walking toward the barn door as Lad followed.

The sunlight beckoned Sam to leave the confines of the dusty barn and its sneering obnoxious inhabitants. As he trod along the straw-covered ground, his boot caught the edge of a hidden hoe, which caused the handle to come flying up and smack him hard in the face.

"Aw! What shanny left this hoe lyin' around like this?" Samuel rubbed the painful, self-inflicted strawberry wound that grew on his forehead. Bursts of hee-haws from the four men surrounded him like flies on honey.

"Let's get out of here, Sam." Lad placed his hand on Sam's shoulder. "Let me take a look at that on the front porch."

ANOTHER WEEK LATER, work gloves adjusted, Lad entered the barn and walked toward the grooming station where Neville brushed the mules. "Is that the last one? Are you ready to walk the geldings to the pasture?"

Neville pat the mule's rump, put the brush down, placed his hands on his hips, and slid a sideways glance at Lad. "Yep. What do you plan to do with these animals after you replace them with the steam tractors?"

"We'll more than likely sell them. At their age, they're not much good, other than dog food."

"Ya know, I bred and raised these geldings on this here farm. Their fair share of work has been done, and now you're gonna sell them for dog food! Just doesn't sit right with me." Neville shook his head and yanked the mule's rein to lead it to the fenced pasture as Lad followed with two more mules until all were outside.

"Well, it's better than working them to their death." Lad slid his hand across the swayed back of one of the mules. "All right. Meet you at the barn after lunch, and we'll work on the horses next." Lad wiped his brow and adjusted his hat. He began walking toward the outhouse as Neville locked the gate behind them. "Too much brown gargle this mornin'. Gotta run to the necessary."

Lad slammed the door behind him, lowered his trousers, sat down on the privy, and relieved himself. As he read torn pieces of newspaper used for therapeutic paper, a loud thud rapped on the door. "Be done in a second." Lad tidied up, fastened his belt buckle, and lifted the door latch. But it wouldn't budge. *What the heck?* He fidgeted with it again and pushed his weight into the door. *Locked. Did someone lock me in?* Lad pound on the door and yelled. "Anyone out there? Open the door!"

"I'M SORRY I'M RUNNIN' LATE. All the mules are back in their stalls, sir."

"Thanks, Neville. You did that all by yourself? Where's Lad? Haven't seen him all day," Samuel said, putting away his tools.

"Don't know. He was supposed to meet me in the barn after lunch to brush the horses. Never showed up." His eyes seemed to dance as he shrugged his shoulders.

"*Hmm.* All right. Well, you and the men have a good evenin', and I'll see y'all tomorrow."

"Sure enough." Neville tipped his hat and headed out of the barn.

That's strange. Lad would've informed me if he were leaving the grounds. After he double-checked the animals' stall security, Sam locked the barn doors and turned toward the farmhouse. *Lad's horse is still here. Where in the world could he be?* Surveying the grounds from where he stood, the farm was still. The superintendents and their horses had gone home. All was quiet when he heard a faint *thump, thump, thump … open the door!*

"Lad! Where are you?"

"In the necessary! Would you open the door?"

Running toward the outhouse, Sam could not believe his eyes. An ax wedged itself into the door latch. He yanked on the handle to free the latch. The door flew open, and Lad came tumbling out.

"Well, about time!"

"How long were you in there?"

"Since the shank of the mornin'. Can't believe nobody's come lookin' for me. Especially Neville."

"Well, I've been assistin' Harold since he needed a hand with the equipment because Grier stayed home today feelin' a little wamble-cropped. *Hmm,* somethin' smells bad, and it ain't the necessary, either. This ax didn't just fall into this latch. It was placed there by someone."

"What are you goin' to do? Ask who did it. Good luck with that." Lad smirked.

Angry, Sam swung the ax at the outhouse door and left it hanging. "Let's go home."

25

Love Revealed

"We're home," Sam called out as he and Lad entered the Sower farmhouse, hung their hats on the foyer rack, and removed their fringed buckskin jackets.

From the kitchen, a scurry of little feet scampered toward the tired, anxiety-ridden men. "Papa, papa!" Amanda and Billy reached out to Lad, each clinging to one of his legs.

Close behind them, Sarah approached wiping her hands on her apron. She paused a moment to examine Lad's distraught demeanor. His head hung low, and his voice lacked the exuberance and laughter, which on normal occasions, accompanied him at the end of the workday when he arrived home to relax with his family.

"Oh, dear. It looks like you both can use a big hug." Sarah wrapped her arms around her husband's neck and kissed his cheek. "All right, children, give your pa some time to unwind." She pried the children off Lad's boots. "Go upstairs and wash up, then join us for supper."

Samuel envied Lad and Sarah's patulous relationship since he and Jia-Li had to conceal their love. At least for his brother-in-law, he had the daily encouragement and support from Sarah, whose ostensive amorous embrace and comforting words affirmed the bravado he needed to redeem his manhood. Although Samuel's family conceded to be amiable and impartial, he and Jia-Li's relationship would challenge their constitution. Not only were they an interracial couple, but they were also publicly classified as heirs to two distinct social stations. He was the farm mogul's son, and she the butler and housekeeper's daughter.

"Come into the kitchen and have a tall glass of cider and unload your worries." Sarah whisked ahead of them as they followed.

Samuel grunted. "Are our lowly dispositions that obvious?"

"My dear bub, of late you both have been wearing your hearts on your sleeves ever since Pa acquired farm two."

Upon entering the dining room, Samuel caught Jia-Li's love-struck glance as they often did when he came home. The men sat down at the table as the women brought them a beverage.

Sarah sat next to her husband. "Please do share your day with me, my love. It's not good to keep emotions bottled up."

"Ugh." Lad rubbed the back of his neck. "Those Maxfield men have us over the barrel. Their pranks will be the unraveling of us, and we can't seem to find any evidence that reveals them as the culprits. I fell off a barn stool today, and I think I pulled a neck muscle. The seat collapsed beneath me, and after examining the legs, I noticed deliberate saw marks on them."

Samuel gulped the sweet apple drink. "We're starvin', by the way. Other than breakfast, we've had nothin' to eat all day. Did we forget our haversacks this mornin'?"

Jia-Li darted to the kitchen door and peered down the foyer at the entry table. "No, Mr. Samuel. They are not on the table."

"That's what I thought. We fetch our belongings like clockwork as we walk out the door. You gals always make sure our lunches are ready before we leave," Samuel said, shaking his head in dismay. "When Lad and I checked our saddlebags, our haversacks were nowhere to be found."

"Did you confront your assistant supervisors?" Sarah asked.

Lad huffed. "Those Maxfield men would never cough up to this deviltry."

Sarah patted her husband's arm and encouraged her husband and brother with Numbers 32:23. "Be patient, darlins'. Be assured the Bible tells us sins will be found out of those who disobey the Lord."

"Yeah, I hope that day will be soon. These shenanigans are wearing on us." Samuel said as his stomach made rumbling sounds.

"Well, at least we can take care of your immediate needs," Jia-Li said. "Supper is ready. I will go call on the others."

Two weeks later, the late autumn pumpkin-colored sun dipped halfway below the horizon, signaling another week's end at farm two. The workers had gone home, and Samuel and Lad completed their final rounds of securing the grounds. No peculiar incidents occurred in a while, causing a song to spring up in Samuel's mind. He began whistling the tune *Old Dan Tucker* as they moseyed over to their horses.

"Maybe there's hope for this place yet," Lad chuckled while tightening his saddle's stirrups. His mare's hind legs shuffled as he did. "Whoa Abby. Anxious to get home, are you now?"

Samuel did the same and Fire neighed. "Looks like our ponies are rarin' to leave this place like we are. Shall we go home, brother?"

"You bet," Lad said.

Both men grabbed their saddle horns, stepped into their stirrups, and hurled themselves into their seats as they have done a million times over. As lightning strikes and obliterates an unsuspecting tree, both horses reared jerking their passengers high into the air. The men landed hard and heavy on the ground. The steeds bolted and scurried down the road headed in the direction towards home. Bewildered and shaken, Samuel and Lad picked themselves off the ground, rubbed their bruised and aching bodies, and dusted off their clothing.

"Lord, what just happened there?" Lad asked.

Samuel rotated his shoulders and returned his hat upon his head. "Can't rightly say — one thing for sure, our horses were spooked by something or someone, and it's not us. I guess we'll find out when we get home. Are you all right?"

"My Sunday-face will be a bit bruised." Lad smirked, rubbed his derriere, and tried to make light of the incident. "Guess will be riding the old mules home for the evening."

"Yep. Let's fetch them. I'm not about to walk home."

The men retrieved two mules, saddled them, and returned to Sower Farm. Upon their arrival, they found Fire and Abby lingering outside the barn scratching to get inside to find security in their stables. After placing the mules in the corral, Samuel and Lad approached their horses. The fatigued steeds snorted and huffed from the four-mile sprint home.

"Whoa, boy," Samuel said in a low, calm voice.

He and Lad gathered their horse's reins and walked them to their stalls. Once inside with the gates closed, they began removing their horse's saddles.

A flabbergasted grumble came from Lad in Abby's stall next to Fire's. "Darn them Maxfield men!"

Sam stopped unbuckling his saddle, rushed over to Lad, and peered over Abby's stall door. The saddle lay on the ground, and the padded blanket on her back pulled away. "Did you find something?"

Lad plucked a dime-sized burr off Abby's spine as she winced from the pain. "Now tell me, Sam. How in the heck did this nettle get under the pad?" He placed the bloodied thick spiked thistle in Samuel's hand.

"Well, it sure didn't just fall there. I wouldn't be surprised if there is one under my saddle too." The men returned to Fire's stable and removed his saddle and pad and found another strategically placed thorn. Samuel shook his head with fury, and he removed the evidence. "I do smell a rat."

SAMUEL AND HIS BROTHER-IN-LAW entered the kitchen downtrodden and parched. Planting himself at the table, he removed his hat and kicked up his heels on the chair across from Lad. The Suen family occupied themselves with supper's preparation, as his parents and sister discussed business and sipped on tea. Without hesitation, Jia-Li brought him a glass of cool beverage.

His mind filled with the day's vexation, he reacted in what should be a typical response for two people in love.

"Are you all right, Samuel?" Jia-Li asked as she stood next to him.

Samuel wearily searched Jia-Li's warm, compassionate eyes. "Oh, my love, I only need your kind embrace." Inadvertent arms wrapped around her waist as his head leaned into her torso.

At first, Jia-Li's brows arched as shock pierced her countenance at his outward affectionate display. She scanned the room at the stares fixated on them. Samuel had no clue he captured the room's attention.

Sensing her lack of reciprocation and percipient to the sudden stifle, Sam turned his head with caution to be met by the family's befuddled semblances.

The family's gander shifted from Jia-Li to him, who remained petrified. Sights converged on his embrace, so he released his grip on her and repositioned himself in his seat.

"I guess I…" He gagged as he tried to find the right words. "We, owe y'all an explanation." Instincts grabbed her hand for assurance and strength. "I am in love with Jia-Li, and she loves me. I knew this since the time I spilled coffee on her blouse last year." To defuse the intensified atmosphere, Samuel grinned.

Arms around her waist again, he leaned his head upon her torso, and she tried her best to relax.

Entwined in his arms, she stared into his eyes and held his head close to her heart. "I am not sure what I would have done without Samuel when Father was hurt. I love Samuel very much."

Both turned their gaze to the family members.

Samuel examined their facial countenance for any clues of disapproval. Silence again for what seemed like minutes.

"Well, congratulations are in order then," his father finally belted out. With the patriarch's approval, the families blessed the young couple with their endearment and continued with the evening's dinner and family affair. Samuel and Jia-Li rejoiced with laughter to be candid about their relationship as the weight of secrecy lifted from their shoulders.

26

A Second Family

November's vibrant canary, tangerine, and Cardinal foliage that sprinkled the bustling university's landscape, now faded to muted scarlet and earthy browns as the leaves prepared to depart from their arboreous abode. The students were feverishly experiencing the frustrations of mid-terms before they adjourned for the four-day Thanksgiving respite. David and his roommate, Clarence Harrington, immersed themselves in their studies at the library, with an occasional break to rest their minds and feed their scarce appetites at the student cafeteria. Piles of hard-back books surround them on the table like a fortified wall illuminated by the natural light which poured in from the library's massive windows. The musty smell of old books written by past sages of the faith, as well as the scent of newly bound manuscripts from modern-day ministers graced the well-endowed learning facility.

"David, are you ready to get some sustenance?" Clarence stood from the table, twisted his torso left to right, and tilted his neck and head until he heard the joints crack to relieve the tension in his spine and shoulders.

"Give me a minute, brother." David dragged his left index finger through several paragraphs in his text until he found the answer he needed. He jotted down the information on his tablet. "Aw. I'm beginning to wonder if it were better to remain in the simple confines of Biblical ignorance than delve into the complex debates of Calvinism and Arminianism." David ran his hands through his hair and pulled on its roots.

"Where ignorance is bliss, 'tis folly to be wise," Clarence said, one brow cocked.

"Yes. Thomas Gray's poem, *Ode on a Distant Prospect of Eton College*." After scratching his head, David closed his book. He packed his belongings, put on his overcoat, wool scarf, and bowler hat. "Don't concern yourself, Clarence. I'm fine. This is as good of a time as any to pause from my spiritual appetite and take care of my carnal needs." He chortled.

They scurried over to the student cafeteria, chatting about the theological exposés which intrigued them. Trays clanked above the students' dense reverberating conversations that bounce off the dining hall's stark walls and tiled flooring. David inspected the limited choices of campus cuisine, and his thoughts retracted to the wonderful home-cooked meals his family concocted in preparation for Thanksgiving. He envisioned his mother's hands and apron covered in flour as she methodically created her sumptuous Dutch apple and pumpkin pies. His thoughts turned to the barn where his father fattened up the chosen turkey for the festive event. Ah, the divine imagery of mouthwatering dishes accompanied by tantalizing aromas teased his senses, unlike the pungent scent of savor lacking cafeteria food infused with his classmate's musty body odors of colognes and toiletries.

"The holidays are going to be more difficult for me than studyin'," David said as he reached for a plate of mass-produced mashed potatoes and breaded chicken.

"Your gloomy countenance tells me you're not planning to go home for the holidays."

"You can't be serious?" David chortled as they shuffled in line, pushing their trays forward. "By the time I arrive in Snelling, I would have to turn right around and head back to school the next day. I'd rather stay here on campus and suffer the cafeteria's homogenized attempts of Thanksgivin' traditions than to be bound to a train and its restless passengers discussin' their holiday plans of grandeur. That type of vacation would be an annoyance at best for me and will cause me more fatigue and frustration than I need right now."

"*Hmm* ... I see. Well, brother, can I offer up an invitation to spend the holidays with my family and me? It may not compare to the glorious California lifestyle you've described, but Marion has a charm all its own, which I'm sure you'll find quite festive and comforting." Clarence gloated. "My mother and sisters have favorite culinary recipes, as well. I assure you, you'll gain the weight back that you lost here on campus the last few months."

With gladness and gratitude, David patted Clarence's back. "My brother, I would be honored to spend the holidays with you and your family, only if it's not an imposition upon them."

"Not at all. Thanksgiving is a time for kinfolk to gather, and you are our brother in Christ. The Bible tells us that God adopted us through his Son, Jesus. So there you have it. We're related. Besides, Mother affords every opportunity to exercise her gift of hospitality. She would love for you to stay with us during the holiday." The jubilant roommate's eyes glistened at his accepted invitation.

AFTER THE GRUELING TESTS HAD CONCLUDED, the two friends returned to the dormitory and packed their bags for the short eight-mile train ride to Marion, Indiana, scheduled the next day.

"Ready to turn in?" Clarence rolled over in his twin-sized bed and leaned over his oil lamp to blow out its flame. "We've got an early rise tomorrow mornin'. Don't want to miss our train."

"Yes, sir. Just finishin' this letter to my family so I can put it in the post before we leave." Ensconced at the student desk in his nightclothes, David signed the letter, placed it in an envelope, and set it beside his carpet bag. "Good night. Lookin' forward to what tomorrow brings." He blew into the oil lamp on his nightstand then planted his head upon his pillow. Soon David fell fast asleep, counting his blessings.

At the bright yellow painted Marion depot, Clarence's father, Clayton, met them in his horse-driven buggy and drove them to their home nestled in the slow-growing mid-western community.

"Someone has rumored that natural gas has been discovered in this region. I can only imagine what kind of industry that will draw to our town. There's talk that some of the farmers are thinking of selling their lands to allow the construction of these factories," Clayton said.

"Father, you aren't considering this for our property, are you?" Clarence jerked his head as if a rug were pulled from underneath him.

Clayton chuckled. "No, no, not at all, son. I'm just trying to impress your young friend with the east coast's modernization efforts. We aren't as backward as the westerners may think of us."

"Oh, no need to impress me, Mr. Harrington. The east coast is far more technologically savvy than we are on the west coast. Resources are at your fingertips. The only difference between us is that we westerners have no choice but to advance ourselves in order to survive the harsh unsettled conditions of California. New territory requires modern ingenuity. As for me, I prefer the quiet, unhurried country life reliant upon God's good graces."

The buggy whisked its way past the downtown community then through the undisturbed, dusty streets between small plots of farmland eight miles outside of town. They stopped in front of a quaint, wood-framed cottage with a narrow porch and a blacksmith shop. A small garden lay to one side of the home and surrounding it sprawled a back and front forty of harvested corn.

"Whoa." Clayton tugged at the reins. "Welcome to our humble abode, David."

After setting the brakes, Clayton stepped off the carriage and secured the horse's reins around the post near the watering trough. His wife and two teenage daughters dashed out of the house and scampered onto the front porch to greet them with a big wave.

Clarence jumped out of the buggy, grabbed his carpetbags, and high-stepped toward the ladies as David strung along behind.

After dropping his small suitcase on the ground, Clarence wrapped his arms around his mother's shoulders. "It's so good to be home, Mother."

David's demure nature pushed heat from beneath his collar to his face as he watched his roommate kiss his sister's cheeks and turn to include him.

"Allow me to introduce you to my lovely mother, Catherine, and my two younger sisters, Clara and Cora." Clarence placed his right hand on David's shoulder to guide him toward the ladies. "Aren't my parents the clever ones to start a new family tradition of naming their brood with names that begin with the letter 'C'?" Clarence guffawed. "This is my roommate, David. He hails all the way from California."

"California … you are a long stretch from home. Well, we welcome you to partake with our family. I hope we can provide some comfort to ease your longing for home." Warmth filled David's heart to hear Catherine's sweet and sincere voice. "Come inside. You'll be roommates again and share Clarence's room. Put those bags away, gentlemen, then join us in the parlor for supper."

"I'm blessed to have Clarence as my roommate and having you as a second family. Thank you so much, Mr. and Mrs. Harrington, for allowin' me to share this Thanksgiving with you," David said.

His peripheral vision caught the eldest daughter, Clara glancing at him, which caused his heart to skip a beat. She seemed to be inspecting him from his polished boots and tailored coat to his hat. *Dear Lord. I've never had a lady look me over. Smile, be pleasant, and exercise manners worthy of a gentleman.*

"Hello, Cora." David removed his hat and tilted his head toward the youngest sibling. "Good day to you, Clara." He proceeded to acknowledge the older sister, who had her eyes fixed upon his hands.

A sweet smile of approval appeared on Clara's youthful visage as she admired his mannerisms. She shifted her focus to his face as he returned her gaze. Embarrassed, her pale rose petal cheeks contrasted to her ivory skin tone as she lowered her lashes and curtsied.

"Come, David. I'll show you to my room," Clarence said, grinning at him and his sister as if he had discovered a secret. "You'll have plenty of time to get to know my family."

27

Emerald Eyes

Supper at the Harrington home on the eve of the great feasting holiday tout a simple affair compared to the culinary scale David became accustomed to back home at Sower Farms. The kitchen, however, presented a cornucopia of harvest delights, which the assiduous ladies prepared for the festive Thanksgiving meal to be had by all the next day. Several stout pies sat on the counter, awaiting their appointment with Catherine's ironclad oven. A pile of washed sweet potatoes dried in a large bowl beside a medium one that contained fresh-picked green beans and corn from their garden.

Clarence devoured the warm pot-roasted meal set before him on the table. "Aw … I'm so glad to be home again. Campus food does not compare to your luscious home-cooked meals, Mother."

"I agree, Mrs. Harrington." David savored every tender morsel of beef slow-cooked with potatoes, carrots, celery, and onions.

"Why … thank you, gentlemen." Catherine chuckled. "Having two well-bred and domestically trained daughters helps as well."

Upon hearing their cue, Clara and Cora began the process of gathering the dishes and silverware to wash. Clara's linen blouse and simple calico skirt swished about as she maneuvered around the table. Exercising utmost decorum, David did his best to be discreet in his observance of the charming young lady.

Clayton relaxed into his chair at the head of the table. "Now, the men take part in this, too. You boys can go with me to town tomorrow morning to the butcher shop to pick up a plump turkey, then to the bakery to purchase some bread and sweets for tomorrow's meal." Clayton rubbed his belly.

"Gladly," David said.

A spark glistened from Clarence's eyes as if a brilliant idea came to his mind. "Clara, would you like to go with them instead of me? I know how much you love going to the bakery," he said to his sister as she headed toward the kitchen washbasin with her hands full. Then in an unscrupulous yet elusive manner, Clarence winked at David without the others noticing. "I can do your chores and spend time with Mother."

Oh, I see. You're playing the matchmaker! I know what you're up to. Amazed, David shook his head and smirked.

"What a wonderful idea. Please, Father and Mother. Is that all right with you?" Clara insisted as she returned to the dining room with an intrinsic glow about her.

Is Clara's excitement as her brother suggests, or can she possibly be attracted to me, and in all innocence, be drawn to the opportunity to explore our acquaintance under her father's chaperoning prudence?

"Why, of course, my dear. The selection of bread and pastries does require a woman's culinary tact," their father said in agreement.

"I'll have plenty of help, Clara." Their mother reached over and squeezed her son's hand as if to release the pent-up longing in her heart during his absence the past semesters.

When the sun breached the horizon the next day, Clayton, Clara, and David took the buggy into the growing township of Marion. Redbrick buildings lined the narrow, graveled road. Their first stop was to visit the town's esteemed German-owned bakery named The Bäckerei.

The alluring sweet yeasty aroma of fresh-baked bread lingered within a block's radius from its location. Those passing by were drawn into the store. Tables stacked with warm baked products and pastries filled the center of the room as the clerks waited behind the back-wall counters to process their customers' orders. The baker and his wife had a captive audience as they demonstrated how to knead the dough by hand and craftily create braided loaves, rolls, sticky buns, and all sorts of delightful pastry specialties.

Clara grabbed a wicker basket at the entrance and began gathering an assortment of palatable delights. Clayton and David followed close behind as they assured her of their choices. Samples were plentiful at each station to relish and coax the customer into purchasing a few.

"Ooo … try this one, David. This is my favorite," Clara suggested as she pointed to a cream-filled sample.

David plucked one from the tray and placed it in his mouth. Closing his eyes, he allowed the creamy pastry to fill his senses. "Ummm … that is delicious. Please add this to the basket, Clara." Euphoric, he fixated upon her sweet smile.

"Of course, I will. I knew you'd like it." Her emerald eyes captured his. Blushing, she turned to place a half dozen pastries into her basket.

"All right, we best be making our purchase, Clara, if we want to have that turkey cooked by supper." Clayton checked his pocket watch.

"Right away, Father." Clara and David hurried to the counter to pay for their items as Clayton returned to the buggy. The clerk wrapped the baked goods and placed them in a large, tan paper bag.

"Here, allow me to carry that, Clara." David took the bag from the clerk.

"Why, thank you, David." Clara put her change away in her reticule.

The items in his left arm, David extended his right arm toward Clara to escort her to the buggy. With grace, she accepted and placed her hand around his elbow. He ogled at the new style of bustle attire she wore, which accentuated her hourglass figure. The small, frilly bonnet accessorized her sparkling eyes amidst the contrast of her reddish-brown ringlets, which flowed from beneath gathered curly locks.

"Your brother stated that Marion certainly has its own captivating charm. I believe he is correct," David said as they both walked toward the carriage. He never had the opportunity to exercise his courtship manners. This was quite a different sensation with Clara stationed at his arm rather than his mother or sisters. His innards burned and caused him to swoon in the pools of her eyes. White billowy clouds seemed to surround them as they approached her waiting father.

David recognized her father's disturbed countenance as he watched them from the buggy's padded seat. The immediate reaction turned and knotted his stomach.

Clara dropped her hand to her skirt's side as her father's contemplative glare pierced through the imaginary clouds. Clayton's lips tightened, and his brows pressed, which sent warning signs as he reached for the bag in David's hand and placed it behind the seat.

Composure maintained, David extended his hand to Clara to help her step into the buggy. "Ladies first." He simpered as he savored every warm touch they made while attempting to conceal his pleasure from her father.

After an enamored glance, she lifted her laced skirt above her ankle-high boots to place her foot on the carriage step. A glimpse of her slender, stockinged calf sent his mind and heart ablaze with carnal thoughts he never realized lurked inside him.

Get a hold of yourself, David. One glance at her father's stern features recomposed him as he settled next to her, absorbing the heat which emanated from her body.

The fragrant lilac scent rising from her corseted breasts' cleavage tempted him to steal a glance. *Lord, help me. So this is what temptation is about.*

By her quick exchange of conversation, he discerned she struggled as well.

"So what size turkey shall we get this year, Father?"

The horse pulled forward into a steady trot toward the butcher shop two blocks away. The oak and maple trees, which lined the streets, still had some fall color left on their thinning branches. The colors described the burning emotions inside him defused by elements such as her father's scrutiny and his spiritual conscience. Was this lust or love?

"I think a twenty-pound turkey will do," Clayton said and began to whistle the tune *Yankee Doodle* as the horse trotted down the bustling streets. He also seemed to want to overlook the moment.

Again, her father secured the brakes of the buggy and was quick to escort his daughter into the building filled with carved varieties of meats and sausages as David walked alongside them.

"Happy Thanksgiving, folks!" The butcher welcomed. "What would be your bidding this grand day?"

"Happy Thanksgiving to you also, sir," Clayton responded. "Do you have a turkey available to feed six hungry townspeople?"

"Yes, indeed." The portly man turned and entered a back room. He returned to the counter with a beheaded, plucked, and gutted turkey cradled in his arms. "Will this fine specimen do?"

Clayton and Clara inspected the glistening white-skinned fowl. "My, it will make for a splendid feast." She sniggered.

"With that said, we shall take this lovely prize," Clayton said as he dug into his pant pocket and slipped money into the clerk's hand.

The butcher covered and wrapped the turkey in paraffin paper and twine. He handed it to David. "Thank you very much. Have a blessed Thanksgiving Day," he said.

"We wish the same for you. Many blessings, sir." The trio chimed in as they brought the prize catch to the buggy.

Merry singing and laughter intercepted the romantic liaison between David and Clara. Clayton bolstered the original version of "Coming 'Round the Mountain" as David and Clara repeated after him.

Clayton, "She'll be coming around the mountain when she comes."

David and Clara, "When she comes."

Clayton, "She'll be coming around the mountain when she comes."

David and Clara, "When she comes."

Clayton, "She'll be coming round the mountain, she'll be coming round the mountain, she'll be coming round the mountain when she comes."

David and Clara, "When she comes."

They continued singing the following verses in the same manner.

"O, who will drive the chariot when she comes?

When she comes.

King Jesus, he'll be the driver when she comes.

When she comes.

She'll be loaded with bright Angels when she comes.

When she comes.

She will neither rock nor totter when she comes.

When she comes.

She will run so level and steady when she comes.

When she comes.
She will take us to the portal when she comes.
When she comes."

28

A Momentous Thanksgiving

The days leading up to Thanksgiving encompassed attitude readjustments between the Sower and Suen family now that becoming in-laws may be inevitable. Mary unexpectedly felt awkward as the loyal staff served her, so she began cleaning and serving herself. By law, the Suens would become family, and family should not be relegated the duties of butler, cook, and housemaid she reasoned with herself.

Domestic work is an honest and decent career, so they have no reason to be ashamed or for you to carry guilt. The still small voice in her head argued in return.

How did her son's emotional involvement with Jia-Li escape her notice or the awareness of any of the family members, including Huang-Fu and Liang? Were the signs always beneath their noses, and she and the other family members' sub-conscience chose not to acknowledge Sam and Jia-Li's fond attractions to one another? No matter. She would not have discouraged their relationship even if they announced their relationship early on. The young couple maintained their secret relationship and exercised courageous fortitude despite the realization their union's complexity may pose in the judgmental society in which they lived. She admired their strength to pursue the challenges ahead of them.

Mary considered herself a loving, compassionate, and impartial person. Societal confluence wrestled with her unprejudiced beliefs. She wanted to be fair and do what is right in the Lord's eyes. But how? *Dear God, show me the way.*

"Please let me do my job, Mrs. Sower. There is nobody I enjoy working for more than you. Your graciousness has blessed my family. Nothing has changed just because our children are in love." From behind the kitchen counter, Huang-Fu wagged his index finger at her to make a point. "I serve you with a grateful heart because you give us so much and treat us with kindness. You are family to us.

"You and Mr. Sower must conduct your business. My family is honored to be part of your operation. All is fair, Mrs. Sower ." The butler reasoned in a graceful manner as he brought the tea kettle to her and filled her cup at the dining table.

"Yes, yes, you're right, Huang-Fu." Her guilt subsided as she watched the aging butler run to and fro in her home with joy in his step. "There is one thing I do want to change, though. We've been together now for such a long time. Since we do consider one another as a family, then I expect we all use our first names. Please, no more formalities. I insist!"

Confused, Huang-Fu and Liang turned to each other, and back to Mary. "All right, Mrs. Mary."

"No…just Mary."

The humble butler's jaw dropped, and eyes widened. "Mary?" He turned to Liang to encourage her to do the same. "Mary." He motioned with his hand as if pulling the word from her mouth.

Liang shook her head in agreement and repeated. "Mary, ah yes, Mary!" She returned a smile.

Mary's heart bloated with contentment for their new heightened relationship and understanding. *Get thee behind me, guilt, and do not deceive me. My conscience is clear. The Lord has blessed my family and me. So I will bless others. The Suens are grateful and are honored to be employed at Sower Farms. I am thankful to You, my Lord, my God.*

The traditional Thanksgiving Day table sprawled with abundance under the oak tree in front of the farmhouse. Adorned in crocheted linen, fine china, and silverware, it sought attention as a grand Victorian duchess would require dressed in her fine apparel. This time, the Sower s planned to enjoy the holiday with not only the Hampton family but also the Suens.

Jonathan and Huang-Fu fussed over the turkey and duck on the spit as the women brought out the side dishes of corn, stir-fried vegetables, bread, and fruit pies and placed them on the elongated table. Parading his bounty, Jonathan placed the overstuffed bird and its trimmings in the center, and Huang-Fu set the duck beside it. They all sat down and joined hands as the proud patriarch prayed.

"Father, there is much to be thankful for. You extended great mercy and grace to my household this year, healin' Huang-Fu from his almost fatal attack, movin' Lad, Sarah, and our grandchildren to our farm, and continuin' to heal Isabelle by bringin' movement back to her limbs. We also thank you for watchin' over David while he is attendin' college and teachin' him of your wondrous ways. Furthermore, you graced us with the opportunity to expand our business. Finally, you blessed us with the lovin' relationship between Sam and Jia-Li.

"Father, we hope we can give you glory in all the things we do. We pray for your blessin's upon this bounty of food you provided. In Jesus' name. Amen." Peace and beatitude filled Jonathan's heart as he peered at the three generations before him.

"Amen," the voracious family replied as Jonathan and Huang-Fu began carving the succulent roasted fouls. The Thanksgiving meal was sumptuous, and the atmosphere glowed with warm affection for one another.

After dinner, Samuel stood, hands shaking, to make an

announcement and a special request. "As y'all know, Jia-Li and I are in love. In all my life, I never met a woman as captivatin' as her. Jia-Li has inner beauty as well as outer beauty. To me, she is more precious than rubies.

"Mr. and Mrs. Suen, I would like to request your permission to marry your daughter, if she'll take me."

A glowing smile broadcast from Huang-Fu as he glanced across the table at his only child whose countenance radiated like the sun. "Nǚ'ér, do you love Samuel?"

"Oh Fùqīn, Mǔqīn, I do with all my heart." Jia-Li trembled with felicity.

"With that said, Samuel, we bless you both." Happy tears flood Huang-Fu and Liang's eyes.

Samuel knelt on one knee next to his euphoric bride-to-be and brushed her supple hand with a tender kiss. "Will you marry me, Jia-Li?"

"Oh, Samuel, yes. I want to be yours forever!"

They stood and embraced one another. Samuel reached into his vest pocket and opened a small black velvet box, which contained a diamond and pearl engagement band and slipped it on her finger. "This ring symbolizes our love. The rough cut diamond represents me, and the pearl of the orient is symbolic of you, my darlin'." He slipped the precious jewel on her slender finger, and they kissed.

The families toasted to their engagement and immersed them with their blessings.

"So, do you have a date in mind?" Jonathan asked.

"We do, Pa. We hoped to be married by February 27th before the planting season begins."

"Well, we better get busy then with plans for your special day," Mary said as she counted the months with her fingers.

Magenta clouds touched by the last glimmer of daylight and an autumn chill prompted the family to move the festivities indoors and further discuss the wedding preparations.

"We've decided on a Christian ceremony here at the farm. However, Jia-Li requested she wear the traditional two-piece Chinese wedding gown," Samuel said, placing his arm around his fiancé's shoulder as they sat on the parlor couch.

Radiance flowed from Jia-Li's being. "It's called a Cheongsam. Red is symbolic of the Chinese culture for good luck and is meant to keep away evil spirits. We know of a Chinese tailor in Columbia who will embroider an elaborate gold and silver Dragon and Pheonix on to the dress. It symbolizes the balance of male and female power. We want to make you aware of this now so you won't be shocked when I am not wearing a white western gown."

"Oh my, this shall certainly be a unique wedding," Naomi chimed in with a twinkle in her eyes.

"And of course, we have agreed on a blend of Western and Eastern cuisine," Jia-Li was quick to add.

"Originally, I chose David as my best man, but he probably won't be able to leave his studies. The next closest of kin is you, Lad. I would love for you to take his place," Samuel said.

"Well, of course!" Lad swallowed the emotional lump in his throat. "I haven't had kinfolk in such a long time. Your request touches me."

"Naomi, you are my closest friend in America. I can't imagine my maid-of-honor being anyone else other than you." Jia-Li's eyes sparkled as she held Naomi's hands.

"Why, I'd be hurt if you didn't ask. Gladly, dear friend, and now, soon to be, sister-in-law," Naomi said.

"And guess whom we selected to be our ring bearer and flower girl? You little Amanda and Billy!" Samuel scooped up his niece and nephew from where they played on the floor, twirled them around, and kissed them on their heads. Giggles and laughter abound as Samuel tickled them.

The evening wound down, and the Sower s retired to their rooms and the Suens to the cabin. Samuel lay awake on his cot in his father's office, imagining him and Jia-Li's children and what life would be like for a blended family. *Will we be accepted in our community, or will we be subject to the adversities of prejudice?* His heart ached with the thought of his precious loved ones under attack by those with hatred filled consciences and evil intentions against the Chinese who sought a better way of life as the European immigrants have when fleeing the tyranny of their homeland. Overwhelming joy from his engagement suppressed the anxiety of the unavoidable social unacceptance.

29

Wedding Plans

Brilliant rays seeped through the barn's board gaps from the lightning bolts outside and rain pelted its metal roof as Harold, Leonard, Grier, and Nevil discussed failed pranks during their lunch break. With Christmas fast approaching and the distraction of Samuel's marriage plans in February, even their dastardly deeds had no effect on their employer's blissful disposition. The head supervisor's increased awareness of the daily routines at Sower and Sons Farm dispelled many of the Maxfield men's shenanigans.

"Oh, darn." Nevil stomped the ground. "Lad fixed the loose hinge on the corral gate. The oxen didn't even have a chance to figure it out. Too bad. Watching Lad and Sam chasin' them down in this gully washer would've been a hoot." He positioned a hay bale next to his co-workers, sat, and dove into his lunch, wrapped in a dusty blue bandana.

"Yeah, well, Sam fouled my plans, too. I jimmy-rigged a few of the floorboards on the front porch of the main house next to the chairs where they sit during lunch. I was hopin' a loose board would rear up and smack him when he stepped down. My plan didn't work. The boards only creaked.

"Instead, Sam hammered the planks back into place. The nurse saw him and notified Mr. Maxfield. Her report must've been a daisy because Sam ended up gettin' a bottle of the ole' bosses good bug juice for his goodwill handiwork. That one backfired on me." Grier huffed.

"Well, you boys save some of those ideas for his return. Sam's focused on his wedding plans, and nothin' will tear him down. We must think up something good for the groom and his Coolie bride. We'll make him realize his honeymoon is over once he's back. Ugh, he really chaps my hide." Harold rolled the snuff around in his cheek and spat into the spittoon next to him. "Yep, they'll wish they never leased this property."

THE RAIN WHICH POURED on the two-day horse and buggy ride to the small town, Columbia, did not dampen Samuel, Jia-Li, and Liang's spirits. They rolled past cabin-size granite formations tucked between oaks and pines, which miners unearthed using dredging machines during the town's gold rush period almost twenty years earlier.

Nǐ hǎo … ǔ-anh … dzàijien! The majority of the Chinese men who stayed behind to forage the remains of the glistening fortune exchanged Mandarin greetings.

"We've arrived, ladies." Samuel pulled the horse's reins and stopped the buggy in front of Ah Chung's Hotel on the north edge of town. They planned to board here while they relegated wedding preparations amongst the Chinese merchants. The stress of judgment was less likely to occur here than at the Fallon or City Hotel, where the white staff snubbed foreigners of dark skin.

"Do you suppose we'll have time to attend Ah Mow's Chinese theater next door?" Jia-Li asked as she stepped into the hotel.

"Of course. Whatever my lovely fiancé desires are my command." Samuel pecked her cheek.

"Nǐ hǎo," the hotel clerk greeted.

"Xìnghuì," Jia-Li said, then rambled on as she spoke Mandarin and requested two rooms, one for her and her mother, and the other for Samuel.

By the clerk's quizzical visage, Samuel surmised that Jia-Li explained their engagement. One brow cocked, the skeptical clerk opened his hand for payment then plopped the keys on the counter.

"Xièxiè." Jia-Li and her mother bowed, cueing him to do the same.

THE TOWNSPEOPLE DRESSED COLUMBIA IN FRESH GARLAND and red bows, which hung from the brick storefront buildings' eaves. Christmas gaiety permeated the atmosphere, and the anxious shoppers, bundled in warm overcoats and capes, shuffled through the surviving town. The aroma of roasted chestnuts, nutmeg, and cinnamon filled the streets as the vendors invoked passersby to sample their delicacies. The *clip-clop* of hooves echoed as teams of horses arrived and departed the Wells Fargo station. The bank was busy, too, as the customers withdrew holiday shopping money.

Sssss … humpf. Whispers and stares followed as Samuel walked a couple of feet ahead of Jia-Li and her mother toward the Chinese mercantile store located at the town's Chinese camp.

"*Mǔqīn*, look at that white man with his Chinese employees purchasing supplies," Jia-Li spoke in a low voice. She wrapped her quilted Chinese jacket tighter around her simple long-sleeved cheongsam to avert the crisp cold air. "No one seems to mind." She let out a giggle. "People must think we are Samuel's *Jìnǚs* … prostitutes."

"Tiān a, Nǚ'ér!" Liang snapped. "Do not think about such things. Although you are probably right." She snickered.

Baskets filled with yams, bok choy, rice, potatoes, carrots, broccoli, snow peas, and ginger lined San Ling Sing's storefront boardwalk. Freshly slaughtered and plucked ducks and butchered pig portions dangled from hooks in the window. Samuel opened the door for the ladies and introduced them to the store owner waiting behind the counter with a wall lined with shelves of Chinese herbs behind him.

"Hello, sir. My name is Samuel Sower, and this is my bride-to-be Jia-Li and her mother, Liang." Samuel tipped his hat. "We are to be married in February and would like to purchase a Cheongsam."

The bronze-face merchant grinned and chuckled as he studied them. However, he became reticent as Samuel placed his arm around Jia-Li's shoulder, came close, and towered over him. Samuel hoped to display his passionate adulation for her and overbearing protection, much like a lion protecting his pride. The merchant seemed to understand Samuel's unspoken message, put his prejudices aside, and began to assist with courteous service.

"Ah … I see," the merchant replied, eyeing Jia-Li. "Congratulations to you both. One moment and I shall fetch my assistant in the back room. He is the tailor, and he will need to take your measurements, young lady. Meanwhile, please have a seat, Mr. Sower ." Samuel waited as the thin, balding garment maker emerged from the back room and guided Jia-Li to stand on a footstool while he measured her.

Afterward, the dressmaker directed mother and daughter to select from bolts of brilliant colored silks. They chose the strawberry red popularized by Chinese brides. The tailor showed them a sample of the dragon and phoenix he planned to embroider on the gown with gold and silver thread.

"This was my specialty back in homeland China," he said. "I haven't touched silk threads while in America. Not enough Chinese weddings here since most are men."

Jia-Li and Liang gasped, their countenance concerned.

"Not to worry, ladies. I assure you, your wedding gown will be ready by February." He smiled, his cheekbones raising his wired glasses.

"Ladies, if we are done with business here, how about some lunch and hot tea at Ah Hie's Chop Shop?" Samuel asked.

The trio paid in advance for the tailoring service and gown, provided their shipping address, and concluded their business. The aroma of stir-fried beef and vegetables guided them to the restaurant a few doors away.

"AH, THAT WOR WONTON SOUP HIT THE SPOT. Good choice for this cold wintery day, Jia-Li." Samuel wiped the drippings from his lips.

The waiter approached and bowed. "Can I get you folks anything more?"

"How about another pot of green tea for the ladies?" Samuel said.

He planned to visit the *Columbia Gazette* located on Washington Street to have fifty wedding invitations made on their printing press while the women continued to dine.

"Ladies, you may want to wait for me here while I conduct business with the printer. I fear the white man is not as accepting and gracious toward mixed marriages as your culture might be. I would rather spare you from any prejudice remarks." Samuel did his best to explain the possible situation.

"Samuel … as my future husband, I trust your judgment. We will wait for you." Jia-Li nodded and wrapped her palm around the warm teacup.

Admiring Jia-Li's sparkling eyes, he squeezed her hand and kissed her warmed cheeks. "I'll high tail it back." He slipped on his overcoat and headed to the printing press shop.

THE STORE OWNER WORE A WHITE APRON stained with ink from his hands after he set the type letters or leaned on the cumbersome contraption.

"How can I help you, sir?" The owner peered at Sam from behind the machine.

"Yes, sir. I want to place an order for fifty wedding invitations. I need them by January fifteen. Will that be enough time?" Samuel cunningly drew the attention away from the content of the invitation but rather upon the owner's abilities to meet the deadline.

"Why, yes! I can have your order ready for pick up a week from today. Please, write down what you would like the invitation to say on this form," The owner explained.

"I have already written down all the information for you on this piece of paper." Samuel waved an envelope in his hand and laid it on the counter. "Everything you need to know is here. Please send my order through the stagecoach line to the address written inside. I will pay for the cost now. So what do I owe you for your services, kind sir?" Samuel motioned, moving the subject to a close.

"Fifty invitations will come to fourteen dollars, which includes the cost of freight." The eager owner did not bother to read the contents of the note, trusting in the happy young man who was excited about his wedding day.

Without hesitation, Samuel laid down his cash, shook the owner's hand, and handed him the paper that read:

> *Mr. and Mrs. Huang-Fu Suen and*
> *Mr. and Mrs. Jonathan Sower*
> *request the pleasure of your*
> *presence at the marriage of their children*
> *Jia-Li Suen*
> *to*
> *Samuel J. Sower*
> *On Saturday, February 27th, 1875 at five o'clock in the evening*
> *Sower Farm*
> *41 La Grange Road, Snelling*
> *Please R.S.V.P. by February 14th, 1875*

The owner opened the envelope, unfolded the paper, and filed it amongst his orders he had to complete. It was not until the day he was to print the wedding invitation when he read its contents. *Well, I'll be damned. That young man is marrying a China girl.* Because Samuel paid in advance, and the press had been set, it was too late to cancel the order. Therefore, the owner printed the invitations and sent them out as promised one week later.

30

A Complete Christmas

Preparations for Christmas began at Sower Farm. The men hung the pine and cedar boughs and garland with bright red bows and erected a select noble fir in the parlor to be trimmed by the family after supper. In the kitchen, the women and children were busy creating edible masterpieces. The emulsified scents of fresh greens, cinnamon, nutmeg, cloves, ginger, and mint, blend with the flavorful aromas of baked pies, cookies, and breads prepared by loving hands.

This holiday became the Hampton children's most favorite time of year. Pinafore secured on Amanda's calico dress and a terry bib pinned on Billy's linen shirt, the siblings helped Sarah bake and decorate the cookies. Isabelle's face framed in a frilly bonnet, her blue eyes glisten as she sat in her high chair, flailing her arms and kicking her legs with delight. Snickers and grins gleamed from candy-coated smiles. Little fingers plastered in dough and frosting performed an enchanting ballet on the tabletop laden with copper cookie cutters. The children aspired for this annual baking moment with their mother.

After Sarah completed the first batch of warm confections, she allowed the older children to choose a colorful sugary icing-glazed cookie amongst the different Christmas shapes.

"Goody, Mama." Amanda squealed as she took a bite of a

bright yellow star.

"Which one do you want, Billy?" Sarah brought the plate of warm cookies to her son.

"Christmas tree, Mama." He pointed his chubby finger at the sweet delight.

"Okay, take it then."

Sarah turned to pour some milk into cups for the children as they ate their cookies when an unexpected sound like a yelp came from Isabelle.

"Ma … Mama." Isabelle cried as her erratic limbs moved frantically.

Shocked at her first words, the tray that carried the cups nearly dropped from Sarah's grip. Milk splattered as the containers danced. Mouths agape, Amanda and Billy froze in astonishment as the table absorbed most of their beverages. Sarah put down the tray, grabbed the plate of cookies, and rushed to Isabelle's high chair.

"Yes, dear. Mama is here. Would you like one, too?" Elated, Sarah fixed her gaze on Isabelle's face as she held the platter, trying to coax her daughter to speak again.

Swinging her legs and reaching for the sugary temptations, she stuttered, "Ma … Ma … Ma!"

Overjoyed at the sound of her daughter's voice, Sarah placed the baked delights on the high chair tray. "Okay, take the one you want, sweetheart."

Isabelle tried her best to control her right arm toward the red bell-shaped cookie and, at last, grasped it, forcing some cookies to the floor. The bell in her hand, she brought it to her mouth with unrefined effort. She held on tight to the cookie and struggled to coordinate her muscular movements. The grand accomplishments far outweighed the menial mess made in the kitchen due to the moment's excitement. Isabelle squealed with gratification as Sarah, Amanda, and Billy cheered.

CHRISTMAS DAY ARRIVED, and the families gathered in the parlor around the tree to make musical merriment. Quadrilles, square dance, exchanging partners, and doing the do-si-do performed by family and friends invigorate the moment. After a bountiful holiday meal, the highlight of the day called for opening gifts wrapped in pretty paper and bows.

The jubilant laughter and chatter in the sitting room overwhelmed Mary as she sat by the warm hearth, trying to absorb the festivities. The joyous occasion deemed almost perfect. Her heart sank a notch as thoughts drifted to David and the last post she received from him just before Thanksgiving. He mentioned an exorbitant amount of homework, plans to spend the holidays with his roommate's family, and his longing to be home. How she missed her youngest and worried for his well-being.

Engrossed in thought, she failed to regard her husband, who exited the room, returned, and placed an envelope on her lap. His peck on her cheek drew her back to the moment.

"I miss him, too, darlin'," Jonathan said as if able to read her mind. His focus concentrated on what lay on her bustled taffeta skirt.

Mary stared at the envelope as the family continued their merriment.

"Ha. David … a letter from David," she yelled above the clamor. "Jonathan, when did this come in?"

"Yesterday, dear. But the instructions said, 'Do not to open until Christmas mornin'.'"

The family hushed and turned their attention to Mary as she read the letter.

"Dearest Family,

I hope this note finds all of you in excellent health and enjoying the pleasantry that Christmas brings. Although my mind fills with the wisdom of our good Lord, my heart quite often reminds me of home. I do miss everyone desperately during this time of great joy and celebration of our Lord's birthday.

Clarence Harrington, the roommate that I mentioned in my previous letter, has invited me to spend Christmas with his family here in Indiana. They have been a tremendous comfort to me. I thank the Lord for his friendship and encouragement to distract me from becoming homesick too often. Otherwise, I am well. Although dormitory food does not compare to meals back home, it has helped me to discard a few unwanted pounds. Clarence's mother and sisters' cooking shall fatten me up.

Please send my congratulations and blessings to Sam and Jia-Li. I truly wish I could be home for their wedding day, but as you are aware, I will be well into the second semester during that time.

Bestow my love to all, especially to my precious nieces and nephew. Happy Christmas!

Your beloved son and brother,
David

"Ah. Now my Christmas is complete. All of my children and grandchildren are accounted for and doing well." Mary sighed and held the letter to her heart.

"EXCUSE ME, MAY I HAVE EVERYONE'S ATTENTION," Lad announced. "I would like to present my beautiful wife with a special gift that I think everyone in this room will appreciate." Lad handed Sarah a scroll tied with a silky dark evergreen ribbon. Sarah untied the bow, unrolled it, and read the contents to herself.

"Oh, my. Lad, how wonderful." Sarah hugged her husband's neck then passed the paper over to Jonathan and Mary to view. "We are now proud owners of forty acres of land on the banks of the Merced River on Merced Falls Road just about three miles from here."

"I plan to start building our small cabin home after Christmas," Lad added, grinning from ear to ear.

"Glory to God. This is wonderful news. Congratulations to you both." Jonathan cheered. "Count me in to help."

Sarah walked over to Isabelle, lifted her from her high chair by the fireplace, and carried her to the Christmas tree where Lad stood.

"Now, I have a special gift to give to you, my love, and I know the family will appreciate this as well."

"Okay, Isabelle, let's show Papa what you can do." Sarah knelt and put Isabelle's feet on the ground as she braced her under her arms until she steadied. One at a time, Sarah removed her hands as Isabelle stood on her own two legs. The family held their breath, froze, and did not make a sound. Isabelle stood motionless for what seemed like minutes until her limbs wobbled. With stealth, Sarah grabbed her before she fell.

"Very good, darling girl! Very good." Sarah cuddled Isabelle.

Lad embraced them both. Tears stung his eyes, and a lump formed in his throat. Taking the grinning little cherub from her mama's arms, Lad managed to choke out his pleasure. "Isabelle, I am so proud of you."

"Pa … Pa," Isabelle stammered into Lad's ear as he hugged her.

Lad locked into Isabelle's eyes as he held her. "Did I hear you say, Papa?"

"Pa … Pa," she repeated with exuberance.

$$31$$

Giant Steps

Peering through the office window's open shutters, Mary surveyed the horizon beyond the bare fields. A dark greenish-gray low-hanging shroud from the mountains crept toward Snelling. Threats of moisture along with an orchestral lightning display would, on normal occasion, accompany a weather front such as this. Like an ocean wave, it barreled through the sky to first reach the land Lad and Sarah purchased a few miles east of Sower Farm. The thought of her menfolk working beneath the fury of this ominous beast gave her reason to worry. A shiver caused the hair on her forearms to stand. So she tightened her Sontag's straps about her waist for a warmer and secure fit, as if to lessen her anxiety.

"You fellers better bundle up today. Those clouds look as if they can burst open at any moment. I'd hate for y'all to catch pneumonia before the wedding," Mary insisted.

Lad, Jonathan, and Samuel huddled around the desk discussing the Hampton's three-bedroom ranch-style home they planned to build on the forty-acre parcel near the Merced River. Patrick Fay delivered the lumber to the property the Monday following Christmas. Cleared and staged, the Chinese farmhands readied the grounds for immediate construction after the holidays.

"Now, Ma, don't you worry. We will. Besides, I would rather be workin' in this cool temperature than in the blazin' hot sun any day. This weather is a far cry from the blizzard conditions I endured when the railroad employed me." Samuel hugged his mother and kissed her on her cheek. He wrapped a knitted scarf around his neck and plunged his arms into his wool-lined suede coat.

"I don't think rain, snow, sleet, or hail will stop Sam from building my home. His mission is to get his bedroom back in time for his wedding day." Lad teased as he sat near the hearth to warm himself and yank on his boots.

The *clip-clop* of horse's hooves and the creaking of wagon wheels drifted in through the window.

"That must be Yung, Sheng-Li, and Anguo." Jonathan stood next to his wife and scanned the wayside path. "All right, dear, we'll return by supper." Squeezing her shoulders, he kissed her. "Let's go, boys."

At the front porch, Jia-Li and Sarah met them with a basket full of bread, meats, jams, crackers, and canteens of water. Mary joined her daughter and future daughter-in-law as the men piled into the wagon.

"I sure hope they can complete my home by the end of January. You and Sam must be anxious to rearrange his bedroom," Sarah said, worry lines cresting her brows.

"Yes. That would be convenient. If it is not ready, we can always stay in my room. My parents wouldn't mind. Sam may feel a little uncomfortable, though, with their bedroom adjoining ours. The walls are very thin, and even the slightest whisper can be heard even with the doors closed. However, it's only for a short while until we can build a place of our own."

Sarah's face turned pink with embarrassment as they discussed the young couple's private matters. Maturity called her to redirect the subject. "I suppose staying in the cabin would be like old times when we were children. Imagine the four of us slept in that same room for a year."

Her arms locked in theirs, Mary chided. "Now, my dears, I trust our men will accomplish what they set out to do. Things will turn out just fine." She quoted Romans 8:28, "And we know that all things work together for good to them that love God, to them who are the called according to his purpose."

"Amen. Now, if you ladies will excuse me, I have some packin' to do in the barn," Sarah said.

Five-year-old Amanda watched her mother prop her little sister on a quilt spread over the straw in the barn. She and her siblings wore the thickest and warmest woolen clothing to fend off winter's cold. Since her grandmother and the housekeeping staff busied themselves with wedding preparations and invitations, and her Aunt Naomi consumed herself with both farms' finances, her mother opted to mind her, her brother, and sister while she organized their belongings.

"Amanda, I need you to play with your brother and sister on this blanket while I pack. I'll be by those boxes over there."

"Yes, Mama." Holding Billy's mitten covered hand, Amanda sat next to Isabelle as her mother began to sift through their possessions. She imagined her little sister running around the barn with her and Billy. *Why can't you walk yet, Izzy? I sure wish you could do things like us. I know you want to. Hmm, what can we play?* She examined her little sister's feeble legs. *Oh, I know!*

"All right, Izzy, let's play 'Hide and Seek.' I'm going to shut my eyes and count to ten while Billy hides somewhere in the barn. Once I open them, I'll search for him, and I'll need you to help me. When I'm close to where he's hiding, I want you to shout out 'hot!' Okay? Can you say 'hot'?" Amanda spoke with brightness to Isabelle. "Hot." She tried her best to pronounce the word with accuracy.

"Ha … ha … hot," Isabelle repeated.

"Good, Izzy. Hot. Now say it louder."

"Hot!" She shouted and clapped her hands.

"Once I find him, it'll be his turn to count and my chance to hide. Try to help Billy find me by saying 'hot.' All right, are both of you ready?" Amanda stood and closed her eyes as her little brother scurried around the stalls, hay bales, wagons, and boxes for a good place to conceal himself

"One, two … uh, five, nine, seven, ten. Ready or not, here I come," she hollered, opened her eyes, and began to search about the dusty building.

"Is Billy behind the bale of hay?" Amanda asked aloud as she peeked over the bundles of straw.

"No." Isabelle giggled.

"Is he upstairs in the hayloft?" She scrambled up the ladder and scanned the room but did not locate him.

"No." Isabelle hooted. Therefore, Amanda climbed down with care.

"Is he in the buggy?" Amanda peered inside.

"No!"

"*Hmm.* Is he near Mommy?" Not one clue of Billy as Amanda inched closer to her mother, who continued her work and, on occasion, slipped her a sideways glance and smile.

"Hot!" Isabelle became restless, kicking her legs.

"Is he behind these crates?" Amanda crept about.

"Hot! Hot!" Unable to contain her excitement, Isabelle placed her hands on the ground, swung her legs behind her and knelt. Instincts brought one foot under her, followed by the other until she was squatting. With every ounce of mustered strength and steadiness, she straightened her limbs and pushed to a standing position.

"Mama … look at Izzy." Amanda froze so as not to frighten her little sister.

Her mother gasped and also stood still. "Shush, Amanda."

One foot at a time, Isabelle took a step, then another. Soon enough, she had walked ten paces until she arrived at the empty crate at the row's end where Billy hid.

"Hot, hot, hot," Isabelle screamed as she held on to the crate and laughed at Billy, who crouched inside, trying to stifle her.

Amanda and her mother ran around from behind the crates. They glanced over at the blanket spread out on the hay, and back to where Isabelle stood with a wide smile which stretched from each side of her wool bonnet. Their jaws dropped and eyes enlarged.

"You're walking, Isabelle." Her mother tiptoed toward her, opened her arms, and reached out. "Now, come to Mommy."

Isabelle glanced at her legs as worry washed over her face. A slow-creeping broad grin and glistening eyes swallowed her anxiety-stricken countenance after she realized her legs no longer wobbled.

Amanda's little sister focused on their mother's awaiting arms and slowly let go of the crate. She tottered into their mother's applauding embrace. Mother held her so tight, she gasped for air.

"Oh, my little girl. You just walked some giant steps. Thank you, Lord. Thank you!" They twirled around, and giggles engulfed the barn.

"You found Billy, too!" Amanda squealed with laughter.

Billy popped his head out of the crate. "Ah … that's not fair. Isabelle gave me away."

Mother guffawed at her brother's serious disposition and stood Isabelle on her feet. "I think we can pardon your little sister this time." She pointed to Billy. "Show him why Izzy. Go to your brother."

As a cowboy lassoes a steer and pulls close to it, Isabelle did the same. Step by step, she waddled over to Billy as he stomped his feet and clapped his hands to encourage her. Once there, Billy jumped out of the crate and hugged his little sister. Laughter filled the barn, and the rest of the afternoon was spent playing more games instead of doing work.

The rain never came, and later in the evening after supper, Sarah allowed Isabelle to demonstrate to the family her new accomplishment. Amanda looked forward to playing outdoors when summer arrives. This time she will have the pleasure of interacting with both her siblings.

32

The Special Guests

Late January after supper, the Sower s, Suens, and Hamptons gathered in the parlor to discuss the plans for the wedding. Samuel stood ogling beside his demure and exotic bride-to-be as they stood by the hearth before their family. The sparkle in Jia-Li's eyes excited every ounce of his being. The anticipation of the grand event consumed his every thought.

"We've gathered y'all here to iron out the details for our unconventional and yet traditional wedding plans in which everyone will have a role to play. I think it's best to allow Jia-Li to explain her family's customs." His hand pressed the small of her back to bring her forward. Her body trembled beneath his touch. Chinese culture discourages their women from speaking unless the other party is addressing them directly, so Samuel understood her apprehension. He held her hand to provide support and strength. "Please give my beautiful fiancée your undivided attention."

The room was hushed to allow Jia-Li's sweet and almost child-like voice to resound. "Samuel and I are so very happy to have our family involved in our wedding. Your participation means so much to us. We've found our two cultures to complement one another, so we hope to combine both Western and Eastern traditions. One of the Chinese customs is to have the groom prepare the matrimonial bed for our bridal chamber. Sam must do this with the aid of a family with many children." Jia-Li turned to the Hamptons. "Sarah and Lad, now that your family is settled in your new home, would you mind taking on this task?"

Brows raised, curiosity consumed Sarah, and her face blushed. Half-suppressed, indecorous laughter escape her being. "We'd be more than happy to assist, but the suggestion seems rather daring. What do you have in mind?"

Samuel surmised his sister's wandering thoughts. "Now, now. It's not what you're thinking, Sarah." He guffawed. "The tradition is quite innocent and enchanting if I say so myself." He placed his arm around Jia-Li's shoulder and allowed her to continue.

"The first thing the parents must do is scatter red dates, oranges, almonds, pomegranates, apples, and other fruit on our bed. Afterward, the children are to scramble for the goodies. This is a favored Chinese omen for fertility." Jia-Li's connotative intentions caused bashful smiles and giggles amongst the group.

"Now, I'm not one to believe much in signs, but I sure fancy that tradition," Mary said. "It's similar to allegories the Bible uses for fertility, such as Psalm 127:3, 'Lo, children are an heritage of the Lord: and the fruit of the womb is His reward.'"

"I'm sure the children will love the idea," Sarah said.

Samuel's eyes glistened as consummating with his bride filled his thoughts. The past year had been difficult for him to contain his manly compulsions. Jia-Li was not one of them abandons who sleazed about the Hell on Wheels' tent brothels that followed the railroad during construction. Like a new bud on a vine whose petals were about to open, he wanted to admire and cherish Jia-Li's innocent beauty and not rend it before it had time to blossom fully. "I can hardly wait for you to see our new bedroom ensemble, sweetheart. Our room will allure and entice you so that you won't be able to resist its beckonin' call."

He visualized in her eyes the decorated room and the prospect of having a family. He felt the rapid pulse in her hands as she held his.

"I can imagine our children jumping into our bed on a cold winter mornin' as they try to wake us. Their angelic faces will look like yours, my love." With his hand, he caressed her cheek. The entire room seemed to fade away.

"Ah, but they will have their father's warm and gentle smile." Using her fingers, she stroked his lips. He bent his head forward to kiss her.

The sound of family members clearing their throats caused the transfixion to be broken between the two lovers, who reluctantly released their clutches from one another. Warmth rushed to his face as Samuel commenced speaking about their plans.

"As for our reception, I've ordered a twenty-by-thirty-foot canvas tent and will place it on the farmhouse lawn. Rows of linen-dressed tables will seat 100 guests." He glanced at the window overlooking the home's front yard. "I pray there'll be no rain on our special day."

"We requested Pastor McSwan to perform the ceremony on the porch steps." Jia-Li sought affirmation from the family member's nods.

"We'd like y'all to stand beside us, as well. The east meets the west," Sam said. "This wedding will be the talk of the whole town for many years." He stroked her hand and kissed it.

He imagined what their future would hold as a mixed marriage with a blend of cultural traditions. *I hope the community accepts us as our family has done so.*

A FEW DAYS AFTER the wedding invitations' reservation deadline, Naomi purposed to purchase her bridesmaids' dress material. At Jacobi's store in town, while she considered the bolted variety, she overheard two women chattering among themselves in another aisle. She recognized the voices, so she shuffled to the row's end and glanced their way.

"Well, hello, ladies," Naomi greeted the town acquaintances, Roberta and Odelia.

The women gasped and snubbed their noses at her. "Good day, Naomi."

"I'm perusing the fabric for my gown for my brother's weddin'." Her forced grin quivered as she recalled the few reservations received from the invitations sent a few weeks earlier. The majority were from the Suen's friends and relatives. "I don't recall seein' your names on our reservation list."

"Well, we're sorry, but we have another engagement that day." Roberta searched through her reticule for her timepiece. "Oh my, look at the time. We must go, sister."

"Uh, yes. I'm so sorry, dear. We are in a terrible hurry. Have a fine day," Odelia remarked as her spiteful eyes twitched. Turning on her heels, she grabbed her sister's elbow, and they scurried to the counter.

"The poor family," Roberta whispered aloud into Odelia's ears so that Naomi could overhear her disapproval. "I don't think anyone in this town wants to attend their wedding. How could they allow their son to marry a China woman?"

"Huff." Odelia snorted as they continued to cackle between themselves. They paid for their items and left the store, slamming the door behind them.

Heart-pounding anger pulsed through Naomi's veins, horrified at the women's hateful remarks.

A dreadful gloom shrouded Mr. Jacobi's countenance as he witnessed the entire conversation. "Don't you pay no mind to those women, Naomi."

As she recalled the guest list without his name, Naomi's hurt resolved to frustration. *How could he? After all the many years as his employee, he had told me I was like a daughter to him. My entire family are faithful patrons of his establishment. Does he think that attending my brother's wedding would jeopardize his business?*

Naomi responded sharply, "I don't recall seein' your reservation either, Mr. Jacobi."

"Now, now, Naomi, you know I have a business to run, and the veekends are the busiest of days. Please send my congratulations to Samuel and his fiancée," he said, stumbling over his German accent.

"Ha! You'll have to tell them yourself, Mr. Jacobi. A good day to you, sir."

Naomi stormed out of the store, not bothering to open her parasol in the pouring rain. The hem of her bustled skirt dipped into the dirt road puddles, and her toes swam in her soaked boots' damp wool socks as she climbed into the buggy. She would plan to purchase her material in Merced on the next sunny day. In the meantime, she returned to the farm to inform her parents of the horrible ordeal.

JONATHAN STOOD FROM HIS OFFICE CHAIR and slammed his fists on his desk, furious at Naomi's earlier encounter. "Well, if this is the town's response, then I say they are not worthy of attending my son's weddin' celebration. Their ignorance goes to show how narrow-minded and prejudiced people can be. Sam is not plannin' to marry outside of our faith as King Solomon did when marryin' foreign wives who had other pagan beliefs." Jonathan paced as he thought of a plan while Naomi and Mary sat by the hearth, gritting their teeth.

"Keep your voice down, Jonny. We don't want to trouble Sam and Jia-Li with this nonsense," Mary said.

"This is what we'll do, ladies. I'll instruct Yung, Sheng-Li, and Anguo to invite as many as they could find at the Chinese camp, and the grand celebration shall commence, as Samuel requested. You bet the whole town will be talkin' about this wedding for decades."

And so it happened. The Chinese superintendents went to the edge of Snelling a week before the wedding and invited many of their friends from the camp, both esteemed and despised. With the approval of the bride and groom's parents, the Asian guests arranged a festive celebration, in addition to the Christian traditions the engaged couple had planned.

Ninety-five percent of the reservations consisted of Chinese men. The few women amongst them were those of ill repute. No matter, they were honored to be included in this grand affair, and Jonathan wanted to make it known that he considered these guests more esteemed than the ones they had originally invited.

33

Traditions

While in bed on his stomach and head turned toward the window, Samuel waited for the early glow of morning light. Alas, the cool misty rays of the California sun peeked through breaks in the cloud's thin layers and illuminated his room. Scattered thoughts of the day's preparations ran through his mind all night and left him sleep-deprived. The first item he must tackle is to remove his bedding and replace it with new linens and the wedding quilt passed down from his grandparent's nuptial day.

The wood floors creaked as several footsteps came closer to his bedroom—*tap, tap, tap.* "Sam, are you awake?" his mother asked.

"I am. One moment." He dangled his legs over the edge of his bed, put on some slacks over his long underwear, and admired his wedding attire, which hung in his armoire.

Upon opening the door, his parents' radiant faces greeted him. "Good mornin', son. Did ya get some sleep?" His father patted his back.

"It is indeed, Ma and Pa. Not a wink. I've a thousand things on my mind." The anxious groom chuckled as he turned to reach for the wedding quilt on his dresser. "I'm so glad you're here. I'm sure you both would like to see my bed dressed in our family heirloom."

"Of course, we do." His mother ran her palm over the white French provincial quilt in Samuel's arms. The twinkle in her eyes suggested she might be recollecting her nuptial day.

"All right, Mary … this is Sam's special day." His father tugged on her elbow.

"Come on, Sam, I'll help you." His mother removed his old blanket and grabbed one corner of the quilt and he another. After stretching it over the mattress, they propped pillows with coordinated shams next to the headboard.

"Last, but not least, Jia-Li's family tradition." Samuel took the fruit, nut, and spice-laden basket and scattered the contents over a thin white veil on top of the quilt. "There. Now it's ready for the kids to gather so God will bless us with lots of children." Samuel captured his mother's and father's attention and winked.

Samuel knew his parents did not believe in omens or superstitions to conjure blessings. They believed in the Almighty God and his Son Jesus as the sovereign being in their lives. Quilts, fruits, and children jumping on the bed, embroidered dragon and phoenix, and all other traditions do not instill peace and happiness. God does. Yet they relished the freedom to enjoy the different cultures around them and not allow their faith to be stumbled.

IN THE KITCHEN, POTS AND PANS CLANKED as Naomi scooped scrambled eggs and corned beef hash onto plates for Samuel and her parents. "Good mornin' y'all. Breakfast is ready. Please grab your plates. I thought I'd give Huang-Fu and Liang a break since they'll be quite busy today for the wedding. I expect the hired Chinese chefs to arrive at around ten o'clock."

Samuel hugged his sister. "Thank you, Naomi. I'm sure the Suens are grateful for your helping hand." He inhaled the appetizing aroma and picked up a plate. "Sure does smell good."

Mary and Jonathan gathered their meals and sat down at the table with Samuel. "Will you not be joining us, Naomi?" Mary asked.

"I've already had breakfast. Y'all relax while I run upstairs to decorate

Samuel and Jia-Li's bedroom. Don't come up before I'm finished, brother dear."

Jonathan chortled. "I'll make sure he stays put until you return."

"Thanks, Pa. I don't want Sam to ruin the surprise before it's done." Naomi grabbed several bags filled with greenery and whisked herself out of the kitchen and up the stairs to Samuel's room.

AFTER BREAKFAST, THE HAMPTON FAMILY ARRIVED. They scurried into the kitchen where everyone sat, except the Suen family, who remained in their cabin, preparing for the appointed time.

"Uncle Samuel!" The children rushed in with baskets filled with fresh mistletoe and holly berries.

"Oh, here are my favorite nieces and nephew. Come and hug your uncle."

"Billy and I picked these for you and Aunt Jia-Li to decorate the bedroom." Amanda's pearly white baby teeth shined beneath her rose-pink smile.

"They're beautiful. Let me find a container to put them in. Then you, Billy, and Izzy can help me place them in my room. I also want to give you three something you'll enjoy." Samuel grabbed a pitcher from the cupboard, filled it with water, and arranged the evergreens in it. "All right, follow me upstairs."

The young children clapped and wiggled to see their handiwork appreciated. Holding the container in his left arm, Samuel scooped Billy in his right arm. Amanda followed, and her parents followed close behind carrying Isabel. They walked up the stairs and into his room.

"Oh, Uncle Samuel, your bedroom is beautiful. It looks much different from when Mama and Papa stayed in it," Amanda chirped as her wonder-filled eyes round the room. "Oooo ... and are those goodies on the bed?"

"Those are for you, Billy, and Isabel. So gather them up in your baskets and bring them home. They are a gift from Aunt Jia-Li and me to you."

"For me?" Billy wrapped his arms around Samuel's neck.

"Yes … for you." Samuel sat Billy on the mattress, Amanda climbed up, and Lad seated Isabel. The children squealed and laughed as they gathered the bountiful harvest and placed them in their baskets.

"Naomi did a wonderful job decorating your room. Jia-Li is going to love what she's done." Sarah admired the boughs and garland braided with white lacy tulle and winterberries. The aroma of the evergreens, fruits, and spices filled the air in the romantic yet whimsical bedroom. The garland draped around the door entrance and windows, on the bedpost, and the furniture.

"Oh my, look at all the goodies we've gathered, Mama and Papa," Amanda said as she and her siblings sat on the bed next to the baskets full of delectable items.

"Wonderful." Sarah gasped.

Samuel placed his nephew in Lad's arms and Isabel in Sarah's as he helped Amanda carry the baskets. "It appears the children had a bundle of fun. If Jia-Li's family tradition holds true, then I dare to think that the Lord will bless us with a quiver full as He has for the both of you." Samuel glowed.

"The children would be happy with cousins to play with them. Thank you, Sam," Sarah said.

"No, sister. It's I who is grateful for your help and support." He hugged her. "Now, if you'll excuse me, there are many other tasks I need to finish before the ceremony."

"Don't let us get in the way. We'll join in the preparations shortly." Sarah gathered her family and trotted downstairs.

34

Talk of the Town

The expansive canvas tent sat centered on the farmhouse lawn. The red-carpet-covered porch steps and brick walkway created a center aisle ending on the tent's opposite side. The head table rest to the far left. Five more rows of tables ran parallel to the head table, totaling six, and were divided up, three on each side of the carpeted path.

Several Conestoga wagons filled with Chinese guests from the camp arrived. The men dressed in fine silk shirts of black and red and matching trousers. Moreover, the five women, known as 'one hundred men's wives,' also came adorned in their finest silken dresses, jackets, and hair embellishments.

Samuel and Pastor McSwan waited at the top of the porch steps as Lad, Sarah, Jonathan, and Mary greeted the guests and directed them to their seats. However, as the visitors mingled, loud voices vaulted at the end of the walkway. Tu, the former supervisor, arrived in a belligerent drunken state, dressed in tattered clothes, pushing people aside.

From the porch, the groom tracked his father rushing over to settle the commotion. "Should I assist them?" Samuel asked the pastor.

"No. Between your father and the superintendents, they'll take care of the matter. Besides, all the guests are seated, and we are ready to begin the ceremonies."

"Tu, how did you come in here without proper wedding attire?" Fists planted on his hips, Jonathan snarled as his superintendents, Yung and Sheng-Li, tried to restrain the disgruntled man. "Send him off to Merced Falls Road. I hope he finds his way to camp on his own and pray he isn't caught."

The men grabbed Tu's arms and escorted him to the edge of the farm, which led to the main thoroughfare headed toward town.

After Jonathan returned to his seat at the head table with Mary and the Hamptons, the clatter of cymbals and Chinese drums filled the tent as the procession entered from the end of the walkway.

Clang, clang, clang, clang. The rhythmic beat hushed the crowd. *Boom-boom, boom-boom.* The drum song matched Samuel's beating heart. As the musical parade passed through, four ushers followed, carrying a sedan chair for the bride. The colorful dancing Chinese lion constructed of paper, silk, sequins, and bamboo superseded them. Two men inside the costume animated the creature as they shook its beastly head and wagged its hind parts.

The procession met Samuel at the foot of the porch steps. One of the men who carried a cymbal motioned him to lead the parade to the Suens' cabin, where they would fetch the bridal party. The dashing groom adjusted his top hat and tugged at his silver and printed vest beneath his dark wool Davenport frock coat and matching slacks then joined the group.

NEXT DOOR, JIA-LI'S BODY TREMBLED full of emotions as she and her entourage prepared for the special day. Her parents, maid of honor, Naomi, flower girl, Amanda, and ring bearer, Billy aided her to remain calm and assured. Liang and Naomi had affixed the phoenix crown upon the bride's styled hair. It added the perfect complement to her silky red and embroidered wedding skirt and jacket. A thin silk veil of the same color hung from the headdress, which covered her face.

"My lovely Nǚ'ér," Liang said as she adjusted her daughter's headdress, "Samuel loves you very much and would go to the ends of the universe for you. It is easy to submit to one another when you truly love each other. And if you esteem your husband better than yourself, and he does the same for you, then the result will be a lasting and abundant life together. Above all, if God comes first in your marriage, then He shall give you the strength and wisdom to endure life's challenges. Your father and I only wish we knew the Lord sooner in our relationship. Gratefully, I see how the Almighty has guided and blessed us with this beautiful union with the Sowers. We are so happy for you and Samuel."

"Thank you, Mǔqīn. I shall keep your advice and sound words close to my heart. I appreciate you and Father's sacrifice to raise and protect me as your only child and daughter. My prayer is to be an excellent wife like you and that I can bring honor to our family and ancestors. I love you so much, Mǔqīn." Jia-Li embraced her mother, and joyful tears filled their eyes.

SAMUEL LED THE PROCESSION TO THE FRONT of the Suens' cabin. The ushers set a string of firecrackers ablaze to announce the groom's arrival to fetch his bride.

The cabin door opened and Huang-Fu, also dressed in silk wedding attire, stood grinning with pride. First, he allowed Amanda and Billy to come out. The flower girl wore a child's green ball gown and held a white basket filled with rose petals. She dropped a few at a time on the ground and paced to the processions anterior. The young ring bearer trailed behind as he carried a lacey pillow with the wedding bands attached. Next came the bride's mother, Liang, wearing a jade-colored Chinese silk skirt and jacket, followed by her maid of honor, Naomi adorned in a teal Victorian bustled gown.

The moment Samuel long-awaited arrived. He suppressed the joy which churned inside him and longed to burst into shouts of happiness. Huang-Fu turned and tugged on a curtain that fell to the floor, revealing the most precious gift a parent can give, their child. The proud father extended his hand to his daughter and led her out the door. Before the groom, he presented the bride. Although Samuel could scarce see the lines of her covered face, his eyes took in every inch of her dazzling exotic beauty in the gown meticulously custom sewn for their glorious occasion.

THROUGH THE THIN, RED VEIL, Jia-Li studied Samuel's handsome facial features. *Oh, my Lord, You have blessed me immensely with this magnificent groom. Am I dreaming? Is this moment real? Samuel is more than I could ever ask for in a husband. You truly are a God of miracles.*

Jia-Li bowed, giving respect to the man she loved beyond measure, then her father whisked her over to the sedan chair where she would recline and be carried to the decorated altar at the farmhouse. Once seated, the joyful entourage proceeded back to the groom's house, down the red-carpeted aisle, and concluded in front of the porch steps.

Both families awaited the couple's arrival. The Sowers stood to the right of the porch and the Suens to the left. Pastor McSwan stationed himself in the center.

SAMUEL WAITED AT THE FOOT OF THE STEPS as the ushers set the sedan chair on the ground. Excitement burst from within as he reached to touch his bride for the first time that day. Jia-Li rose to her feet and placed her palm upon his. Together they walked up the stairs.

Pastor McSwan began the wedding vows. "Dearly beloved, we are gathered here in the sight of God, and in the presence of this company, to unite Samuel J. Sower and Jia-Li Suen in holy matrimony. Marriage was ordained by God in Eden and confirmed in Cana of Galilee by the presence of the Lord and is declared to be honorable among all men by Apostle Paul. On this occasion, we ask for God's blessing upon Samuel and Jia-Li as they state their matrimonial vows.

"Do you, Samuel, take Jia-Li to be your lawful wedded wife, to have and to hold from this day forward, for better for worse, for richer for poorer, in sickness and in health, to love and to cherish, till death do you part, according to God's holy ordinance?" Pastor McSwan asked.

"I do," Samuel replied.

"And do you, Jia-Li take Samuel to be your lawful wedded husband, to have and to hold from this day forward, for better for worse, for richer for poorer, in sickness and in health, to love, cherish, and to obey, till death do you part, according to God's holy ordinance?"

"I do," Jia-Li responded.

"You may now place the rings on each other's fingers and say your vows," Pastor McSwan instructed.

Samuel placed the gold band next to the engagement ring on Jia-Li's finger and began his vow. "With this ring, I thee wed, with my body, I thee worship, and with all my worldly goods I thee endow. In the name of the Father, and of the Son, and the Holy Ghost. Amen."

Jia-Li followed suit and repeated the same vow.

"I pronounce you as husband and wife. You may now kiss your bride." Pastor McSwan invoked a smile as Samuel lifted the veil.

Jia-Li's adoring face glowed, and her sweet lips enticed him to seal their love forever. *She is mine.* Enveloping her into his arms, he dove deep into her almond eyes, then immersed her in his most passionate kiss.

"Please welcome Mr. and Mrs. Samuel J. Sower!"

The newlyweds marched down the steps and through the aisle as the guest sprinkled rice upon them for good luck. Samuel, Jia-Li, and their families sat at the head table. The reception began as several Chinese waiters served champagne.

The best man, Lad, rose to speak and interject 1 Corinthians 13:7. "I would like to make a toast to my brother-in-law, Samuel, and his beautiful bride, Jia-Li. May God bless their marriage with unfailing love for one another, which bears all things, believes all things, hopes all things, and endures all things."

Everyone raised their glasses and shouted, "Gān bēi!"

The cheers prompted the waiters to begin serving the wedding feast along with the guest's choice of western utensils or eastern chopsticks. Roasted suckling pig, shark's fin soup, deep-fried crab claws, squab, Peking duck, lobster, vegetables with sea cucumber, and fish. For dessert, they served hot sweet red bean soup and two types of dumplings.

After dinner, Samuel and Jia-Li cut the wedding cake, and the waiters distributed a dish to the appreciative guests. The finality of the day concluded with a display of colorful, incandescent Chinese fireworks, which no doubt taunted the disparaged residents of Snelling.

This day will be the talk of the town. As Samuel admired his beautiful wife, his heart beat as rapid as the drum song, and his mind roared like the dancing lion as consummation filled his thoughts. *Time we leave this party.*

As the evening wound down and the waiters poured the last of the wine, Samuel and Jia-Li left the festivities to find respite in their anticipated bed-chamber. The following day they would depart for their honeymoon in downtown San Francisco and would return to the farm a week later.

35

Reflections

"Last year began with some difficult challenges for our family, Mary. However, the good Lord was faithful to bring all of us through those circumstances as we learned to put our hope and trust in Him." Jonathan reflected upon the events of 1874 as he and Mary sat in their wingback chairs next to the fireplace in his office.

Their farmhouse was once again quiet. Samuel and Jia-Li were on their honeymoon. Sarah, Lad, and their children were nestled in their new ranch home. Naomi had left early to do some bank errands in town. David was entrenched in his studies at the university. Huang-Fu and Liang were busy about their chores, and the farmhands were preparing for the next season of planting.

"Yes, dear. I pray 1875 is off to a better start. It sure does seem to be." Mary put her crochet down for a moment to glance at him. "God, once again, has shown himself to be faithful to His word in Romans 8:28, 'And we know that all things work together for good to them that love God, to them who are the called according to his purpose.'"

"He sure has. Although, Jesus never promised us Christians that the journey of followin' His example of a sinless life would not be without its bumps, obstacles, and attempts from the devil to throw us off the path to the Father. We add to these mishaps when we, as Christians, fall prey to the enemy's schemes and are tempted to make a bad decision or wrong turn in a direction which is not of the Lord's will," Jonathan added as he thought of his children's life journeys toward the goal of living chaste.

He continued, "Naomi, as a child, once made a poor choice of entangling herself with savory peers to whom she lacked the wisdom and strength to combat their misguided schemes. God tested Sarah's faith as she met tragedy through the unfortunate circumstances of Joshua's death, her difficult marriage, and her daughter's illness. Samuel went astray when tempted to fulfill his desires for gold and lascivious livin'. Now, David must challenge himself with the giant course of education to obtain his career goals in ministry and maintain this pathway.

"Adam and Eve's bad decisions have certainly left us with sin-cursed minds, bodies, and a corrupted world. I am grateful the Lord is forgivin' and can overlook our sinful ways as long as we turn our hearts and minds to Him and follow His direction. True repentance brings us back to the right path to God," he concluded.

"Yes, indeed, dear. Thank the Lord for His grace and mercy toward us and the mistakes we've all made. For now, all is well. Let us enjoy this moment of reprieve and get plenty of rest in the Lord. Our Christian journey shall not be complete until we go to be with him. I'm sure there'll be more challenges ahead for you and me, our children, and our grandchildren."

"Yes, my love. We certainly must rest, but also stay alert, always trustin' in God. We need to remember Deuteronomy 7:9, 'Know therefore that the LORD thy God, He is God, the faithful God, which keepeth covenant and mercy with them that love Him and keep His commandments to a thousand generations...'

"Yes, Mary. I believe we are the generation he speaks of in this passage," Jonathan concluded as they both joined hands and prayed for their family.

The Parable of the Lost Sheep

Luke 15:1-7

[1] Then drew near unto him all the publicans and sinners for to hear him.
[2] And the Pharisees and scribes murmured, saying, This man receiveth sinners, and eateth with them.
[3] And he spake this parable unto them, saying,
[4] What man of you, having an hundred sheep, if he lose one of them, doth not leave the ninety and nine in the wilderness, and go after that which is lost, until he find it?
[5] And when he hath found it, he layeth it on his shoulders, rejoicing.
[6] And when he cometh home, he calleth together his friends and neighbours, saying unto them, Rejoice with me; for I have found my sheep which was lost.
[7] I say unto you, that likewise joy shall be in heaven over one sinner that repenteth, more than over ninety and nine just persons, which need no repentance.

The Parable of the Lost Coin

Luke 15:8-10

[8] Either what woman having ten pieces of silver, if she lose one piece, doth not light a candle, and sweep the house, and seek diligently till she find it?
[9] And when she hath found it, she calleth her friends and her neighbours together, saying, Rejoice with me; for I have found the piece which I had lost.
[10] Likewise, I say unto you, there is joy in the presence of the angels of God over one sinner that repenteth.

The Parable of the Prodigal Son

Luke 15:11-32

[11] And he said, A certain man had two sons:

[12] And the younger of them said to his father, Father, give me the portion of goods that falleth to me. And he divided unto them his living.

[13] And not many days after the younger son gathered all together, and took his journey into a far country, and there wasted his substance with riotous living.

[14] And when he had spent all, there arose a mighty famine in that land; and he began to be in want.

[15] And he went and joined himself to a citizen of that country; and he sent him into his fields to feed swine.

[16] And he would fain have filled his belly with the husks that the swine did eat: and no man gave unto him.

[17] And when he came to himself, he said, How many hired servants of my father's have bread enough and to spare, and I perish with hunger!

[18] I will arise and go to my father, and will say unto him, Father, I have sinned against heaven, and before thee,

[19] And am no more worthy to be called thy son: make me as one of thy hired servants.

[20] And he arose, and came to his father. But when he was yet a great way off, his father saw him, and had compassion, and ran, and fell on his neck, and kissed him.

[21] And the son said unto him, Father, I have sinned against heaven, and in thy sight, and am no more worthy to be called thy son.

[22] But the father said to his servants, Bring forth the best robe, and put it on him; and put a ring on his hand, and shoes on his feet:

[23] And bring hither the fatted calf, and kill it; and let us eat, and be merry:

[24] For this my son was dead, and is alive again; he was lost, and is found. And they began to be merry.

[25] Now his elder son was in the field: and as he came and drew nigh to the house, he heard musick and dancing.

[26] And he called one of the servants, and asked what these things meant.

[27] And he said unto him, Thy brother is come; and thy father hath killed

the fatted calf, because he hath received him safe and sound.

²⁸ And he was angry, and would not go in: therefore came his father out, and intreated him.

²⁹ And he answering said to his father, Lo, these many years do I serve thee, neither transgressed I at any time thy commandment: and yet thou never gavest me a kid, that I might make merry with my friends:

³⁰ But as soon as this thy son was come, which hath devoured thy living with harlots, thou hast killed for him the fatted calf.

³¹ And he said unto him, Son, thou art ever with me, and all that I have is thine.

³² It was meet that we should make merry, and be glad: for this thy brother was dead, and is alive again; and was lost, and is found.

The Parable of the Barren Fig Tree

Luke 13:6-9

⁶ He spake also this parable; A certain man had a fig tree planted in his vineyard; and he came and sought fruit thereon, and found none.

⁷ Then said he unto the dresser of his vineyard, Behold, these three years I come seeking fruit on this fig tree, and find none: cut it down; why cumbereth it the ground?

⁸ And he answering said unto him, Lord, let it alone this year also, till I shall dig about it, and dung it:

⁹ And if it bear fruit, well: and if not, then after that thou shalt cut it down.

The Parable of the Good Samaritan

Luke 10:30-37

[30] And Jesus answering said, A certain man went down from Jerusalem to Jericho, and fell among thieves, which stripped him of his raiment, and wounded him, and departed, leaving him half dead.

[31] And by chance there came down a certain priest that way: and when he saw him, he passed by on the other side.

[32] And likewise a Levite, when he was at the place, came and looked on him, and passed by on the other side.

[33] But a certain Samaritan, as he journeyed, came where he was: and when he saw him, he had compassion on him,

[34] And went to him, and bound up his wounds, pouring in oil and wine, and set him on his own beast, and brought him to an inn, and took care of him.

[35] And on the morrow when he departed, he took out two pence, and gave them to the host, and said unto him, Take care of him; and whatsoever thou spendest more, when I come again, I will repay thee.

[36] Which now of these three, thinkest thou, was neighbour unto him that fell among the thieves?

[37] And he said, He that shewed mercy on him. Then said Jesus unto him, Go, and do thou likewise.

The Parable of the Mustard Seed

Luke 13:18-19

[18] Then said he, Unto what is the kingdom of God like? and whereunto shall I resemble it?

[19] It is like a grain of mustard seed, which a man took, and cast into his garden; and it grew, and waxed a great tree; and the fowls of the air lodged in the branches of it.

The Parable of the Growing Seed

Mark 4:26-29

[26] And he said, So is the kingdom of God, as if a man should cast seed into the ground;

[27] And should sleep, and rise night and day, and the seed should spring and grow up, he knoweth not how.

[28] For the earth bringeth forth fruit of herself; first the blade, then the ear, after that the full corn in the ear.

[29] But when the fruit is brought forth, immediately he putteth in the sickle, because the harvest is come.

Do Not Judge

Luke 6:37-42

[37] Judge not, and ye shall not be judged: condemn not, and ye shall not be condemned: forgive, and ye shall be forgiven:

[38] Give, and it shall be given unto you; good measure, pressed down, and shaken together, and running over, shall men give into your bosom. For with the same measure that ye mete withal it shall be measured to you again.

[39] And he spake a parable unto them, Can the blind lead the blind? shall they not both fall into the ditch?

[40] The disciple is not above his master: but every one that is perfect shall be as his master.

[41] And why beholdest thou the mote that is in thy brother's eye, but perceivest not the beam that is in thine own eye?

[42] Either how canst thou say to thy brother, Brother, let me pull out the mote that is in thine eye, when thou thyself beholdest not the beam that is in thine own eye? Thou hypocrite, cast out first the beam out of thine own eye, and then shalt thou see clearly

to pull out the mote that is in thy brother's eye.

The Parable of the Laborers in the Vineyard

Matthew 20:1-16

[1] For the kingdom of heaven is like unto a man that is an householder, which went out early in the morning to hire labourers into his vineyard.
[2] And when he had agreed with the labourers for a penny a day, he sent them into his vineyard.
[3] And he went out about the third hour, and saw others standing idle in the marketplace,
[4] And said unto them; Go ye also into the vineyard, and whatsoever is right I will give you. And they went their way.
[5] Again he went out about the sixth and ninth hour, and did likewise.
[6] And about the eleventh hour he went out, and found others standing idle, and saith unto them, Why stand ye here all the day idle?
[7] They say unto him, Because no man hath hired us. He saith unto them, Go ye also into the vineyard; and whatsoever is right, that shall ye receive.
[8] So when even was come, the lord of the vineyard saith unto his steward, Call the labourers, and give them their hire, beginning from the last unto the first.
[9] And when they came that were hired about the eleventh hour, they received every man a penny.
[10] But when the first came, they supposed that they should have received more; and they likewise received every man a penny.
[11] And when they had received it, they murmured against the goodman of the house,
[12] Saying, These last have wrought but one hour, and thou hast made them equal unto us, which have borne the burden and heat of the day.
[13] But he answered one of them, and said, Friend, I do thee no wrong: didst not thou agree with me for a penny?
[14] Take that thine is, and go thy way: I will give unto this last, even as

unto thee.

¹⁵ Is it not lawful for me to do what I will with mine own? Is thine eye evil, because I am good?

¹⁶ So the last shall be first, and the first last: for many be called, but few chosen.

The Parable of the Talents

Luke 19:11-27

¹¹ And as they heard these things, he added and spake a parable, because he was nigh to Jerusalem, and because they thought that the kingdom of God should immediately appear.

¹² He said therefore, A certain nobleman went into a far country to receive for himself a kingdom, and to return.

¹³ And he called his ten servants, and delivered them ten pounds, and said unto them, Occupy till I come.

¹⁴ But his citizens hated him, and sent a message after him, saying, We will not have this man to reign over us.

¹⁵ And it came to pass, that when he was returned, having received the kingdom, then he commanded these servants to be called unto him, to whom he had given the money, that he might know how much every man had gained by trading.

¹⁶ Then came the first, saying, Lord, thy pound hath gained ten pounds.

¹⁷ And he said unto him, Well, thou good servant: because thou hast been faithful in a very little, have thou authority over ten cities.

¹⁸ And the second came, saying, Lord, thy pound hath gained five pounds.

¹⁹ And he said likewise to him, Be thou also over five cities.

²⁰ And another came, saying, Lord, behold, here is thy pound, which I have kept laid up in a napkin:

²¹ For I feared thee, because thou art an austere man: thou takest up that thou layedst not down, and reapest that thou didst not sow.

²² And he saith unto him, Out of thine own mouth will I judge thee,

thou wicked servant. Thou knewest that I was an austere man, taking up that I laid not down, and reaping that I did not sow:

23 Wherefore then gavest not thou my money into the bank, that at my coming I might have required mine own with usury?

24 And he said unto them that stood by, Take from him the pound, and give it to him that hath ten pounds.

25 (And they said unto him, Lord, he hath ten pounds.)

26 For I say unto you, That unto every one which hath shall be given; and from him that hath not, even that he hath shall be taken away from him.

27 But those mine enemies, which would not that I should reign over them, bring hither, and slay them before me.

The Parable of the Wedding Feast

Luke 14:15-24

15 And when one of them that sat at meat with him heard these things, he said unto him, Blessed is he that shall eat bread in the kingdom of God.

16 Then said he unto him, A certain man made a great supper, and bade many:

17 And sent his servant at supper time to say to them that were bidden, Come; for all things are now ready.

18 And they all with one consent began to make excuse. The first said unto him, I have bought a piece of ground, and I must needs go and see it: I pray thee have me excused.

19 And another said, I have bought five yoke of oxen, and I go to prove them: I pray thee have me excused.

20 And another said, I have married a wife, and therefore I cannot come.

21 So that servant came, and shewed his lord these things. Then the master of the house being angry said to his servant, Go out quickly into the streets and lanes of the city, and bring in hither the poor, and the maimed, and the halt, and the blind.

22 And the servant said, Lord, it is done as thou hast commanded, and

yet there is room.

²³ And the lord said unto the servant, Go out into the highways and hedges, and compel them to come in, that my house may be filled.

²⁴ For I say unto you, That none of those men which were bidden shall taste of my supper.

Deuteronomy 7:9

Know therefore that the Lord thy God, he is God, the faithful God, which keepeth covenant and mercy with them that love him and keep his commandments to a thousand generations;

About the Author

Rosanna Cerezo Sharps enjoys sharing God's Word to better understand and develop our relationship with the Heavenly Father, and to provide directives for life's challenges through its application. By vicariously experiencing another person's difficulties as they strive to maintain their course on the "narrow path"† to God, one can summarize his or her spiritual journey. Realizing "there is nothing new under the sun"*, she hopes to convey a picture of this process through the character's lives in her historical fiction trilogy *Golden Harvest*. The author prayerfully crafted the story, which allegorically applies to the timeless parables and other scriptural passages found in the Bible to help enlighten the pathway for God's people.

Rosanna studied Psychology at Southwestern College and theology at Calvary Chapel Bible College. She taught Bible studies for women, youth, and grade school children at several Calvary Chapel churches, including the church her husband pastored in Rio Vista, California. They have a musically gifted son whom she homeschooled. Her passion is to study God's Word and pray, to love her family, writing, fellowship with other Believers, singing worship songs, reenacting historical periods, travel and enjoying God's creation, and being creative through crafts such as crocheting, knitting, and painting. Currently, she and her husband are sole proprietors of a book and variety store in the historic town, Columbia, California, where all her attributes can be utilized by God to creatively plant the seed of His gospel to peoples around the globe.

† Matthew 7:13-14
* Ecclesiastes 1:9

Snelling town folk gathering in front of Simon Jacob's Store
in the 1870s

Methodist Episcopal Church

Drawing of Kelsey Ranch in 1881

Drawing of Henry Nelson's Flour and Wool Mill on the Merced
River in the town of Merced Falls

A typical late 19th century cargo hauling business pulled by horse, mule, or oxen

Yosemite Valley Railroad steam train at the Snelling Depot

Drawing of John Milton Montgomery, 1860-1863. Wealthy San Joaquin Valley cattle baron. Montgomery Street in Snelling is named after him.

Photo of Henry Nelson, owner of Nelson's Flour and Wool Mill
located in the town of Merced Falls

Old Snelling Schoolhouse

Carson Hill School 1888

A typical cabin home built in the late 19th century

A typical small mountain farm

Typical late 19th century
Chinese child attire

Typical late 19th century
Chinese women's attire

Typical late 19th century Chinese men's attire

Twenty mules pull combine wheat harvester